# Welcome to Santa Barbara,
## Mr. Zalman!

"Oh God," Ed Rome moaned. "I'm dying and I don't even own a house."

"Are you all right?" Zalman heard Yip call. "I'm calling the police. The police are definitely on their way."

Jimmy Federal ran back along the edge of the driveway and crouched by his car. "I've got a slug with your name on it, sucker!" He yanked open the tailgate on the station wagon, rummaged around, pulled out a flare pistol, and fired off a cartridge in the direction of the shots. There was a solid "whump," then a small explosion of white light in the distance, and immediately a large cypress began to burn furiously. "Ah hah!" Jimmy Federal howled manically. "You can run but you can't hide! . . ."

**Books by Gabrielle Kraft**

Bullshot
Screwdriver

Published by POCKET BOOKS

# SCREWDRIVER

## Gabrielle Kraft

**POCKET BOOKS**

New York    London    Toronto    Sydney    Tokyo

Another *Original* Publication of POCKET BOOKS

POCKET BOOKS, a division of Simon & Schuster Inc.
1230 Avenue of the Americas, New York, NY 10020

ISBN: 0-671-63725-8

First Pocket Books printing November 1988

10  9  8  7  6  5  4  3  2  1

POCKET and colophon are trademarks of
Simon & Schuster Inc.

Printed in the U.S.A.

"I'VE LOOKED BETTER," JERRY ZALMAN GRUMBLED, STAR-ing into the bathroom mirror at the thick piece of white surgical tape stretched over his broken nose. "Okay, okay, I admit it. I'm not what you'd call a handsome guy. Rugged, maybe rugged, but not handsome. Still, I've always fig-ured, hey, not so bad. Not the tallest guy in the world, but . . ."

"Five foot four and a half isn't that short, Jerry," Marie Thrasher called from the bedroom, flicking through the TV channels and stopping momentarily on the Home Shopping Network to sneer at some cubic zirconia earrings. "Would you look at those?" she squealed. "Who would wear those? I mean, if you were wearing things that big and you weren't Liz Taylor, do you think anybody in the known world would think they were real?" She fluffed up her red curls angrily.

Zalman ignored her comments on the cubic zirconia ear-rings. "Five foot *five* isn't that short, Miss Thrasher," he countered, lying by the usual half inch. "I'm taller than you, doll, and don't you forget it. But jeez, a guy has a big piece of tape over his nose, it kinda takes the zing out of shaving." Zalman studied himself more closely. He was a good-looking guy with curly black hair that constantly threatened to get out of hand, quizzical brown eyes, and a mocking grin that girls never quite trusted.

Marie flicked onward, trapped in the late-night remote control zone. "Comes off tomorrow, sweetie," she said as she passed up a few seconds of mindless video violence and settled briefly on *Top Hat*. "Look at that." She sighed. "Why doesn't *my* life look like that?"

"Because life is in color," Zalman said, "and color stinks." He continued to regard his nose in the mirror. Behind him a framed poster of Jimmy Cagney from *The Public Enemy* snarled at Paul Muni as Scarface. Zalman, a short, successful Beverly Hills lawyer, collected original lobby cards and key art, and the bedroom and bath in his Hollywood Hills home looked like a plush reminder of Warner Brothers' best.

"You've been a brave little soldier, Jerry, no kidding," Marie sympathized. "Will you quit it, please?" Marie's cowardly Doberman, Rutherford, was trying to escalate his way onto the bed by slowly insinuating himself one paw at a time. The phone rang, and Zalman sprang into the bedroom.

The Dunhill clock he kept by the bed read 11:30. He shook his head. "Must be a client." He grinned at Marie. "They always get needy just before midnight. Yes?" he said with professional gruffness as he picked up the phone.

"Jerry? Jerry, is that you?" a woman's voice trilled.

Zalman felt his stomach do the China Syndrome. It was the worst thing in the world, the worst thing that could possibly happen to a guy with a taped nose watching TV with his girlfriend and her dog at 11:30 on a Sunday night. It was his ex-wife. The first one.

"Jerry?" she breathed, her throaty voice stirring up dim memories of long hot nights in Palm Springs and long cold days in court. "Jerry, honey, don't hang up. I know I shouldn't be calling you, but gee, honey, I just don't know where else to turn. . . . You there, Jerry?"

"You bet," he said heartily, glancing over at Marie, who

was deeply engrossed in *Top Hat*. Rutherford had made his way onto her lap, and she was tapping his front paws together in time to "Cheek to Cheek."

"Can't this wait until morning?" Zalman said, trying to keep his voice down. "Call me at the office."

"Jerry? Please . . ." *Oh, boy,* he thought, *that hesitant, tremulous quaver, that little hint of a rough edge curving away under all that silk.* . . . "Jerry, I don't want to make trouble for you, honest, but I need your help. It's about my husband. Well, actually it's about my father-in-law."

Zalman breathed a tightly controlled, barely audible sigh of relief. She was married. Thank God she was married again. "Look, let's talk tomorrow, huh?" he suggested, forgetting to keep his voice down. "It's still the same old number, same old place, on Beverly Drive?"

Marie looked up sharply, muted Fred and Ginger, and stared off intently at the far corner of the ceiling. She began to whistle "Abide with Me" under her breath.

Zalman flinched. Of course he was going to tell her about the phone call. It was just that he never liked to be on the defensive. The whistling he took as an especially bad sign. Marie was paying elaborate nonattention to him. "Talk to me tomorrow," he said into the phone. "Tomorrow afternoon."

"Promise, Jerry?" the little voice begged. "You're not trying to get rid of me, are you? You always said that if I—"

"Listen," Zalman interrupted sharply, "if there's one thing an ex-wife shouldn't do, it's remind her ex-husband of what he always said, okay? Talk to me tomorrow." He slammed down the phone and reached over onto the bedside table for his cigar case.

Marie resumed flicking through the channels, leaving the sound off. "Any particular ex-wifey?" she asked caustically. "Should I prepare for the worst?"

"With her, the worst was a long time ago, believe me." Zalman sighed. "Damn, my nose itches like hell under this thing, I can tell you," he said in a futile attempt to change the subject.

"Why don't you tell me what her name is?" Marie said sweetly, refusing to be deflected. "I think I'm getting jealous. I always want a sandwich or something fattening when I get jealous, and all of the sudden I've got a monster appetite. So what's her name?"

"You'll laugh," Zalman said moodily.

"At her name?" Marie was delighted. "Oh, goody gumdrops, what is it? Lulabelle? Esmeralda? C'mon, Jerry, what's her name?"

Zalman glowered as he puffed his Macanudo to life. "T-R-A-C-E-E," he spelled. "Tracee."

"TRACEEEEEEE!" Marie giggled helplessly. "You're right. I'm laughing. But you gotta admit, it's pretty funny. She surfs, I presume? Like a totally awesome wave knocked her flat at the Rincon, and now she's thinking personal injury? That's why she's calling you up in the middle of the night and you're getting nervous?"

"I'm not getting nervous!" Zalman snapped. "Not in the slightest! Why should I be nervous? What do *I* have to be nervous about? Hell, wouldn't *you* be nervous if one of your ex-husbands called you up at eleven-thirty on a Sunday night?"

Marie stuck out her tongue. "Hah! For your information, Mr. Bluebeard, I only have one ex-husband, and it's highly unlikely I'll ever hear from him again unless he creates the perfect salsa, makes the cover of *Bon Appétit,* and calls up to gloat, that swine." Rutherford turned over to have his belly scratched and panted happily. Then he clambered off Marie's lap, sauntered over to the sliding glass door that led out to the patio and pool area beyond, and made a sticky noseprint on the glass. When both of the humans in the room ignored him, the Doberman lay down, rolled over, and waggled his paws in the air.

"Saved by the dog!" Zalman said gratefully, leaping off the bed. "I think ol' Ruth here wants to go out, don't you, buddy?" Rutherford howled happily. "Honey, I don't know why she called." Zalman sighed as he pulled open the sliding glass door and let the dog out into the crisp Southern California night air. "She says she's got a problem. That's the first thing they teach you in law school, Marie. Everybody's got a problem, and these days they call their lawyer first. Before they tell their husband, their wife, their priest, before they phone up Phil Donahue, before they call a press conference, something happens and bingo bango bongo, they phone up their attorney."

"You're still her attorney?" Marie squawked. "You're divorced! You haven't seen her in years—at least I hope it's been years, 'cause if it hasn't been years, what am I doing sitting on your bed watching your nose heal if it hasn't been years?" Marie fairly frothed with righteous indignation.

Zalman blew a smoke ring and watched it float away over his small walled garden, quiet and peaceful in the midst of the big city's madness. He turned to Marie and gave her the broadest grin the tape on his nose allowed. "Listen, light of my life. If Tracee can afford me, you'd better believe I'm still her attorney. Maybe there's a chance I can recover some of the dough she blew getting her bikini line waxed." He winked, let Rutherford back in the house, and with that man and dog went happily off to the kitchen in search of a midnight snack.

First thing Monday morning, Zalman drove over to Dr. Jimmy Chang's office in Century City to have the tape taken off his nose. Chang was Zalman's secretary Esther Wong's brother-in-law. Most of the time he stuck to tuck-and-roll jobs on starlets' faces, and he usually wouldn't bother with a simple broken snout, but Zalman liked to go first class. Besides, Chang needed a little legal help with a new beak emporium he was setting up in Santa Monica, so Zalman had managed a flat trade, a no-cash deal that would make both parties concerned very happy.

Chang's waiting room was done in tasteful shades of pink and gray, with a vaguely atomic wallpaper design that reminded Zalman of the old Googie's coffee shop on the Sunset Strip. The fifties looked better and better, he mused as he contemplated Chang's selection of magazines.

Chang poked his head out of the office door and motioned to Zalman to come into the back. "So, Jerry, how's it feel?" he asked as he bustled into the office. He was wearing a pair of gray slacks and a gray-on-gray striped silk shirt underneath a regulation white doctor's coat that looked like it had been tailor-made. Zalman wondered what it was that made Chang's clothes look better on him than they would have looked on anybody else. Chang rubbed his hands together in anticipatory glee and adjusted his nine-out-of-ten-doctors' headlight on his forehead, then flashed it blindingly in Zalman's face.

"Itches like hell, I can tell you," Zalman growled, trying to ignore the light.

Chang gently pulled the tape from Zalman's nose. "Looks great, Jerry," he said, stepping back to admire his handiwork. "Boy, I do nice work! You'd never know it had been touched. Now, it'll be scaly for a few days. . . ."

"Scaly!" Zalman yowled in horror, leaning forward to look at himself in the mirror. "A scaly nose now? That's great! I gotta have a scaly nose? This is too much, Jimmy! I can't walk around looking like a goddamn crocodile belt!"

"Been covered up for a while, Jer." Chang shrugged. "Skin's gotta normalize itself. Listen, I got a major rhino-plasty schedule this week. How's about you and I get together next week on the hospital? You can run through the papers."

"Sure, Jimmy," Zalman said, standing. "Set it up with Esther; we'll have lunch over it." He rubbed his newly uncovered nose tenderly.

"Take care of it." Chang grinned as he left the room, white coattails flying like a gull's wings. "It's worth a fortune."

Zalman went downstairs and climbed into his perfectly restored 1968 silver-gray Mercedes 280 SE. "Great," he muttered, "a goddamn scaly nose." He revved the engine fiercely and peeled out of the underground parking lot, frightening a pair of blue-haired old ladies who waved their canes at him angrily. He turned onto the Avenue of the Stars and called Esther Wong on his car phone. "So, doll," he said when she answered, "any new business?"

"Oh, hi, Mr. Z.," Esther said vaguely. "I was hoping you'd call. How's your nose?"

"Don't ask," Zalman said grumpily. "Scaly. Mostly my nose is scaly."

"Oh, dear," Esther cooed sympathetically. "But other than scaly, how does it look?"

"Just like the old nose . . . but scalier."

"Well, it will get better in time, I'm sure," Esther commiserated. "Everyone says Jimmy does very nice work. Now here's the thing. Somebody named something called . . ." Esther's voice trailed off.

"The name, Esther, think!" Zalman commanded. He could practically hear the tumblers in Esther's brain click, ever so slowly, into place.

"Tracee!" Esther said triumphantly. "Her name was Tracee. She said she talked to you last night?"

"Yeah, she did." Zalman sighed. "I was hoping she'd forget, but I'm obviously flat out of luck. What did she say?"

"Weeeeelllll," Esther hemmed, stumped by this new challenge. As usual, messages weren't Esther's best thing, which put her at some disadvantage as a secretary, but Zalman liked her anyway. Although her minimal cranial capacity meant she couldn't be counted on for everyday things, like typing and dictation, filing and taking messages, she did know how to handle troublesome clients and tearful wives and could always be counted on when things got tough. In short, Zalman found her invaluable, although he hadn't surrendered the right to get mildly irritated at her frequent memory lapses.

"She lives in Santa Barbara," Esther remembered finally. "And she's coming in this afternoon. We made an appointment for four-thirty, which I hope's okay, because she's probably already on the road. She said she was going to swing by Bijan to pick something up. She said it was important . . ." Predictably, Esther's voice trailed off as she lost the thought.

"Yeah, fine," Zalman muttered, peering at his nose in the rearview. Didn't look all *that* scaly. "Bijan, huh? Wives don't shop for their husbands at Bijan, so she must want a divorce. . . . Okay, see you after lunch, dear." Zalman rang off and headed down Wilshire toward Le Croque, where he ate lunch three or four times a week. But at the last minute he thought better of it and went over to his friend Moe's hot dog stand on La Brea for a pair of franks. If he went to Le Croque, he'd just have to listen to a lot of smart cracks about his scaly nose, and he wasn't in the mood for that. He also wasn't in the mood for a meeting with his ex-wife, but it looked like there was no way out of it. He'd been halfway hoping she'd be struck by lightning at the last minute, or that an earthquake would open an impassable fissure in the Pacific Coast Highway. Anything. Something. But alas. Zalman gritted his teeth.

In fact, Jerry Zalman wasn't the kind of guy who liked to think about the past, at least not his own past. Because he was an attorney in Beverly Hills he listened to a lot of stories about the past, but somehow other people's sad stories were always a lot more palatable than his own. Case in point. He'd married Tracee in college. Nobody told him not to do it, because it wouldn't have done any good. When a guy who says he's five foot five starts going around with a blonde who's six foot two, the results are pretty darn predictable. Jerry Zalman, then in the midst of a brief flirtation with the anti–Vietnam War movement at UCLA, had been a bright guy, an ambitious guy, a guy with his eye on the main chance, and as soon as his best buddy Doyle Dean McCoy got sent to San Quentin for kidnapping, Zalman decided to El Paso the entire war situation. McCoy, who claimed he was just trying to scare the dean of men when he picked him up, carried him to the broom closet, and locked him in, thought that kidnapping was pushing the truth a tad. But Zalman, who could read handwriting on walls with brilliant clarity, decided it was time to devote his restless energies to things other than the picket line. Besides, he was mixed up with the selfsame Tracee by that point, and she, a girl with a ditzy but firm head for figures, wanted him to get on with the business of their future.

Two years later, when Zalman got out of law school, he joined the L.A. County D.A.'s office, but right from the start it was obvious that he wasn't going to fit in. He had too many ideas, he had too many opinions, he was simply too smart in the mouth. Next he tried a very conservative law firm in downtown L.A. where, despite his talent for attracting and winning lucrative cases, it quickly became clear that Zalman wasn't partner material either. Once again, too smart in the mouth. So he went out on his own, even though he couldn't afford it.

Like many a young lad he borrowed the money from his father, although, unlike many a father, Earnest Zalman won the $50K it took to set up his son on Beverly Drive shooting craps in Reno. But once Zalman was on his own, free of the conservative-minded gray faces downtown, he found that, for him, the legal dodge flowed like water off the hood of a highly waxed Mercedes. A lot of ladies came to Zalman for their divorces because Tracee had a lot of friends who somehow seemed to need divorces, and pretty soon Jerry Zalman was known all over Beverly Hills, Brentwood, and Bel Air as the guy to see when a girl wanted a little postmarital understanding. At the same time a lot of wiseguys started going to Zalman because he quickly became known all over town as a stand-up guy who paid his poker debts promptly, invariably picked up the lunch tab, and never made you feel like a damn fool just because you went and did something damn foolish. Zalman also had an enviable reputation as a guy who could settle things out of court, which, as any wiseguy knew, was the way to go if you wanted to hang on to your life-style. Within two years Zalman paid his father back the $50K and gave him a gold Rolex for interest.

But Zalman's marriage to Tracee didn't work out. Despite many interests in common—namely a fondness for Chinese food—Tracee had the brain of a not-too-bright newt, and Zalman got bored, even though Tracee, with her long blond hair and long blond legs, looked like his dream

girl. So one sad spring the lovebirds parted without undue
animosity, Zalman paid Tracee a whopping sum, she
moved to New York to forget, and quickly became a Rockette, second girl from the end, stage right.

Meanwhile, Jerry Zalman continued to work hard. He
bought himself a lovely cantilevered house in the Hollywood Hills, got married again, got divorced again, got a
little bored again, and quite accidently found the dead body
of one Sticky Al Hix while in the company of Miss Marie
Thrasher, the pint-sized daughter of a policeman. But that
was yesterday's news. . . .

Now Zalman sat on a stool outside Moe Zelnick's hot
dog stand on La Brea and ate his weenies despondently
while watching West L.A. traffic spew acrid fumes into the
air. He also thought how nice it would be to see Tracee
again after all these years when he had a scaly nose. It'd be
great. Of course, he'd known he'd run into her someday,
but he'd always pictured it a little differently, maybe like
something from *The Way We Were,* a chance encounter on a
New York street corner, she still beautiful but a little worn,
he deepened and mellowed by the bittersweet pathos of
life, distinguished, maybe a little gray at the temples,
taller . . . a scaly nose definitely wasn't part of the fantasy. He sighed, finished his weenies, polished off his egg
cream, went around back to the men's room, picked the
loose skin off his nose, and felt like a miserable teenager.
But when he was through he realized that at least he didn't
look like a lady's handbag anymore, and that made him
feel a lot better.

Zalman went back to his office in Beverly Hills and did
a little phone work with Esther Wong, who was grouchy
because she had tickets to Randy Newman at the Roxy and
didn't feel like staying late at the office. After that Zalman
cajoled her into doing some filing just to round out her day.
He felt a lot better, his mood warmed by the sense of security that can come only from sitting behind a huge desk in a
beautifully decorated room full of very expensive Persian

rugs and Victorian furniture. He tapped his fingers on the desk and waited for his ex-wife to appear.

Sure enough, Tracee buzzed in at 4:30 on the dot. She was still six-foot-two all right, which meant that she had to bend down to let Zalman kiss her on the cheek because he wasn't the kind of guy who'd stand on his tippy toes for any woman. She was still gorgeous. Her hair had reached new shades of rich, golden allure, a flaxen cascade direct from Fort Knox that was perfectly complemented by her understated beige outfit. It was the kind of thing only a blonde could wear, something cunning in cashmere with a casual little wrap of wheat-colored fur that melted into her hair so that you couldn't quite tell where fur left off and hair began. Zalman, who scanned Esther Wong's copy of *Vogue* every month just to keep in touch, figured the whole shot came straight from Calvin Klein and that his ex-wife was wearing a cool five thou on her long, lean back. Maybe ten. He thought about his fee schedule and merrily slid it forward.

Tracee flowed down on one of Zalman's armchairs and crossed her mile-high legs gracefully. "Jerry, honey," she said throatily, "thanks for seeing me. No kidding, Jerry, I really need your help. . . ." She batted her heavy-lashed eyes helplessly.

Zalman patted her on the arm with professional neutrality and retreated behind his big partners' desk. "Can I get you something to drink, dear?" he asked. He felt a swift sense of relief. Even though they'd been divorced on a quasi-friendly basis he'd wondered if he'd feel, well, that old black magic when they met again, and he was glad to see that he didn't care at all. Oh, Tracee was good-looking, no doubt about that, but her conversational repertoire was so limited! If you were going to be married to someone, Zalman figured that you had to be able to talk about something other than manicures, massages, mini-lifts, and Chinese food.

Tracee shook her head, her hair drifting along her

shoulders like a field of grain. She shrugged off her wrap and furrowed her pretty little brow, then thought better of it. Furrowing is known to produce wrinkles.

"It's good to see you again, dear," Zalman said, leaning forward on his desk with practiced concern. "I'm sorry to hear you have a problem. Why don't you go ahead and tell me all about it?"

Tracee furrowed her brow again. "Gee, I just don't know where to start. . . . Well, after you and I, you know, split up and I went to New York and became a Rockette? Well. Okay, so I'd been on the line for about a year, and it was really loads of fun, but, well, a girl doesn't want to spend her whole life doing high kicks, you know. I mean, a girl has to think about her future. Well, there I was, trying to think about my future when I met this darling guy. We started going out together, and pretty soon we decided to get married, even though he didn't have any money, which is kind of a problem in New York. He'd been living with some friends in this really nifty loft where they were all doing this conceptual art stuff?"

"You mean like having a forty-nine Ford in your living room?" Zalman asked.

Tracee nodded her head enthusiastically. "Exactly. But the thing was, my boyfriend wasn't into being an artist, he was into healing."

"Into healing?" Zalman asked warily. "You mean like snakehandling?"

"Silly. No, he was into making up all these special teas, all these different blends, you know, something to take when you, ummmmm, had your, ummmmm, cramps, or when you needed a lift . . . but everything strictly herbal. So I said, 'Well, honey, these things are so good, all the girls at Radio City are crazy for them,' and pretty soon I realized that if we put them up in cute little fabric bags and took them around to Bloomie's and Dean and De Luca and out to the Hamptons even, well, we just might be onto something."

"And were you?" Zalman prompted. Tracee's nattering had nearly put him to sleep, but he figured that once she got through with her life-and-hard-times she'd get to the juicy part.

Tracee smiled broadly and adjusted her legs ever so minutely. "Yip Tea," she said succinctly.

"Yip Tea!" Zalman echoed, astounded. "You married Mr. Yip Tea?" He was beside himself. That huge settlement he'd struggled manfully to pay, and she'd married Mr. Yip Tea, health food brewmeister to the New Age masses. The cruelty, the injustice of it all was more than a lawyer could bear.

"Well," Tracee said modestly, "he wasn't Mr. Yip Tea when I married him. I must say that I helped to make him into Mr. Yip Tea, because selling the tea and putting it up in the cute little bags was all my idea. I sewed up those little bags myself, at night, after I got home from Radio City! But finally we had so many orders we had to start hiring people. But now listen to the rest, Jerry honey."

"There's more? I can't wait."

"So Yip and I got married, and we started with the teas, and pretty soon Yip Tea went national and Yippie started doing the commercials. You've seen the commercials?"

Zalman nodded, trying not to grind his teeth down to nubbins. Unless you were from the planet Zot or you hadn't watched any TV for the last few eons, you had to have seen the Yip Tea commercials. A pleasant-faced young man with curly blond hair and a gaggle of spaniels at his feet is sitting by a roaring wood fire, Crosby, Stills and Nash whimpering in the background. "Hi," he says, raising a steaming mug of tea at the camera. "I'm Yip, and this is Yip Tea. You really oughta be drinking Yip Tea; I know you're gonna like it. I figure it's a rough, tough world out there, and when you get home you oughta do a little something for yourself, okay? So have a cup of Yip Tea and relax!" He smiles cheerfully, holds up his steaming cup and . . . fade out on Yip, still smiling.

That's all there was to it, except for some reason "It's a rough, tough world" became a catchphrase. For close to a month folks all over the U.S. of A. were going around saying "It's a rough, tough world" to each other and laughing their damn fool heads off. Then Bland, a major rock and roll star who just happened to be managed by Zalman's sister, Lucille Zalman Hanning, had a double platinum album called, naturally, "Rough, Tough World" and donated the entire proceeds to the homeless of East London, Bland's hometown. Bland was Peter Jennings' "Person of the Week," and suddenly Yip and Yip Tea were everywhere, peeking from the cover of *People*, laughing with Larry King, talking to Ted Koppel.

"So then what happened?" Zalman asked, although he had the sinking feeling he didn't really want to know.

"Well," Tracee continued, "so one day Yip and I are at my apartment doing our yoga and there's a knock at the door. It's his father, can you believe it? And guess who his father is?" Tracee stared expectantly at her ex-husband.

"You know I hate guessing," Zalman said through clenched teeth.

"Oh, come on, Jerry, just a little guess?" Tracee said happily.

"Adnan Kashoggi."

"Who? Oh, you're joking again, silly. Well, it turns out that Yip's father is E. Y. Knotte!"

Zalman nodded placidly, got up, went to the wet bar in the corner of his office, and mixed himself a Bullshot, a hefty shot of vodka backed up by a steaming cup of bouillon. He knew that he badly needed a powerful drink that would numb his brain cells before he murdered his ex-wife, then tossed her broken body out onto Beverly Drive to be trod upon by trendy shoppers.

E. Y. Knotte was one of the richest men in the civilized world. Ever since the advent of McDonald's many men had struggled to put the fishwich in a strong competitive position with the burger, but E. Y. Knotte had done it. Now, it's a known fact that nobody likes fish because A) it tastes like fish, and B) it smells like fish. Other than that fish is a very good food, low in fat, low in calories, and good for the little gray cells. But nobody likes it. They always say, let's have fish because it's healthy, but when they get to the restaurant they order hamburgers because that's what they really want.

E. Y. Knotte had changed all that. Realizing that nobody likes fish, he'd made a tiny little patty out of various kinds of fish, then smothered it with shrimp, which everybody likes because shrimp are expensive, and then dripped hot cheese over the entire melange and called it a "Shrimpkin." This became known in business schools across the land as a Great Moment in Marketing. Despite the fact that it was fried in lard, despite the fact that the cholesterol level was close to the level of the trade deficit, despite the fact that its nutritional value was about that of a breath mint, people across the length and breadth of the country perceived the Shrimpkin as a healthy food that was good and good for you and thought themselves very clever to have given up all those greasy burgers for all that healthy fish. And E. Y. Knotte became a very wealthy man indeed.

"I thought you said that Yip didn't have any money," Zalman said, bolting his Bullshot and pouring another. He could feel his blood pressure zooming skyward.

"Well, he didn't. I mean, his father did, but he didn't, and I didn't know about his father because Yip never told me. He and his father weren't speaking, is the thing of it. His father, E.Y., who is just an old cutie if you ask me, was mad that Yip was in New York, being artistic and working on himself and discovering the need for personal growth and all. But when Yip proved himself by getting rich on his own, well, his father forgave him for being artistic. See what I mean?" Tracee stopped, out of breath.

"Say good night, Gracie," Zalman muttered. "Well, dear, that's a very interesting story, but what's the problem? It sounds like you and Yip should be happy as clams, whatever that means." Tracee looked a little blank from all that talking, so Zalman prodded her gently. "You have a problem, and that's why you came to see me . . . ?"

Tracee nodded her golden head and frowned slightly. "Well, Yip and I went back to Santa Barbara, where E.Y. has a lovely home, except of course we built a little house right near him so everyone could have privacy. But here's the problem part. I'm not quite positive about this—I mean, I don't have any evidence—but a few weeks ago I think that somebody tried to kill E.Y. It's just that he had this teensy accident with his car? He got in and put it in drive, and naturally when you put a car in drive you think it's going to go forward, right?"

Tracee twisted a blond lock around her little finger. "But E.Y.'s car went backward, and he rammed right through the garage wall and out onto the patio and right into the pool! It was terrible! Luckily he had his seat belt on because I made everyone in the house swear to me personally that they would always wear their seat belts, and so even though the car went into the pool he just waited until it sank, and then he climbed out of the window and floated up. But he could have been killed, and I think somebody tried to. E.Y. doesn't believe it, he just says it was an accident, and Yip doesn't believe it, and Rhonda, who's E.Y.'s wife, doesn't believe it, and neither does Lisa, his secretary. But I think something's wrong, and I like E.Y., so I need you to help me, okay, Jerry?" Tracee finally ran down like a Walkman with dead batteries and sat in the armchair, snapping the jeweled clasp on her beige leather handbag.

Zalman, who was still standing at the bar, suddenly remembered his scaly nose and sneaked a quick peek in the mirror in back of the rows of glasses. He didn't think it looked too bad, maybe like a little too much sun on the tennis court.

"That's a very interesting problem, Tracee. Have you been to the police?"

Tracee shook her head vigorously. "Are you kidding? The police? E.Y. would have a conniption fit. See, he and Rhonda are very Santa Barbara, sort of snooty social? Well, Rhonda is. E.Y.'s so rich he can do anything he wants, and he does. She's always going to these awful charity things where they wear funny headdresses or dress up like Old Spain? She always wants me to go, but I'm too busy with Yip Tea, that's what I tell her. That's why I called you, Jerry. I need your help."

Zalman went back and sat down behind his desk. "Well, in that case, let me put it to you straight. What's in it for me?"

Tracee smiled happily, snapping her handbag with fervor. "I just knew you were going to say that, Jerry honey, and it so happens that I've got something you want."

"I'm not touching that line, Tracee. Why don't you just tell me what it is?"

"The Toulouse-Lautrec." Tracee smiled innocently and regarded Zalman with the gaze of a cherub.

Zalman nearly leapt from his leather armchair. "What?" he howled, gnashing his teeth with rage. "You want to pay me with my own lithograph? My own lithograph, which my own father gave me? You got a lot of damn gall, Tracee!"

"It's mine," she said righteously. "You gave it to me."

"It was a moment of weakness! Moments of weakness don't count!"

"They do with gifts, honey. Any girl can tell you that. It's worth your fee, wouldn't you say, Jerry honey? Maybe thirty thousand? More next year? It'll, what do you call it, appreciate in value?"

"You know damn well it'll appreciate, Tracee. Don't you play that game with me! You . . . you stole it from me!"

Tracee shook her head. "You know that's not true. You gave it to me, and you know it. And I'm offering you a chance to get it back."

Zalman knew she had him. He didn't regret his marriage to Tracee, but he did regret giving her the Toulouse-Lautrec lithograph, a small but beautiful gem his father had won in a high-stakes poker game with a Broadway producer and had given to Zalman on the occasion of his marriage to Tracee. Zalman and Tracee had been young in those days, and love had stretched out in front of them like an unbroken field of golden wheat. Zalman, unskilled in the game of marriage, thought that giving the lithograph to Tracee meant that she would be very happy, and that made him happy, and he thought that the Toulouse-Lautrec would stay right where it was, on the wall over the fireplace in their rose-covered cottage of love. This concept soon proved to be a delusion, however, for Tracee regarded the litho as her personal property, and when she moved out, Toulouse went with her.

"Besides, I don't have any money, Jerry. I mean I don't have any cash. I mean, I could probably get it eventually, and of course I've got charge accounts everywhere, if you wanted a nice set of Gucci luggage or something like that, or we could hock my furs and jewelry, but that seems sort of tacky, don't you think?"

Zalman nodded helplessly. "Tacky," he repeated dully. "Very tacky."

"I thought you'd think that. The litho seems so much cleaner. I mean, we did used to be married and all. Money shouldn't pass between us, Jerry."

"Oh, heaven forfend!" Zalman agreed.

"Well, here's what I think, and actually I think it's a pretty good deal. You come up to Santa Barbara and stay with us for a few days. Bring a girlfriend, if you have one," she said magnanimously.

"What do you mean, if I have one? You think I'm a leper?" Zalman was incensed. "Of course I've got a girlfriend!"

"Well, there's no need to get so upset about it, Jerry. Nobody said you didn't, and I'm sure she's just as nice as

23

she can be, whoever she is. So you two come up to the house and spend the weekend and see what you think. I'll tell Yip why you're there, but we won't tell E.Y. or Rhonda or the others, okay? I know what I think, but I want to know what you think, and if you decide there's something funny going on, you'll help me. If you think I'm just being silly, I'll give you the litho anyway, just because I think it's the right thing to do. Jerry, that's a pretty good offer, wouldn't you say?" Tracee beamed at him and replaced her fur over her shoulders, the orange L.A. sunlight glittering off her hair.

Zalman sat silently and looked at her. He'd always thought Tracee was dumb, but he was beginning to think that maybe she'd made remarkable intellectual strides in recent years. Ruefully, he had to admit to himself that she had him. "Let me get this straight, Tracee. You think maybe, just maybe, somebody tried to bump off your father-in-law? Is that right?"

Tracee nodded emphatically.

"And you want me to come up to Santa Barbara and poke around and see if I agree with you?"

Tracee nodded again. "That's right."

"And for this you're willing to give me back the Toulouse-Lautrec lithograph?"

Tracee nodded a third time and held up her ringed hand. A ten-carat diamond winked at Zalman gleefully. "Yes, but if there *is* any trouble you have to help me. I love my Yippie, don't you dare misunderstand. But he isn't, well, forceful the way you are. You know all about things like this—icky crime things, I mean. I just want your opinion, is all. So you help me and I'll give you back your picture. Is it a deal?" Tracee looked at him expectantly.

Zalman got up, went around, and stood next to her. "Deal," he said. And they shook on it.

ZALMAN SAW TRACEE OUT TO THE ELEVATOR, WENT BACK into his office without speaking to Esther, who was now filing her nails, and flopped down in his chair. He spun around and looked out the large plate-glass window behind his desk and stared down at Beverly Drive spread five floors below his office like an upscale version of Uncle Milton's Ant Farm. He made a steeple with his fingers, put his feet up on the windowsill, and meditated on the wacky ways of the wealthy, quite a few of whom were meandering below him, spending their ill-gotten gains in the chic shops lining Beverly Drive. Beverly wasn't as well-known as Rodeo, but it held a certain glitzy allure all the same.

"Esther!" he yelled over his shoulder. "Get ahold of McCoy for me!" It was only 5:30; McCoy was probably lumbering around his mobile home out in Newhall, tossing bones to the ill-trained, cowardly mutts he palmed off on construction sites for guard-dog duties.

Zalman knew he was taking a gamble. Tracee might renege on her bargain to deliver the lithograph, but he was betting she'd come through. She'd always been true-blue. Besides, Zalman badly wanted the lithograph back and was willing to take a chance. It wasn't the principle of the thing, Zalman assured himself, it was the actual cash value. It was worth a little of his time, a relaxing weekend at Tracee's house in Santa Barbara, and a little of McCoy's time doing some legwork to see what he could discover about the E. Y. Knotte ménage.

Esther buzzed. "McCoy's on the line, Mr. Z.," she said.

Zalman punched his speakerphone and began to pace the length of his office. He did most of his best thinking on the hoof. "Dean, how's it going?" he said. "You'll never guess who's back in town. You'll enjoy this, I know."

"Luciano?" McCoy's gravelly voice echoed over the phone. "Albert Anastasia? Dutch Schultz? Who, Zally?"

"Tracee."

"*Tracee!* Your Tracee?"

"My ex-Tracee, and don't you forget it. Now, guess whom she married after she stripped me of all my worldly possessions and left me alone and poverty-stricken."

McCoy began to laugh. "This is going to be good, isn't it? Okay, Zally, I'll play. Who'd she marry? I can use a good yock."

"Numero uno, she married Mr. Goddamn Yip Tea. Numero dos, Mr. Goddamn Yip Tea's father is E. Y. Knotte, the Sultan of Shrimp. Like it?"

McCoy howled with laughter. "Hot damn! Life is unfair, wouldn't you say, pal o' mine? Tell me more. She wants you to handle her divorce so she can gnaw the financial flesh from Yip's bones? Is that it?"

"Shut up, Dean," Zalman snarled. "You've had your little laugh. Actually, that was my first thought, but our Tracee claims it's true love with her and the hubby."

McCoy began to hum "Love in Bloom."

"Shut up, Dean," Zalman warned again. "Tracee, whom you no doubt recall has the brain of an underfed paramecium, believes someone tried to kill her father-in-law, whom she described as an 'old cutie.' Seems there was a little accident with his car not too long ago, and the aforesaid car went backward instead of forward, and both E. Y. Knotte and the car ended up in the swimming pool. Tracee, who begged for my help, has offered me a deal I

am unable to refuse. I go up to her place for a few days—
and Marie goes with me, I'll point out to you before you
make any snide cracks—and I help Tracee figure out if her
suspicions are valid. For this, for my help and expertise,
Tracee is willing to give me back my Toulouse-Lautrec
lithograph. You remember my Toulouse-Lautrec?"

"The litho Earnest gave you? That you gave to Tracee?
Sure I do." McCoy laughed. "Boy, does she have you
where she wants you. Hey!" McCoy hollered in the background, "cut it out, you dogs!" There was a momentary but
audible decrease in the low-grade Doberman snarling that
accompanied all McCoy's phone conversations like doggy
Muzak, then the decibel level resumed. "Damned curs,"
McCoy grumbled. "Well, Zally," he prodded, "what're you
gonna do?"

Zalman ground his teeth. "Dean, you're absolutely right.
She has me by the proverbial shorts, but you shouldn't kick
a guy when he's down. It's my litho, I want it back, and I
intend to get it. Besides, a weekend with E. Y. Knotte is a
price I'm willing to pay. Personally, I think it's unlikely
that someone's trying to knock off E. Y. Knotte. As I recall, Tracee was very rarely right about anything. But what
I want you to do is get me some background on the whole
crowd. Get a line on who lives there, who works there, the
wife, the secretary, the whole gang. You know the routine.
Okay?"

"You must really want that Lautrec. Sure, I'll get right
on it and see you tomorrow. Usual rates?"

"Yes, Dean," Zalman said patiently. "Usual rates."

"All right, buddy." McCoy chuckled. "But I gotta call
you on one little point, about how Tracee was never right
on nothing? I mean, it seems to me that she knew enough
to marry Mr. Goddamn Yip Tea, which was a pretty good
move for someone with the brain of an underfed paramecium, now wouldn't you say?"

"Good-bye, McCoy," Zalman said pleasantly in a highly
controlled voice.

"Adios, pal," McCoy said, still laughing, and hung up.

Zalman stared angrily around his office and thought about dinner. He decided he'd like to take Marie someplace very expensive, maybe Spago, and order up some champagne and eat up some caviar. His eyes flicked over the walls of his office appraisingly, and his restless gaze finally settled on the long mahogany bar and the Victorian gilt-framed mirror that hung over it. He sprang from his chair, stalked over to the bar, and took the mirror down. *That,* he thought with satisfaction, *is where I'm going to hang* my *Toulouse-Lautrec*.

AT SIX P.M., AS THE SEMI-DESERT HEAT OF THE DAY BEGAN
to subside a little, Zalman left the office, drove back to his
house, had a quick swim, changed into fresh summer-
weight khaki slacks, a blue Oxford cloth shirt with French
cuffs, and a blue sports coat, then drove over to Studio
City to pick up Marie. She lived alone in a small stucco
two-bedroom house on a side street, with a beautifully
tended yard that she did herself, and her "collection."
Marie, who owned and operated a prosperous script-typing
service on Ventura Boulevard in the San Fernando Valley,
had a houseful of odd items she'd picked up at swap meets
and garage sales, and it always gave Zalman a little jolt
when he walked through her door. The living room looked
like F.A.O. Schwarz at the height of the Christmas season:
Antique toys and gigantic stuffed animals were everywhere, and circus posters lined the walls. This was coupled
with an assortment of furniture that looked like it had formerly been in the possession of Dagwood and Blondie
Bumstead. Zalman sneaked a quick peek in the living
room, shuddered, and went down the hall to the kitchen.

"Honey? I'm home," he called. "You hungry?"

She was in the kitchen, sitting at the green Formica
kitchen table she'd made Zalman haul home in his Mercedes from the Saugus Swap Meet. She was drinking a

glass of white wine. The table fit in perfectly with the huge cream and green enamel Magic Chef stove and, of course, the Star Trek collection that graced the breakfast alcove, not to mention the magnetized toy robots on the refrigerator. Rutherford, as usual, was lying in the middle of the floor, asleep.

The dog opened one eye when Zalman came in, then closed it again. Marie looked blearily at Zalman.

"Jerry," she said tiredly, "your nose. It's scaly. . . ."

Zalman sighed, shrugged philosophically, and resolved not to let anything spoil the evening. "What's the matter, doll?" he asked. "You look whipped."

"I've had the world's worst day," she said, draining her glass. "I'm sorry I'm not dressed, Jer, I just don't think I can handle Spago tonight. I don't think I can handle anything except a shower and a frozen Stouffer's. I think there's some lasagna in the freezer that isn't more than three or four years old."

Zalman poured her another glass of wine and one for himself. "Why don't I zip down to the Finest Snax and get some corned beef? Maybe a little potato salad, some cream soda. If that doesn't give us heartburn, it's not for lack of trying." He kissed her gently on the cheek. "What happened? You want to tell old Dad?"

"Corned beef sounds great. Oh, God, just the usual insane writers with their last-minute rewrites. This idiot we were doing a script for? What a bozo. Linda had knocked out the thing in record time because he said he had a deadline at Columbia, and then he comes in at the last minute with thirty pages of little picky things, like he's changing *large* to *big*, real earth-shattering changes. Linda wanted to leave early 'cause she was going to Randy Newman. . . ."

"That's where Esther was going," Zalman mused. "Why is it that our employees are going to the Roxy and we're sitting here like lox?"

"So I did it myself, of course. I'd like to kill that guy. . . ."

"Speaking of murder . . ."

"We were speaking of murder?" Marie looked at him with alarm. "Uh-oh."

Zalman winced. "Don't say 'uh-oh' till you hear the worst. Then you'll say 'uh-oh,' believe me."

"Tell me."

"Shouldn't we eat first?" Zalman suggested hopefully.

Marie moaned and put her head down on the table. "It's too late for that," she said. "You shouldn't have told me not to say 'uh-oh.' Then I could have eaten first. Now it's too late. Tell me, get it over with, then I'll be able to eat."

"You're not going to like it. . . ."

"Wait a minute!" Marie insisted, picking up her head and glaring at him suspiciously. "This has something to do with your ex-wife, doesn't it? She calls last night, all in a dither, and now, tonight, you're telling me not to say 'uh-oh.' Jerry Zalman, if it turns out you're still married to her, like in *Mr. and Mrs. Smith*—"

"In *Mr. and Mrs. Smith* it turns out they're *not* married, smarty pants."

"You know what I mean," she said. "Well?"

"We're not still married, that's definite," Zalman said emphatically. "And what's more, she's married to someone else now."

"Thank goodness," Marie said, relieved.

"Funny, that's just what I thought. But that's not the problem. Tracee thinks someone tried to kill her father-in-law, and she wants me to help her find out if her fears are real or if she's just imagining things."

Marie shook her head. "I don't like this," she said darkly. "I really, seriously don't like what I'm hearing here one little bit!"

"Relax, will you? You get to go, too!"

She narrowed her eyes to slits. Zalman had never seen anyone narrow her eyes to slits before, but Marie did it. It was actually quite frightening. "I . . . get . . . to . . .

go . . . WHERE?" she hollered, causing Rutherford to wake up and whimper pitifully at his mistress's voice.

"I knew we should have eaten first," Zalman remarked to no one in particular. "Tracee has invited you and me up to her house in Santa Barbara for a few days while I take a look at the situation and give her my expert opinion as to whether someone's trying to knock off the aforementioned father-in-law. That's it, that's all, end of story, finito, finis, ciao, we pack it in and hit the sawdust trail."

Marie said nothing. She was mulling. Zalman could see she was mulling.

"Honey, I swear there's nothing between Tracee and I—"

"Tracee and me," Marie corrected.

"Tracee and me, then, whatever. It's just that she's got something I want—"

"Ah-hah! That's what I thought! And I don't like it! I mean, we don't own each other or anything, Jerry Zalman, but I have my pride, and I'm not carrying on with a man who's carrying a torch for his ex-wife, even if she does have a silly name! I won't put up with it!"

"Honey, you've got it all wrong—"

"That's what they all say," Marie told Rutherford, who had his snout buried deep in his kibble bowl. "They say, 'Honey, you've got it all wrong.' Or they say, 'I just did it for old times' sake.' Or they say, 'It didn't mean a thing to me, I was drunk.' My mother was right," she added moodily, "it's the woman who pays. . . ."

"Honey, Marie, baby," Zalman pled, "will you listen to me, please? Tracee has something I want, yes, but it's a lithograph by Toulouse-Lautrec."

"Toulouse-Lautrec?" she said, instantly alert. "You mean the real Toulouse-Lautrec, the short painter?"

"Yes, dear, the short painter, as you so charmingly put it. When Tracee and I got married my father gave me a Toulouse-Lautrec lithograph which, I'm embarrassed to say, I gave to Tracee, and she's still got it. But in return for my invaluable legal help in this little matter, she's willing to return it. And I want it! It's mine, and I want it!"

"Well, I can't say that I blame you," Marie said reasonably. She had a strong streak of practicality, and a Toulouse-Lautrec litho was a treasure no true collector could ignore. "A real Toulouse-Lautrec, huh? Boy, this is terrible. In order to get this litho back we have to go spend a few days with your ex-wife?"

"And her husband," Zalman added hastily. "Don't forget the husband. She's a married woman. Can't you just view it as a sociological experiment? A field trip? Sort of like when you were a kid and they used to take you to the Museum of Science and Industry or the Helms Bakery to see the wonders of dough?"

"You're really the Marquis de Sade, aren't you, Jerry? You're trying to drive me barking mad so you can collect on my insurance or something. . . ." Marie shook her head slowly. "I don't believe this is happening to me. This is like something you read in *True Confessions* while you're waiting for the dentist to pull your teeth out. Besides, I thought we were going to Hawaii. Don't I remember something about you taking me to Hawaii?"

"We'll go! We'll go! I swear it. Please, doll, just do this little thing for me. If you go with me, it'll sort of balance things out. Besides, you've got such sharp little eyes and such a devious little mind and such a cute nape of the neck . . ." Zalman began to nuzzle her. He couldn't help it. Marie was the essence of nuzzlability.

"You promised me Hawaii *and* you promised me corned beef," she said firmly.

"Trust me," Zalman said.

33

ZALMAN GOT TO THE OFFICE LATE THE FOLLOWING MORN-
ing because he'd stayed over at Marie's house, which
meant he had to go back to his place to change before
hitting Beverly Hills. Usually he tried to persuade her to
come to his house, because her bedroom made him nervous. It was filled with antique dolls, and their glittery
glass eyes always made him feel uneasy. But it obviously
hadn't been the night to persuade Marie to leave the house,
so he'd ignored the watchful dolls and left early in the
morning.

He found McCoy perched on the corner of Esther's desk
while Chester, Rutherford's brother, sat on the waiting
room couch, gnawing a pillow.

"Get that mutt off the furniture," Zalman ordered.

McCoy eased off Esther's desk and ambled into Zalman's office behind him, whistling plaintively for Chester.
McCoy was a big man, six-two, with a wide, slow grin and
an easy, likable style. He was wearing snakeskin boots
with silver toes, a ratty pair of faded Levi's, and a National
Rifle Association T-shirt with a pack of unfiltered Luckys
in the rolled-up sleeve. McCoy did not belong in Zalman's
office. McCoy did not belong in Beverly Hills. The thing
was that Zalman and McCoy went back a long way together, and over the years their youthful friendship had

deepened into something resembling trust. Now McCoy helped himself to a wake-up beer out of Zalman's refrigerator and nail-fired a Lucky with a kitchen match. He sprawled in a leather armchair.

"You're gonna love this, Zally," he said gleefully through a haze of cigarette smoke. He drained half his beer in one long gulp. "It's better than anything you can see on TV."

"McCoy . . ." Zalman said warningly, settling back in his desk chair and reaching for his cigar case. "Don't kid around. I ain't in the mood, as the girl said to the sailor."

"Okay, I won't rub it in, pal. Well, the Knottes are pretty well known in Santa Barbara. Of course, the old guy, E.Y., is richer than God, and he's also by way of being a character. I guess he figures he's so rich he doesn't have to do anything he don't want to do."

"Man after my own heart," Zalman mumbled, drawing on his cigar. "Go on."

"So the old man's playing cowboy. He's got a lot of Western art, Remingtons, Russells, you get the picture. Collects fancy cowboy guns, likes to show 'em off at parties. In fact, every year he has this big quick-draw contest for all his old cronies. The stewed prune set gets together and blasts off their weaponry, pretends they're Randy Scott or something.

"Now this is where it gets good. E.Y.'s got a bodyguard, name of Mercer Lamont. Now ol' Mercer happens to be a graduate cum laude of San Quentin University. In fact, I think I remember him from when I was in there for my tune-up. Anyway, I phone this buddy of mine, guy I know from the bad old days, knows all the alums, and he says Mercer is a real lame. Like listen to this, the cops nail Mercer with a goddamn stolen truck full of cigarettes which have been hijacked not two hours earlier, and he gives them this long song and dance about how he was walking down the road and this guy gave him a lift and then runs out on him at a diner. So Mercer thoughtfully decides to drive the truck back to San Fran—"

"Is this germane, Dean?" Zalman barked. "Is this whole goddamn rigamarole goddamn germane to E. Y. Knotte?"

"Well, you damn bet it is!" McCoy said defensively, helping himself to a second beer. "So Mercer claims he was framed with the cigarette hijack, which probably would have netted him about twelve minutes in the county lockup except for the original driver got bopped on the noggin with a piece of steel pipe, so it came down as attempted murder, and old Merce gets big time."

"Dean, just cut to the chase, will you?"

"Jeez, Zally, you might as well get your money's worth; it took me a lot of work to find this stuff out. Okay, so Mercer Lamont, a guy who should have been charged with 'unimaginative alibi,' is hired by E. Y. Knotte's son, this guy Yip with the teas. Tell me, Zally, just between us boys, what the hell kind of name is 'Yip' for a grown guy, huh?"

"It's an homage to Abbie Hoffman, Dean. As a retired radical you should understand that. What the hell do I know? What else?"

"I thought this was quite a lot!" McCoy countered, draining the rest of his beer and thoughtfully setting the wet bottle on the Persian carpet. "The old guy's son hires him a bodyguard who's a former resident of San Q? I wouldn't get my old man a guy who's been up for attempted who-hah, would you?"

"What else, Dean?" Zalman pressed.

"Well, there's a pretty young secretary name of Lisa Comden. Don't have anything on her yet, but I'm working on it, and there's a butler, maids, gardeners, that sort of thing. You want me to check these guys out, I gotta go up to Santa Barbara, nose around. But the other winner is the wife, name of Rhonda? Formerly Rhonda Warwick, the actress circa the sixties?"

"Sure. I remember Rhonda Warwick. She was in some spaghetti Westerns, lots of low-cut dresses and cleavage?"

"Right on the money," McCoy said. "Rhonda was the light of love of James M. Maugardus, the big movie tycoon. Maugardus was the head of some damn studio, Fox maybe, I forget. Anyway, he gets bounced out of there on his ass about 1962, goes over to Europe to find his creative voice, and meets Rhonda at Cannes, where's she's plugging some piece of schlock she's in. Then it's off to the races for a couple of years. Maugardus keeps putting her in these real dog movies, and she doesn't do much to improve 'em. The films flop, and Maugardus finally flips his lid, like for real. He goes off to Ding Dong School, Rhonda comes back to the States and marries up with E. Y. Knotte soon after and retires from the screen. Now she's a society hostess."

Zalman nodded happily. "Very good, Dean. Where'd you get all this, anyway?"

"Back issues of *Photoplay*," McCoy said. "You think it's a state secret?" He stretched his lanky frame and helped himself to yet another cold beer out of the fridge. "So you want me to run up to S.B.?" He burped. "I could dig around, let you know about the secretary, personal habits of the household, if they got any interesting relatives or friends—that is, if you want to pop for some more dough. Yup," McCoy said dreamily, "I could use a few days in the sun at your expense."

"No, thank you, no, Dean," Zalman said airily. "This is costing me enough as it is. I expect to run up there myself, eat a few good meals overlooking the ocean, relax, and be back here at my desk, admiring my Toulouse-Lautrec, in three days. Four, tops. So I doubt if I'll need any more investigation from you on this matter, but I will need some dog-sitting. I doubt if the ex–Mrs. Zalman is ready for Rutherford."

"Rutherford can't be a house guest, huh?" McCoy snorted derisively. "Sure, he can spend the weekend with us real folk at the farm. Tell him to bring his jammies now. . . ." And with that McCoy sauntered out of the room, carrying his beer. He whistled for Chester, who'd settled down on the couch with the remains of the pillow he'd been gnawing. "By the way, Zally," McCoy called from Esther's office, "how's your nose?"

"Shut up, McCoy!" Zalman hollered.

ZALMAN AND MARIE LEFT FOR SANTA BARBARA ON FRI-
day, minus Rutherford. Marie was uncharacteristically silent during the first part of the drive, though the day was
glorious and the smog unusually light. Zalman ignored her.
He figured she was simply in the midst of a snit, and,
knowing Marie, he knew her snits were brief. He amused
himself by whistling along to the third movement of
Haydn's Trumpet Concerto in E-Flat as he tooled the Mercedes up Highway 101 and filled his lungs with air condi-
tioning.

Marie continued to glower for about forty-five minutes,
until she spotted something a little way ahead. "Pullover-
pulloverpullover!" she squealed, bouncing up and down in
her seat like an overwrought child. She pointed at a dirt
road through the beanfields off the highway. "In there! In
there! Follow the other cars! There! Now get in line! No,
the other one!"

Astonished, Zalman maneuvered the Mercedes like a
Formula One racer, instinctively following her directions.
"What's the matter with you?" he snapped as he braked to
a shuddering stop in the line of cars. "Where the hell are
we?"

"The Blue Sky Drive-In. Pulluppulluppullup!"

"There's nothing playing! It's the middle of the day!"

"There's a great swap meet here, Jerry, and we're almost the first people in!" Marie said excitedly. "I can get great stuff here! I haven't been here in years."

Zalman handed the bespectacled attendant a dollar and pulled the car into the parking lot. "This is insane," he said warily as a family of bikers draped with chains, studs, and dangling doll heads passed him by. Zalman stared straight ahead.

"Over there, there's a space right next to that low-rider," Marie said, still bouncing up and down.

"I'm not putting my beautiful Mercedes next to a tuck-and-rolled monster that looks like a jukebox with dangle balls!" Zalman told her. He finally settled for a space next to a dusty Plymouth station wagon where a very fat family was eating its lunch off the tailgate. Zalman cringed, but at least the fat family looked harmless. They happily munched long, dripping hero sandwiches, mustard flowing like congealed yellow blood.

"Now what?" Zalman asked as he killed the motor and turned to Marie. Her seat was empty. She was already out of the car.

"Come *on!*" she urged from up ahead, "we'll miss everything!"

Zalman opened his mouth to speak, but she was gone. Her tiny, fully packed figure was half walking, half running down the dusty trail toward the entrance next to the snack bar. Zalman groaned. He had no choice. It was march or die. He had to follow her because it was a cinch he wasn't going to hang around a hot car next to the fat family in a crowded parking lot until Marie decided she'd had enough.

So he spent the next hour dogging her footsteps through the maze of booths, stalls, and blankets on the ground that made up the selling spaces at the Blue Sky Drive-In. It was just the sort of place he would have chosen to spend a contemplative hour—a dusty field filled with plants and jeans and feather baskets with Day-Glo birds that squawked when you pulled their tails and stolen stereos and a carnival barker with a dirty semi in which he claimed to have the original bearded lady. Marie darted this way and that, buying, looking, talking, haggling, stuffing things into her purse and begging Zalman to take the larger items back to the car while she went in search of more.

Zalman thought about suicide on his trips to and from the car but decided the idea lacked élan, especially in a drive-in movie parking lot. Besides, he'd been married twice before and had learned to go with the flow. Finally she had enough, and he bought her a very bad hamburger at the snack bar, took her back to the car, and cleaned her up with some Wipe 'n Dipes he kept in the trunk for emergencies. Zalman, a very neat guy, considered baby technology one of the great breakthroughs of the twentieth century.

"Boy, that was fun!" Marie sighed as she leaned back in the seat and let the cool air-conditioned breeze blow on her face. "I got some great stuff," she said dreamily. "We should come here more often."

"You bet!" Zalman lied enthusiastically as he eased the Mercedes out of the parking lot and back onto the highway. "You going to show me what you got?"

Marie rummaged in her purse. "Well," she said critically, "I think this is by far the bargain of the day." She held up a red and white plastic crab, cunningly fashioned into a brooch. "It was only fifteen cents!"

"You'd never know," Zalman said. "Coulda been a quarter, easy."

"You just don't understand my passions, Jerry," Marie said mildly. "And I made a heavy hit in salt and pepper shakers, too," she said. "I bought most of this woman's collection. She said she started in nineteen-fifty-two when she and her husband drove out to North Dakota to see her sister. I've got a washer-dryer combo, a Waring blender, and this little TV set. See, when you twist this little knob here the salt and peppers pop out of the console. Bunch of others . . . clams . . . Seattle Space Needle . . . Mr. Pea-

41

nut . . ." Marie was lost in a world of her own decoration. "Oh, and remember that package you took to the car for me?"

"The one that weighed forty pounds?"

"Oh, Jerry, honestly! Well, it's absolutely the most beautiful plastic lamp I've ever seen, like thirty years old maybe. Of course, it needs a good cleaning and rewiring and a shade, but other than that—"

"It's perfect, right?" Zalman laughed.

"Oh, Jerry," she said again. "Listen, I'm feeling a little scruffy all of a sudden. Do you think you could stop at the next clean-looking service station you see? Maybe I could put myself back together so I don't have to meet your exwife and all these rich people looking like a refugee."

Zalman smiled his man-of-the-world smile. "I've got a better idea, sugarplum," he told her. "Why don't we go to a motel?"

The motel they found on a back street in the little town of Carpenteria was old and certainly not the top-of-the-line resort Zalman usually frequented, but Marie thought it looked cute, and it had a quiet, sleepy air straight out of the forties that felt comforting.

As Zalman signed in, Nick, the owner, immediately told him that he used to work at Frederick's of Hollywood until he and his wife Mamie and their dog Frou-Frou moved up to live the quiet beach life. Zalman wasn't in the mood for the guy's life story and kept edging for the door, but Nick had to get towels, so Zalman heard all about how Frou-Frou, a half-cocker, half-poodle mix, sat up at the table just like a human being because he loved to lick the heart out of a baked potato.

Finally Zalman and Marie got to their room, which was a tiny whitewashed cubicle with red checked curtains that made it look like an Italian restaurant. Marie headed for the shower, and Zalman got in with her to help soap down her back.

As they slipped into bed the afternoon shadows were

lengthening, so Zalman left the desk lamp on. The yellow shaft of light that fell across the room onto the narrow bed felt like the ray of a streetlamp shining through a window with a hurrying city in the background. Zalman reached out to caress the smooth upper reaches of Marie's thighs, and as he felt her begin to respond he realized, once again, that she was by far the most important woman he'd ever known. . . .

Afterward they lay quietly, listening to the traffic rush by in the distance, and she slept for a few minutes, curled against him like a small animal tucked among its litter. When she woke she stretched and asked for a glass of water. "I miss Rutherford," she said softly as she sipped from the glass he'd brought her. "Do you think he'll like being back with McCoy?"

"You bet he will," Zalman assured her. "He's got all his pals to play with out there. Maybe McCoy will take 'em out and let 'em savage some school kids."

"You're so silly," she said, punching him lightly on the arm. "If Rutherford bit anybody, it would be strictly by mistake. Okay, now that you've had your bestial way with me I guess we'd better go see Tracee and the gang."

"Hey, I want to tell you something," he said, taking her in his arms. "I used to be married to Tracee, but I'm not married to her now, and I don't want to be married to her again. But I *do* want my lithograph back, and am I going to get it? Yes I am!" he cheered. "Rah rah for the Zalman team!" He sprang from the bed, and twenty minutes later they were on the road again.

ZALMAN PULLED UP AT THE DELICATELY CURVED wrought-iron gates that opened onto a long, palm-lined driveway twisting up and away out of sight in the gentle Santa Barbara twilight. The gates, which were closed, spelled out "Knotte Pines" in scrollwork.

"'Knotte Pines?'" Marie giggled incredulously. "It's even better than 'Upson Downs.' This is going to be more fun than I thought!"

Zalman scowled and impatiently jabbed the button on the intercom. It flashed, and he leaned out of the car window and said "Jerry Zalman for Mrs. Knotte" into the speaker. The gate slid open smoothly on its oiled tracks, and Zalman gunned the Mercedes, sending up a fine spray of gravel from the wheels. "Stop laughing," he told Marie. "This isn't funny. As a matter of fact, this is a whole lot worse than I thought."

"What's the matter, honey? I thought 'Knotte Pines' was pretty darn good."

"This is the matter," he answered, waving at the rolling landscape on either side of the car. "Notice we ain't at the house yet? Notice we're looking at acreage here? What the hell's that over there, huh? A goddamn polo field. My ex-wife, who squeezed plenty good bucks out of me, let me tell you—bucks I could ill afford at the time—has married into this, a goddamn polo field? And now she's poor-mouthing and squeezing me for my own lithograph, my own father's gift! I tell you, life is not fair." He frowned darkly and growled like Rutherford having a bad dream.

"Ohhhhh, feeling sorry for ourselves, are we?" Marie cooed cloyingly, arching her delicate eyebrows. "Poor, poverty-stricken Jerry. Fighting our way up Beverly Drive in the snow, are we? What's the matter, doll, did the Chivas fountain run dry? Are we just a teensy bit short on Châteauneuf du Pape, huh, huh? Don't snivel, Jerry, it doesn't become you. Can't you look on this as a sociological expedition, a field trip, sort of like when you were a kid and they used to take you to the Helms Bakery—"

"Wait a minute! Wait a minute! That's my line! That's what *I* told you!"

*"Nyuck nyuck nyuck . . ."* Marie did an excellent imitation of Curly from the Three Stooges. "Just getting a bit of my own back." She smiled as he drove toward the house. "Oh, my God, would you *look* at this place?" she said as they saw the full splendor of Knotte Pines rising up in front of them in the growing twilight like the Love Boat.

It was true. Knotte Pines was classic Santa Barbara, with early California white adobe walls and red clay tile roofs gleaming out of the oncoming dark like phosphorescence floating on the surface of the sea. A moment later Zalman pulled the Mercedes to a stop in front of the entryway and they sat silently, taking in the massive opulence of the place.

There was a large tiled fountain burbling in the center of the circular graveled driveway, and two entwined seahorses spewed water ten feet into the warm evening air. Bougain-villea and morning glories covered the low walls that surrounded the four-story house, and lacy wrought-iron grillwork adorned the low balconies that gave way onto the lawn. To the left of the house lay the garages and servants' quarters, and to the right a manicured emerald-green lawn inhaled the misting water cast off by the sprinklers. A square tower sprang up out of the center of the big house, and the overall effect was massive, imposing, and elegant, a lavish home where happy, rich people played endless games of tennis, croquet, and polo while drinking gin rickeys and pondering their investment portfolios.

"This is very impressive," Marie uncharacteristically whispered to Zalman.

"Grrrrr," Zalman growled again, but before he could get out of the car the front door opened and a tall, thin man dressed in basic butler black appeared on the big semicircular steps.

"Yessss," he hissed, his eyes flicking over the silver Mercedes. Apparently he decided that Zalman's car entitled him to further conversation. "I'm afraid Mrs. Knotte is not expecting you, sir. . . ."

"I'm looking for Mrs. Tracee Knotte. Isn't this her house?" Zalman called.

"Ahhhhh, well." The butler smiled condescendingly. "There you are, sir. This is the residence of the senior Knottes. The junior Knottes live just down the road." His upper lip twitched almost imperceptibly, implying that anyone who wanted to see the junior Knottes was second-rate at best. He picked his way down the steps and minced over the gravel as if trying not to scuff the soles of his shoes. His lantern jaw and pale skin gave him the look of an unhappy cadaver. He freed the thinnest of smiles, momentarily displaying large, horsey teeth. "If you'll just follow the driveway to the fork in the road, sir. Bear to your left and you won't go wrong. Thank you, sir." He inclined his head, minced back to his perch on the steps, and let loose another crinkle-lipped smile.

"Thanks a million," Zalman called genially as he swung the car around the circular driveway and headed back down the road. "Better make that a billion," he added in an undertone.

He followed the butler's directions and a few minutes later pulled up in front of Tracee's house. Tracee was standing in the doorway, waiting for them. She was wearing a simple white cotton dress which set off her gently tanned skin and her mane of golden hair. Her heavy matte gold cuff bracelets gleamed in the twilight as she waved happily.

The house was a long, low Spanish ranch affair with a brilliantly bejeweled stained-glass window over the front door, spraying multicolored lights and shadows over the front steps. It was a large house with slanting red-tiled roofs and whitewashed walls covered with yet more bougainvillea. The sea pounded nearby, its crash a palpable addition to the atmosphere.

"Well, hi!" Tracee trilled as Zalman and Marie got out of the car. "Brunson rang from the big house and said you all were on your way down. I'm Tracee," she said to Marie. "I'm just so glad you two could come. Did Jerry tell you everything?" The two women shook hands, Marie eyeing Tracee with a speculative glance. Tracee's tone was warm and unaffected as she took Marie's arm and smiled. "Look," she said, completely ignoring Zalman. "I'm afraid we'll just have time for a quick drink and a change of clothes. When Rhonda heard I had house guests she immediately asked us up for dinner, and there's no refusing Rhonda, who's my father-in-law E.Y.'s wife, by the way. E.Y.'s just an old bear about being on time. Men are so silly about things like that, don't you think?" she said as they strolled into the house together, Marie laughing in agreement.

Zalman stood at the car door, watching them. "I'll get the bags," he said to the bougainvillea as he opened the trunk and took out his leather Gucci bag and Marie's circa 1940 Vuitton suitcase. "I'll be fine. Don't worry 'bout me. I don't need any help."

He wrestled the bags into the front hall, deposited them, then went into the living room. As he came in Tracee was saying, "I mean, it doesn't matter if we get there at seven or seven-fifteen. They just sit around and have cocktails for an hour, so who cares?"

"I know just what you mean," Marie replied as she looked around. "This is a wonderful room. Did you have someone do it, or . . ."

"No, I did everything myself, and of course I'm always working on it. Does it look . . ."

"Not at all," Marie said firmly. "It's perfect. It's elegant, yet at the same time it's . . ."

"That's just what I wanted!" Tracee said. "You know, not too . . ."

"Exactly."

Zalman looked around. It was a good room, all in white with pale accents of color washing the bare wood doorways and window frames in a flush of pastel color. Two of Andy Warhol's "Endangered Species" flanked a broad white marble fireplace, and the chairs and couches scattered around the room looked deep and comfortable, as if a man could get some serious napping done on them on a quiet afternoon. Through floor-to-ceiling windows the blue-green Pacific glittered far below like a pirate's treasure. All in all, the house had the feeling of a casual summer home dressed up in its Sunday best.

"You don't know how much this means to me, Marie, having Jerry here to help me," Tracee said. "I hope all this is okay with you. It's just that I didn't know who else to ask." Her hands fluttered nervously, and she twisted her thick gold wedding ring.

Zalman watched Marie's eyes sweep the room, then give Tracee a long, slow once-over. "I did think it was weird," she admitted, "but now that I've met you I'm beginning to see it differently."

"I'm so glad!" Impulsively, Tracee bent down and kissed Marie on the cheek. "Come on outside, I'll show you where the pelicans nest." The two women went out through the sliding glass door onto the deck beyond.

"Why am I standing here like a dolt?" Zalman asked the

empty room. He kicked off his loafers and fished in his pocket for his cigar case. He lit a Macanudo, lay down on the couch, and began to blow smoke rings.

"Oh, hi," a voice called. "You must be Jerry! Really great of you to come up here, man."

Zalman craned his head around and looked behind him. A tall, good-looking blond man was standing in the doorway, flashing a toothy but engaging grin. He wore an expensive velour running suit and carried a video camcorder in his right hand. He raised it to his eye, then shot some tape of Zalman staring blankly, cigar smoke wafting toward the ceiling. Zalman recognized the man right off from his TV commercials. It was Tracee's husband, Yip Knotte, the Colonel Sanders of health-food yummies.

"Tracee told me what a great guy you are," Yip said enthusiastically as he sat down on the white marble coffee table across from Zalman's couch, putting his camcorder aside. "You don't inhale, do you?" he asked anxiously, waving cigar smoke away from his face. "Tell me you don't inhale."

"Okay, I don't inhale," Zalman said promptly.

"Glad to hear it," Yip said. "Say, you like tofu?"

Zalman contemplated his cigar and carefully knocked the ash into a huge philodendron on the end table. There were no ashtrays in sight. "That's what we're having for dinner?"

"I doubt it," Yip said morosely, picking at his velour knee with long fingers. "We're dining with my dad, and it's probably going to be a huge slab of bloody meat." He shivered involuntarily.

"Thank God," Zalman mumbled.

Yip glanced outside, raised his camcorder, and shot Tracee and Marie, who were sitting on a pair of gaily striped lounge chairs, their heads together, their knees almost touching. They were deep in earnest conversation, and they both looked very, very serious. He put the camcorder down on the table again and turned back to Zalman.

"Aren't women amazing?" he asked, his tone filled with the wonderment of a child on Christmas morn. "Their ability to form relationships so quickly. To slice through the artificial formality of our alienated, post-industrial society. Like amazing!"

Zalman blew a double smoke ring and watched it drift across the room. "Yeah," he said, "amazing. So we're going up to your dad's? Tracee says he's had a spot of trouble recently. So what do you think about it, Yip?" Zalman was a man who believed in immediately knocking the conversational ball into the other guy's court.

Yip looked uncomfortable. He screwed up his face and shrugged. "Well, uh, I dunno, Jerry. Like, at first I thought it was just an accident, but then Tracee said she didn't think so, and I started to think maybe she was right. You know, Tracee usually is."

"She is, huh?" Zalman sat up on the couch and put his sock feet on the coffee table next to Yip. "Tell me more."

"Well, my dad's a funny guy. He's really tough, old-fashioned, you know the kind. Always talking about how rough he had it when he was a kid and how the rest of us don't know how tough life really is because we didn't live through the Depression. He's made lots of enemies in business, too. So after this thing with the car went down, what with Tracee being worried and everything, well, I thought we'd better get somebody to be around my dad, kind of a bodyguard. So I hired this guy Mercer Lamont, then I come to find out that he . . ."

Zalman waved deprecatingly. "I know all about Mercer's record, for Chrissake. What I want to know is, how come you didn't check up on the guy before you hired him, and how come you don't fire him now?"

"Wow! That's totally amazing. Boy, Tracee was right. You're an amazing guy, Jerry."

"True. But you haven't answered my question," Zalman pressed. "Why don't you just bounce him out?"

Yip rearranged the books on the coffee table and opened

and closed his mouth a few times like an anxious grouper nosing up on Uncle Bud's Day-Glo electronic pulsating surefire fish lure. When he spoke his voice had the high, shrill whine of a lad who's just put a nasty crimp in the fender of Daddy's brand new Rolls. "I wanted to, Jerry, honest! But by the time I found out it was too late! My dad really likes Mercer now, and besides, Mercer isn't a bad guy. He's just not very evolved in the spiritual sense."

"He's very evolved in the criminal sense, Yip, I'll say that for him. Okay, let's pass on Mercer Lamont for now. Is there anybody else in the house who might want to see your dad go down for the count?"

"Well . . . gee . . ." Yip mumbled. "I dunno. . . ."

Tracee burst into the room, Marie right behind her. "It's almost time to leave!" Tracee said breathlessly. "I hate to be a pain, Yipper, but you know how E.Y. is, and Jerry and Marie haven't even seen their room yet . . . Could you get them settled while I fix my face?" She rushed off down the hall, her bare feet pattering on the tiled floor.

"Sure, honey," Yip said to her retreating back. "You never told me if you like tofu," he said to Zalman as he led them down the opposite hall toward the guest room.

"I'm wacky about it," Zalman said.

"Outstanding! I've got big plans for tofu, you know."

"No, I didn't know," Zalman said, wondering if Yip Knotte had a full bag of marbles. Yip led them around a corner and opened a thick oak door.

"Oh, this is lovely," Marie exclaimed, taking in the guest room. It was large, airy, and overlooked a long expanse of lawn leading to the cliffs. Below, the ocean rumbled hungrily. The room gave onto a brick patio, had a spacious private bathroom and the usual accoutrements of comfort including a big TV, a tray of liquor, and a well-stocked bookshelf.

"Very nice," Zalman told his host. "If the room service is any good, I may move in. We'll be ready in a few minutes." He closed the door.

Ten minutes later, Zalman and Marie were in the living room waiting for Yip and Tracee. Zalman was wearing his usual dark three-piece suit. Marie had opted for a skintight pair of black velvet toreador pants, gold-strapped three-inch heels, and a low-cut gold lamé blouse.

"Very nice." Zalman grinned, bending down to kiss her on the cleavage. "Let's talk later?"

"You still owe me Hawaii, Jerry Zalman." She laughed. "And don't you dare try to weasel out of it. Not that this isn't a thrill."

Tracee dashed down the hall, Yip at her heels. She was wearing a blue-sequined dinner dress that clung to her perfect figure like white on rice, and her cloud of golden hair floated around her head like a nimbus. Yip had changed into a black velour jumpsuit with a false boiled white shirt quilted onto the front.

"Is everybody ready?" Tracee asked anxiously. "Oh, Marie, what a pretty blouse! Do you have pierced ears?"

"Yes," Marie said, instinctively reaching up to touch the diamond studs she always wore.

"Oh, good," Tracee said, running back toward her room. "Yippie, start the car, will you, dear? I have to get something."

Yip went off to do as he was told, obviously a situation he found exceedingly comfortable, while Zalman and Marie went outside and stood on the front steps.

"Nice house," Zalman said. "You know, maybe I could go for a beach place."

Tracee reappeared. "I hope you like these," she said warmly. "I've had them for ages, but I don't have pierced ears, so I can't wear them." She thrust a pair of earrings into Marie's hand.

"Oh, they're beautiful!" Marie said as Yip pulled an aqua Country Squire station wagon up in front of the steps. The earrings were black onyx and gold bead drops, and they matched Marie's outfit perfectly. Without hesitation she took off her studs and handed them to Zalman. "Put these in your pocket, will you? Tracee, these are just lovely. Thank you so much," she said, slipping into the back seat of the car.

"I'm so glad you like them." Tracee smiled. "Now Jerry, don't be mean to E.Y., okay?"

"Mean? Me? Surely you jest, woman," Zalman said, getting into the back seat next to Marie.

"You know what I'm talking about," Tracee insisted, with the air of a sixth-grade math teacher. She slid behind the wheel of the big wagon, and Yip moved obligingly over to the passenger's seat. "E.Y.'s a little eccentric, that's all. You're supposed to be on *our* side, so if he starts in about World O' Yip—"

"World O' Yip?" Zalman and Marie chorused.

"Haven't I told you about World O' Yip?" Tracee said innocently, putting the big car in gear. "I can't believe I haven't told you about World O' Yip. . . ."

"It's gonna be great!" Yip enthused as they headed up the hill toward Knotte Pines, the eucalyptus and chaparral hillsides flashing by in the deepening dusk beneath a cold navy blue sky. "See, World O' Yip will be more than a restaurant. It'll be a total health and personal growth concept right here in Santa Barbara. We'll have everything!" he said as Tracee stopped the car in front of the huge white stucco house. "Holistic healing, crystal gazing, hypnotherapy, flotation tanks, a world-class gym, total body packs, massage, you name it. Plus, of course, gourmet food with nutritional emphasis, including personalized diets. World O' Yip will be in the forefront! That's what the camcorder is for," he explained, holding it up. "I'm shooting a promotional video, you know, family and friends at home. I'll tell you all about it later, Jerry. I know you'll be interested."

"Who wouldn't be?" Zalman said caustically as he helped Marie out of the car.

Tracee opened the front door without waiting for the butler and ran inside. "Yoooo-hoooo," she called. "Yoooo-hoooo . . ." She and Yip disappeared, and her voice echoed down a seemingly endless series of corridors. Zalman and Marie, entering the room behind her, stopped and stared around in amazement.

The foyer of Knotte Pines was a complete contrast to the white stucco and tile exterior. E. Y. Knotte clearly suffered from a surfeit of Merrie Olde England. The room was dank, had a high ceiling and gray marble floor, and was lined with a silent assortment of knights in full armor, each holding a sword or mace or shield in a vaguely threatening manner. Flags and pennants featuring heraldic coats-of-arms dangled above them, emitting an aroma of dust and mildew.

"Yikes!" Marie muttered. "What the hell is this, the B-movie version of *Ivanhoe?*"

"Calm down, doll," Zalman said, reaching up and chucking one of the knights under the chin, then rapping on his stomach. A hollow ping emanated from the knight's tin tummy. "See? No problem."

"Listen, do you think there're any salamanders in here? I seriously hate salamanders. . . ."

"This way, please," a sepulchral voice intoned. The butler had crept up behind them on his silent soles. "Mr. Knotte is in the bar, sir . . . if you'd care to follow me."

"What's your name?" Zalman asked as he and Marie followed the butler down a half-timbered hallway decorated with yet more silent knights.

"Brunson, sir," he said, sucking on his teeth.

"Well, Brunson," Zalman said jovially, "this is a cheerful little room, isn't it?"

"I'm sure I wouldn't know, sir," Brunson said, without a flicker behind his pale eyes. He opened a huge, studded door and bowed slightly. "Mr. Zalman and Miss Thrasher," he announced.

"Thanks, Brunson," Zalman muttered as he and Marie went into the room.

"Howdy, pardner!" a reedy voice called. "Welcome to Knotte Pines!"

Zalman stared around the room with a sinking feeling of dread, doom, and despair. This room was decorated in a completely different style. Rather than the dank, cavernous, dungeon effect of the front hallway, the room in which they now stood was straight out of "Gunsmoke" and seemed to be a rendition of E. Y. Knotte's idea of a Western saloon. The room was paneled in walnut. There was a long mahogany bar with a glittering mirror behind it, and over the mirror was a big oil painting of a buxom but somnolent redhead wearing little more than a gauze scarf who gazed out over the room with heavy-lidded torpor. There were also antique slot machines, a pool table, a scattering of poker tables and chairs, plus the usual complement of upholstered bar stools. In addition, there were many glassdoored display cases filled with knives, pistols, and rifles.

E. Y. Knotte was behind the bar. He was a wiry little gent with the sharp, acquisitive eyes of a hungry vulture's chick. He was going thin in front and had carefully combed his brown hair down and over his forehead in an effort to conceal his incipient baldness. He looked close to eighty but was still going strong, with the quick step and brusque movements of a man dedicated to an eternal alliance with his rowing machine. His eyes were a bright but watery blue, and he was still wearing his own teeth.

"Howdy, pardners!" he called again. "Have a screwdriver! It's the specialty of the house! What's that son of mine?" he demanded sharply. "Gone to get hisself a cup of herbal hogwash," he muttered with contempt.

Zalman glanced behind him. Yip and Tracee were nowhere to be seen. "I don't know, Mr. Knotte," he said, taking charge of the situation. He took Marie's elbow, and they strode to the bar, planted themselves on a pair of stools, and shook hands with E. Y. Knotte, whose grip, Zalman noted painfully, was capable of collapsing tennis balls.

"I thought Yip and Tracee were right behind us, Mr. Knotte, but they seem to have disappeared," Zalman said easily.

*"Rumpf,"* E.Y. replied. "Say, what happened to your nose there, young fella?" He leaned across the bar, staring into Zalman's face at point-blank range. "Looks a little scaly. You gotta be careful about too much sun, you know. Skin cancer's a major cause of death among the unsuspecting. I read that in *Reader's Digest.* If I'd known I was gonna last so long I'd of taken better care of myself when I was younger, you damn betcha. You take my advice and get yourself some sunscreen or better yet wear yourself a hat. You ask me, it's a major reason right there why the modern world's the sorry mess it is, nobody wears a hat these days. Whole shebang started going to hell when folks gave up hats. Sun's harmful rays poached their brains like eggs. Well, then, how about that drink?" E.Y. concluded.

Zalman looked critically at E.Y. He was wearing full cowboy regalia, including a pair of pearl-handled Colt revolvers strapped to his hips. He had a ten-gallon Stetson, calico shirt, cheerful red bandanna, blue jeans, and leather chaps. Tooled Tony Lamas and silver rowel spurs that jingle, jangle, jingled completed his chic ensemble. There was no question about it, E. Y. Knotte was perfectly togged out for the 1880s. "I'd think you'd be drinking red-eye," Zalman said.

E.Y. laughed harshly. "That's good, that is! Well, I tell you, son, I drink a screwdriver 'cause that way you get a good wallop from the booze plus you get your vitamins. Even if it is a damn Commie drink, vodka is. Tell you, though," he said, leaning forward on the bar confidentially, "I don't use that damn Stolichnaya stuff no more, not since they set off the big blast over at Cher-no-beel. I hate them damn Commies, but I had to hand it to 'em, they made good vodka, before they went and radiated the hell out of it, the damn fools. Now I don't want it no more!"

E.Y. laughed heartily as he tossed a few plump oranges

into a tall juicer, whirred them around, and poured the frothy nectar into a pair of Waterford glasses. He splashed a liberal dollop of vodka into one glass, looked appraisingly at Marie, and put a smaller slug into her glass. "Just a teeny-tiny one for you, miss," he said, "'cause you're just a teeny-tiny girl!" He laughed mischievously, slid the glasses across the bar to Zalman and Marie, then reached over and pinched Marie on the cheek.

Zalman watched Marie with great interest. It was even money if she was going to punch the old man's lights out or let him tweak her cheek. Marie sucked in her breath and smiled. "You do that again, Mr. Knotte," she said sweetly, "and I'll kick in your kneecaps."

"Good! Good!" E.Y. said with approval. "Like a girl with spunk. All of 'em around here're no better than a sack of jellyfish. Now, don't you two be afraid to ask for more. That's the house rule. You want a drink, speak up and I'll make it for you. I like to play bartender," he added conversationally. "That's why I had the bar done up this way. Nice, isn't it?" he asked, gazing around fondly at his domain. "Kinda homey . . ."

"Homey," Zalman echoed. "Homey. You could say it was homey. Well, Mr. Knotte—"

"Call me E.Y."

"Well, E.Y., Yip says you had some trouble with your car?"

"You damn betcha. Went right into the pool and had me an unexpected bath, is what I did. Hah!" He laughed, refilling his own glass. "Now tell me, son. You used to be married to my Yip's girl, is that right?"

Zalman sipped his drink casually. "You make a good screwdriver, E.Y. Yes, Tracee and I were divorced some years ago. It was a friendly divorce."

"Hah! No such animal. I been married four times, and I can tell you, a friendly divorce is one where nobody gets shot."

Marie choked on her drink.

"I make that too strong for you, sweet thing?" E.Y. asked, his leathery face crinkling into a fatherly grin.

"No," Marie said. "I like strong drinks, E.Y."

"Good girl!" he said. "You'll fit in around here. That darn son of mine with his darn health drinks. Thinks if a man takes a drink at the end of the day he's a damn alkie. Life's too tough to take sober, I can tell you that. Man needs a drink along about sundown. At least he does if he's done my work. My son don't need a drink 'cause he's been sitting on his damn bee-hind all day long." He stabbed viciously at an intercom button. "Mercer!" he yelled into the speaker. "Mercer! More oranges, goddammit."

Thirty seconds later Mercer Lamont shot into the room, a twenty-pound net bag of oranges over his shoulder, looking like a laid-back Santa from La-La Land. He stared at Zalman and Marie with unaffected, childlike interest. "Howdy . . . folks . . ." he said with elaborate slowness, concentrating on the syllables to get them right. He stood about five-foot-ten and weighed in at a taut 170 or so. His tanned arms bulged gently over the short sleeves of his lavender Ralph Lauren polo shirt; his muscular thighs rippled out of khaki walking shorts. He had light brown hair cropped Marine-short and steely gray eyes. Except for the loopy grin of a stoned six-year-old, Mercer Lamont looked like the kind of guy who loved to split concrete blocks with his bare hands, just for something to do. He smiled happily at the guests, clearly entranced by the idea of new playmates. "I'm . . . Mercer . . ." he said shyly. He extended his sinewy paw to Marie. "Pleased to meetcha. . . ."

Marie took his hand and smiled. "Hello, Mercer," she said carefully. "My name's Marie. . . ."

Mercer swung the net bag over the bar with ease and set it down at E. Y. Knotte's feet. "There ya go," he said proudly. He took a stool next to Marie. "You came with Mr. Zalman, Tracee said. . . ."

"That's right, she did," Zalman broke in. "And why don't you call me Jerry?"

"Okay, I will," Mercer intoned, ever so slowly. "Jerry . . ."

E.Y. was busy tossing oranges into the blender. "Okay, Mercer, get ready. . . ."

Mercer got up and went down to the end of the bar. E.Y. filled a tall glass and expertly shot it down the length of the long, smooth bar, and Mercer caught it on the fly, drained the glass in one big gulp, then smiled happily. It was obviously a routine they'd done many times, and like two small boys with a frog in a jar they were absurdly proud of it.

Marie sucked in her breath with exaggerated awe. "Ohhhhh," she sighed in a voice which sounded like Teddy Ruxpin's, "isn't that cute!"

Zalman shot her a sharp glance. He had the feeling he was in for a long evening of googly-woogly from her, and he wasn't looking forward to it.

"Pretty good, huh?" Mercer said, preening. "We saw it in a mooovie. . . ."

"Hi, everybody . . ." Tracee was poised in the doorway, Yip at her side, his camcorder whirring like a wet wasp. Together they looked like a glossy print ad for Bain de Soleil.

"Get that dang thing out of my face!" E. Y. Knotte barked.

"Aw, Dad . . ." his son whined, dropping the camcorder to his side. "Don't you want to be in my video?"

"Now let's not bicker this evening," Tracee said helplessly, looking from her husband to her ex-husband and back again.

"E.Y.," Zalman said with false heartiness, "how about another one of those screwdrivers?" He had the soggy feeling that he was standing in quicksand, and it didn't look like anybody was going to yank him out.

Luckily, E.Y.'s attention was diverted. "Okey-dokey. Got plenty of damn vitamins in 'em. Like I said, you get your booze, you get your vitamins. You should like that, Yip," he prodded.

Yip opened his mouth to speak, but a hard glance from his wife shut it for him. "Shall we sit down, dear?" she said. Wordlessly, Yip followed Tracee to the bar, setting his camcorder gently on the stool next to his.

"Yoooooo-hoooooo," an extended trill echoed from the hallway. "Yoooooo-hoooooo . . ."

"In here, babykins!" E.Y. called. "Got one in the blender for you, Buttercup. . . ."

Rhonda Warwick Knotte appeared in the doorway, and without hesitation every man in the room sprang to his feet. She had a great froth of auburn hair, carefully arranged to look easily disarranged, and her light green chiffon dress augmented the green of her great cat's eyes, eyes that showed only the faintest signs of wear and tear around the edges, eyes that still held the promise of a pool a man could go bankrupt in. The cream of her flawless skin peeked from beneath her gown, and as she flowed across the room there was the slightest echo of a rim shot on each rounded hip.

Rhonda Warwick Knotte hadn't been much of an actress. It was mainly her breathtaking beauty that had attracted audiences until, with customary fickleness, her star was tarnished by time and the public's greedy love transferred itself to another, younger face. But Rhonda Warwick didn't give up. As McCoy had mentioned, she'd sailed for Cannes and begun an affair with legendary though slightly down-on-his-luck film tycoon James M. Maugardus, and the press had thrilled to each new episode as they'd battled their way across the continent. When it finally ended Zalman had still been a lad, so he figured she now had to be pushing fifty, fifty-five. Then, in a masterstroke of publicity genius, Rhonda Warwick married E. Y. Knotte and retired from show biz. Rather than spend the remainder of her days drifting aboard the Love Boat of the Damned or cranking out TV undergarment commercials for the incontinent, Rhonda had become a society hostess who only allowed her face and figure to be used for charitable purposes, preferably if said charitable purposes included a six-page spread in *Town and Country*. In other words, Rhonda Warwick Knotte had fallen into a tub of butter.

Rhonda Knotte sauntered over to the bar and took the stool next to Zalman. "Tracee told me all about you," she said with a faintly suggestive air.

"I find that hard to believe," Zalman said easily. "Tracee and I haven't seen each other for ages."

"You have a lovely home, Mrs. Knotte," Marie put in smoothly. "It's very kind of you to have us for dinner."

Rhonda looked past Zalman and smiled graciously at Marie. "I hope you'll let me show you around after dinner. I do so enjoy giving my little tours. Darling?" she addressed her husband. "Didn't you say you had a drinkie for me?"

Marie elbowed Zalman in the ribs and rolled her eyes.

"Here you go, Buttercup!" E.Y. said, handing Rhonda a tall, icy screwdriver. "This'll set you up."

"Thank you so much, darling," she said as she turned back to Zalman. "You're an attorney, Mr. Zalman? Do you have a specialty?" She sipped her drink, leaving a lipstick print on the edge of the glass.

"Like everyone in Beverly Hills, I do quite a bit of divorce work," Zalman said. "And often I'm able to settle things for my clients without the strain of a court case."

"Settle things? What things?"

"As Yip says in his commercials, it's a rough, tough world, and people often have problems they can't solve. They come to me. Sometimes I'm able to help them find an answer, sometimes not. In plain English, sometimes I can fix things for people. If I can't, well, there's always the legal system. It takes longer and it costs more, which is why they come to me in the first place." Zalman smiled easily and watched Rhonda's face as she stared vacantly into his eyes. He could tell that she hadn't heard a word

61

he'd said. She'd long ago mastered the trick of looking directly at a man and seeming terribly interested, but he guessed she was probably thinking about the next sale at I. Magnin.

"Yes, life can be so difficult, can't it?" Rhonda said as if she were being forced to choose between diamonds and pearls.

E.Y. looked up from behind the bar, his watery blue eyes misting over. "This is great, isn't it?" he asked. "I like to have my whole happy family around me at the cocktail hour." He scowled suddenly and looked sideways at Yip and Tracee. "Just wish there were more of us. A little nipper, crawling around on the floor, that's what the hell I'd like to see."

Tracee smiled weakly and flushed, her cheeks and throat glowing rose beneath her tan. She reached out and took Yip's hand.

"Now, Dad," he said, trying to defend his wife. "You promised. . . ."

"Didn't," E.Y. said petulantly. "Didn't promise a thing. Don't intend to promise nothing either. Don't like promises. They're always broken."

Zalman could see he was in the presence of a regular homespun philosopher, Plato in buckskin, and he felt a duty to his ex-wife to try to change the subject, especially since her present husband was making such a bum job of it. "You're a gun collector, E.Y.?" he asked, indicating the glass-fronted cases that ran along the back of the room. There were many rifles, all of them quite fancy, and though Zalman knew next to nothing about guns, he figured that only the best would do for E. Y. Knotte.

E.Y. nodded, his venom momentarily deflected. "Pistols, rifles, knives, swords. I like weapons. Man has a lot of guns around the house, he figures he can defend his family," he said, as if there were a hoard of Visigoths poised on the outskirts of Santa Barbara, ready for an afternoon's pillaging. "I guess a smart fella like you could see that as soon as you came in, huh, Jerry?"

"Well," Zalman said modestly, "of course, Tracee told me what to expect." This was a complete lie. Tracee had told him next to nothing, and it was that very fact that had led Zalman to believe that he and Marie would be spending a relatively normal weekend with relatively normal people. This had proved a total falsehood, since clearly the entire Knotte household was about as normal as the inhabitants of a locked ward during the full moon.

E.Y. waved a liver-spotted hand around the room expansively. "I'm a quick-draw fan, Jerry. Say, you ever done any shooting?"

Zalman held up his own hand in a gesture of placation. "Personally, guns make me nervous, E.Y. They have a habit of going off."

E.Y. rasped a phlegm-filled laugh. "Let's just say that guns give people ideas, eh? That's why I like to have plenty of 'em around. That way I always have a better idea than the next fella!" E.Y. laughed heartily at his little play on words, and the assembled company joined in halfheartedly. "We're gonna have a quick-draw contest here, me and my pals, in just a few days. You stick around, Jerry, and I promise you'll see some real shooting." He turned to his wife and refilled her empty glass. "Say, where's Lisa? Get on the horn, babykins, and get her down here. It's time for my dinner."

Rhonda nodded, walked very carefully over to the house phone, and spoke briefly into it. "She's on her way," she announced. "Lisa is my husband's secretary," she explained to Zalman and Marie. "A lovely girl and terribly helpful. He just doesn't like to sit down to dinner unless we're all here, his whole little family around him."

"Isn't that sweet," Marie said. "So cozy."

"Isn't it?" Rhonda said, draining her glass. "If there's just a squidge left in the blender, E.Y. . . ." She smiled

63

winningly at her husband, who poured her another drink and gallantly tipped his ten-gallon hat.

A brunette with large, horn-rimmed glasses burst into the room. "Sorry to be late,' she said. "I was on the phone." She was a nice-looking girl, twenty-three or -four, with the straightforward good looks that made Zalman think of the captain of a girls' hockey team on a snowy winter morn. She wasn't spectacular like Rhonda or Tracee, but she had a good firm jaw, and a simple charm shone from her eyes. Introductions were made all around, and as Zalman rose from his bar stool to shake hands he could see that Lisa Comden had been crying. She'd bathed her face in cold water, but the puffiness around her red-rimmed eyes was evident, though she'd obviously tried to hide it by a fresh application of makeup.

Yip, undaunted by his father's admonitions, reached down for his camera and began to shoot everyone in the room. He made a frame with his hands and distractedly gazed about, mumbling, "Shadows . . . if only there were shadows . . ."

Luckily, Brunson announced dinner and everyone trooped into the dining room, which continued the Merrie Olde England motif of the entrance hall. There was a long, ornately carved table big enough to seat ten with comfort. Heavy mock-Elizabethan tapestries depicting hunting scenes of slaughtered stags covered the walnut-paneled walls, and a bank of serving tables with platoons of silver dishes and a massive silver tea service stood guard at the end of the long room.

"What? No trenchers?" Zalman muttered to Marie as he settled her into a chair on E.Y.'s right. Mercer sat on E.Y.'s left, while Zalman's calligraphed place card put him at the foot of the table on Rhonda's right. Yip and Tracee were isolated in the middle of the table; Lisa Comden was on Rhonda's left.

Brunson began to serve the first course, a large shrimp cocktail, in honor, Zalman suspected, of the family

Knotte's financial origins. Rhonda smiled pleasantly, if somewhat blearily, and leaned forward toward Zalman, exposing a pale expanse of bosom as she did so.

"I'm so glad you're here, Jerry," she whispered. "Tracee told me why you've come, and I can't tell you how happy I am about it. That horrible Mercer!" she said, glancing severely down the table at her husband's sidekick. "I'm sure he's the one who fooled around with E.Y.'s car." She nibbled delicately at her shrimp, probing the dead crustacean's plump little body with her fork.

Zalman wasn't surprised to hear that Tracee had confided in Rhonda Knotte, especially since Tracee had sworn secrecy. As an attorney and a fellow who numbered himself among the worldly wise, Jerry Zalman knew that there were very, very few true secrets on the planet Earth. Human beings were simply incapable of keeping their yaps shut. There was something deep in their constitutions, in their very beings, that demanded they tell all, to all, all the bloody time. "What makes you say that, Rhonda?" he asked smoothly. "Is there something you haven't told Tracee?"

Rhonda looked briefly startled, her emerald-green eyes widening momentarily in the flickering candlelight. "Nooooo," she stalled, with the air of someone who isn't quite sure of the correct answer. "Nooooo . . . it's just that Mercer is so . . . terrible! Look at him!"

Zalman followed Rhonda's disgusted gaze down the table to Mercer, whose shrimp cocktail had somehow managed to leap from his plate and end up on the tablecloth. Mercer stabbed ineffectually at the mess, trying to rectify his gaffe.

"Okay, so his table manners aren't exactly up to Miss Manners," Zalman laughed. "And so he hasn't got a very big brainpan. But that hardly makes him a candidate for murderer of the week." Brunson whipped Zalman's shrimp cocktail away and slid a splendid spinach salad in its place. "Now Brunson's another story," Zalman observed out of the corner of his mouth as the dolorous butler glided around the table out of earshot. "Brunson's downright sinister."

"Well?" E.Y. suddenly roared, making everybody jump. "Howsaboutit, you two? A little nipper, crawling around under the table? Better get started! Time's running out!"

"Dad . . ." Yip warned. "I asked you before not to bring this up. Tracee's very sensitive about it, and so am I. We've got plenty of time for kids. These things take time. . . ."

"Shouldn't take that much damn time, you ask me," E.Y. growled, spearing a shrimp the size of a small dachshund from his dish with the hunting knife which completed his Dodge City ensemble.

"For heaven's sake, E.Y., don't use that horrible knife at the table!" his wife cried. "It's so frightening, so . . . pointy. . . ."

E.Y. rasped a laugh. "I like this here little shrimp-sticker, Rhonda honey. It used to belong to William S. Hart," he explained, peering in Zalman's general direction. "He was a famous cowboy movie star back in the silent days. And Bill Hart, he got this little knife from Charlie Russell, the cowboy artist. So you see, it's got plenty of history behind it, and now that I've got it, I intend to put it to good use." Slowly, he bit into the shrimp on his knife, the red cocktail sauce dripping down the knife handle and onto the snowy tablecloth like a coagulating freshet of blood.

Rhonda sighed. Tracee sighed. Lisa sighed. Even Marie sighed. All four women were unable to ignore this blatant flaunting of everything they'd learned at their mothers' knees. But despite his protests, E.Y. quieted down, and the rest of the meal passed quickly. Zalman ate his roast beef happily, although Yip and Tracee barely touched theirs, nibbling disconsolately around the edges.

"Probably longing for tofu, huh?" Zalman needled Yip.

Yip brightened. "Boy, you're an amazing guy, Jerry.

That's just what I was thinking. Tofu is the food of the future, you know, and I'm bringing out a whole new line of tofu-based foods in the next few months. Oh, I know," he said, as though Zalman was disagreeing, "I know there's Tofutti. I know all about Rice Dream. But my 'Yip Cream' will top all of those. 'Yip Cream' will be the best non-dairy dessert ever made," he said fervently. "My new line will revolutionize the natural food market."

"Tell him about your damn health deal," E.Y. sputtered.

"Jerry knows all about World O' Yip!" Tracee said defensively.

"This darn fool son of mine is building this health deal right out over the damn ocean," E.Y. snorted. "Damn thing's gonna fall right in, you mark my damn words."

"Now E.Y. . . ." Rhonda soothed.

"Goddamn health food is un-American, you ask me. Americans want grease and plenty of it! Didn't I prove that with my Shrimpkins?" he roared. "Huh? I damn tricked them into eating fish! Americans want grease! Try a Shrimpkin, you want something good." He stabbed furiously at his meat.

From outside the dining room door there came the unmistakable sounds of a scuffle. Two voices, one of them Brunson's, were raised in argument. There was the sound of furniture hitting the floor and some pained yelping.

"What the hell's going on?" E.Y. demanded irritably, "Brunson, what's going on out there?"

The door burst open suddenly, slamming into the wall with a terrific whack, and a disheveled young man in a gray business suit stood there, his fists clenched. "Lisa," he wailed tearfully. "Baby . . ."

Lisa Comden half stood in her place, her eyes wide, an expression on her face reminiscent of a spotlighted deer. "Ed . . ." she faltered. "Please, not here . . ."

"Jeez, another nut!" Zalman muttered.

"What the hell do you want, Robin?" E.Y. asked angrily,

staring at the young man. "I'm trying to eat my damn dinner here!"

"You old weasel!" Ed Robin cried. "How could you do this to Lisa?"

"Pass the wine, will you?" Zalman called down the table to Marie. "I need a drink."

"Me!" E.Y. shot a crafty glance at Rhonda. "Do what?" he asked in the innocent voice of an aged, tricky fox caught with chicken feathers on his chin. "I didn't do anything. . . ."

"Ed, please," Lisa Comden cried helplessly.

"I love her!" Robin said stoutly. "And you . . . you . . ."

Rhonda tossed off the remains of the screwdriver she'd carried in to dinner. "Explain yourself, Mr. Robin," she said coldly, her eyes shifting from her husband to Lisa Comden and back again. "What are you talking about?"

"Now sugarplum . . ." E.Y. said.

Robin yanked at his pink polka-dot power tie. "That old goat's been after Lisa for months, creeping into her room at night, trying to buy her favors!"

"'Buy her favors,'" Zalman said to nobody. "What is this, Rosemary Rogers?"

"Don't be so smart, Jerry," Marie called.

Rhonda turned angrily to E.Y. "Is this true?" she asked, her voice outraged.

Trapped, E. Y. Knotte did the only thing a man in his position could do. He reached for his gun.

"Jesus H. Christ!" Zalman yelled as E.Y. blasted one of his six-shooters through the dining room ceiling.

"Get him, boss!" Mercer yelled happily.

"Dad, no!" Yip shouted.

As if with one voice, all of the women in the room let out the shrill howl of trapped Siamese cats and dived under the table. E.Y., his head whipping left to right, blasted off another round, this time into one of the slaughtered-stag tapestries.

"The hell with this," Zalman said as he and Yip and Mercer followed the women under the table. Survival was certainly the better part of valor. He found himself face to face with Rhonda's expansive cleavage.

"Robin, you cluck! Stand still and lemme blast you!" E.Y.'s voice thundered. There was another roar of gunfire, followed by the tender tinkling of shattered porcelain. E.Y. fired again.

Rhonda moaned in fear. Zalman discreetly tried to shift his face out of her chest but she clung to him, shivering in terror. "Please," he said, "you're crushing my cigars!"

"Jerry!" Marie stage-whispered. "What the hell's going on?"

"Ask Lisa!" Zalman shot back. "It's her boyfriend E.Y.'s trying to shoot."

Lisa Comden was half buried under Yip. "He's insane!" she whimpered, although Zalman's fine legal mind noted she didn't mention whether Ed Robin or E. Y. Knotte was the Nutty Professor.

Overhead, Robin hollered, "Lisa, you'll get yours, and you, too, E.Y.! I'll kill you, you old . . . you old . . ." He stopped, evidently at a loss for words.

"Lecher?" Zalman called helpfully. "Howsabout Casanova? C'mon, you guys, you're scaring the women, and I don't feel too good myself!"

"I'll be back!" Robin shouted. "I swear it!" Then came the sound of running feet, a slammed door, and silence.

E.Y.'s harsh cackle filled the room. "Damn! That was fun! Come on out, everybody, the coast is clear."

Slowly, the group from beneath the table untangled itself and came up for air. One by one, they flopped down in their chairs. Rhonda poured herself the last of the wine. Tracee moaned softly while Yip buried his head in his hands and did yoga deep breathing.

Marie snuggled up to Zalman. "Are you all right?" she asked. "I thought Rhonda was giving you the Heimlich maneuver down there."

"I'm fine," Zalman laughed. "How about you?"

"I could live without this," she said. "I'll see how Tracee is, poor thing."

Zalman watched as his lady love comforted his ex-wife. *I'll never understand women,* he thought, *never in this lifetime.*

E.Y. was back at the head of the table, happily digging into a huge slab of roast beef. His revolver lay in his butter plate, smoke still wafting from its gunmetal-blue barrel. "Buttercup, we got any horseradish?" he demanded.

Rhonda blinked at her husband, speechless. "Ask Brunson for it," she said shortly. "I'll say good night, if you don't mind." She frosted the assembly with a glacial smile and did the alcoholic glide out of the room, knocking over a large English ivy plant as she went.

E.Y. continued to chew his food, unperturbed, and Zalman rang for Brunson. The inscrutable butler sailed in seconds later, seemingly oblivious to the condition of guests and dining room alike.

"Brunson," Zalman said, "some horseradish for Mr. Knotte, another bottle of wine—better make that two—and have that cleaned up, please." He gestured toward the remains of the ivy plant.

Brunson didn't miss a beat. "Very good, sir." He swiveled expertly on his heel and vanished.

"You're all right, Jerry," E.Y. observed approvingly. "A take-charge guy. I like a take-charge guy for a lawyer. Tell you what," he said, cramming a chunk of meat into his maw, "since it looks like Robin isn't going to be handling my legal business anymore, why don't you take a whack at it?"

Zalman was rarely taken aback, but he had the embarassing feeling there were dollar signs lighting up in his eyes like Uncle Scrooge McDuck. E.Y.'s business, even the odds and ends of E.Y. Knotte's business, was worth a considerable piece of change. Nevertheless, ethics demanded a certain amount of professional protestation.

"E.Y.," he said slowly, "you hardly know me. A relationship of this nature, a legal relationship, can't be entered into lightly. There are certain . . ."

"Considerations?" E.Y. asked mischievously. "Horse puck!" he said flatly as Brunson silently slid a crystal dish of horseradish down in front of him and poured fresh wine all around. "You're a smart guy, Jerry. Hell, Tracee here told me everything I need to know about you. And besides, I like a young guy for a lawyer. Nothing's worse for a geezer like me than having his lawyer die on him. 'Cept, that is, if he plugs him himself. . . ." E.Y. added, emitting his rasping laugh. "We'll talk more tomorrow, okey-dokey?"

"Okey-dokey," Zalman said.

E.Y. pushed his chair back from the table. "Well, boys and girls, that was some party, and I hate to break up the fun, but it's time for my swim."

"Swim?" Zalman asked blankly, glancing at his Piaget watch. It was close to 11:30 at night.

"Yep," E.Y. said, stretching. "I'm a lifetime member of the Midnight Polar Bear Club. Never miss a night."

"You want me, boss?" Mercer asked.

"Nah, go ahead to bed, Merce," E.Y. said. "But don't forget, get on over to Porter's first thing tomorrow and pick up them guns, okey-dokey?"

"You bet, boss." Mercer smiled. "I won't forget."

And with that, E. Y. Knotte left the room, Mercer close on his heels.

Zalman looked over at Marie, and the two of them burst into laughter. "You still owe me a trip to Hawaii, Jerry," she reminded him. "And after tonight's little performance I don't think I'm apt to forget about it, either. . . ."

There was a groan from beneath the dining room table. Zalman lifted the tablecloth and stared underneath. Lisa Comden was still there, lying in a fetal heap. "Oh God," she said when she saw Zalman staring at her, "this is so humiliating. . . ."

71

"Come on out, kiddo," he coaxed gently. "Might as well rejoin the living. E.Y.'s gone for a swim, and Rhonda's said nighty-night. It's as safe as it's gonna get."

Slowly, Lisa crawled out on all fours like a wet Pekingese. She shook her head miserably, stood up, and straightened her rumpled frock. "How could this happen to me?" she asked tearfully. "I was in the upper five percent of my class at Harvard. Things like this aren't supposed to *happen* to someone who's in the upper five percent of her class at Harvard." She sat down and took the wine Zalman poured for her. "How could he *do* this to me?" she moaned. "I'm going to die of shame."

"Relax," Zalman said lightly. "Nobody's died of shame in America since the invention of 'Wheel of Fortune.' Ed's just a guy in love, that's all."

Lisa gulped her wine and gestured for more. "E.Y.'s a dear man, really," she sniffled at Tracee and Yip, who still looked ashen. "He didn't mean anything by it. . . ."

Marie put her arm around Lisa's shoulder. "E.Y. means plenty by it, if you ask me. He was groping my thigh all through dinner till I poked him with my salad fork."

Zalman grinned. "That's what I like about you, Marie, you know how to wield your cutlery. E.Y. *is* a goat. And pardon me, Yip, but I agree with Marie, your dad's not exactly harmless. What'd he do, back you into the file room when you weren't looking?" Zalman asked Lisa.

"Something like that," Lisa said miserably. "I shouldn't have told Ed about it."

"No, you shouldn't have," Marie agreed. "You should never tell your boyfriend when somebody puts the serious moves on you. Just upsets 'em."

Zalman cocked an eyebrow. "I'll keep that in mind, doll. Look." He addressed Lisa. "Relax. Not much damage was done. E.Y. will forgive Ed in the morning. I'll talk to them both and smooth things over. Much as I'd like a piece of the Knotte action, this isn't the way I like to get business.

Okay? Go have a sauna or something. Get a good night's sleep. I'll take care of things. Trust me."

"I suppose you're right," Lisa said, her voice tired and dispirited. "I'll have a swim, but I'm going to make damn sure E.Y.'s not around. And I'm quitting tomorrow. I can't stand it here anymore." She left without speaking to the others, and in her wake Zalman, Marie, Tracee, and Yip stared at one another wordlessly. What was there left to say? Then, from the side of the house, a diving board spronged and a body cannonballed into the water, followed by the sound of rasping laughter.

"Great," Zalman said. "We've got an octogenarian who thinks he's Johnny Weissmuller, a love-crazed secretary, a wicked stepmother, and other assorted loonies. Tracee, it's a good thing we're divorced, that's all I can say, because if we weren't this could spell disaster for our marriage. . . ."

"Jerry," Marie warned, "give it a rest, will you? Poor Tracee's been through enough this evening without your badgering her." Tracee looked gratefully in Marie's direction.

Once again, Zalman stared at his lady love open-mouthed. Was this the same woman who, only a few days before, had had a screaming fit over the possibility of spending a weekend in the same general geographical vicinity as his ex-wife? And was this same lady love now acting as his ex-wife's protector? "Words fail me," he told Marie.

"Thank heavens," Tracee put in primly. She turned to Yip and smiled sweetly. "Can we go home now, Yippie?"

"Of course, dearest," Yip said. "I'll just see where Brunson hid our coats. Back in a flash."

Zalman, Marie, and Tracee sat at the dining room table without speaking. Zalman considered lighting his after-dinner cigar but thought better of it. Yip would probably bitch about smoke in the car, and Zalman figured he'd wait for his cigar until he could enjoy it without any kibbitzing. But one thing he knew: If he had to stay in this rubber room any longer, he was going to foam at the mouth. "Ladies," he said, standing, "are we ready to leave, I hope?" He blew out the candles.

"Where's my bag?" Tracee said dully. "I know I had it when we came in. It's a little blue mesh . . ."

"Blue?" Marie asked. "I thought that was Lisa's. I'm sure I saw . . . oh, I bet it's under the table. . . ." She looked over at Zalman, who instantly began to shake his head.

"Not a chance," he said strongly. "You want to crawl under the table again, you go right ahead. If you think *I'm* crawling under the table for a second time, you're sadly—"

Suddenly, there was a sharp sizzling noise outside the house, followed by the harsh crackle of burning electricity. Tracee gave a little yelp of terror, and in the brief second before the lights went out, Zalman saw her eyes flash open in fear. She'd always been afraid of the dark, he remembered.

"Jeez, what have I done to deserve this?" Zalman moaned, trying to keep it light. "I'm a regular guy. I eat Wheaties, I contribute to charity, I'm kind to old ladies, I—"

"Jerry, for God's sake!" Marie said in exasperation.

Zalman fumbled through his pockets, found his gold Dunhill lighter, and relit the candles. "Don't worry," he said. "It's probably just some terrorists destroying the local power station. No cause for alarm . . ."

"Jerry! Jerry!" Yip's voice was hollow. "Where the hell is everybody?"

Zalman took a candlestick and went out into the hall, feeling a little like Wee Willie Winkie on his way to bed. "Some fun, eh, Yip? Remind me to have dinner with you more often."

Yip's face was contorted in the shivering candlelight. He was holding a flashlight, and his spasmodic gestures kept sweeping the beam into Zalman's face. "Jerry, something's happened," he said in a shaky voice. "Outside by the pool, quick . . ."

Zalman didn't hesitate. He could see by Yip's terrified expression that whatever had happened, it wasn't good. He left the candlestick on a table in the hall, took the flashlight, and followed Yip at a dead run.

Yip went out through a pair of French doors leading to a large brick patio. The moon was full, and the substantial grounds were illuminated in its pale light, the gracious sweep of the bougainvillea casting a sharp image in black and white relief against the soft white glow of the house. A hooded figure in a white terrycloth robe was standing by the pool, looking into the deep end where a body lay floating facedown in the dark water. Yip got there first, though Zalman was close enough behind to hear the shock in his voice when his father looked up out of the hood of his robe.

"Dad," Yip faltered. "Thank God! I thought it was . . ."

"It's Lisa," E.Y. said in a flat voice, drained of emotion. Suddenly, he sounded very tired.

Zalman stopped short, trained his light on the pool, and stared at the bobbing figure as it drifted gently back and forth in the water.

Tracee and Marie came running up behind him, and he heard Tracee gasp and felt her grab convulsively at his arm as she realized what was in the pool. "Jerry, my God," she said. "What happened? Is that . . . is that Lisa?" she asked, her voice faint with horror. She took a small step forward and stared into the pool's murky water. "I think I'm going to be sick," she said softly. "No kidding . . ." She turned away from the sight of the body and covered her eyes with her hands.

"Holy smoke!" Marie breathed. "Just like William Holden in *Sunset Boulevard!*"

"Please, Marie," Zalman said sharply. "This is no time for movie reviews!" Tracee made a little gagging noise, and he shifted the flashlight beam away from Lisa Comden and onto his feet.

"I really feel sick," Tracee said weakly. "Honest . . ."

"Ladies," Zalman said quietly, "I suggest you return to the house immediately, if not sooner. Marie, if you would be so kind as to telephone the police. And, babe," he added softly, "see if you can hustle up to Rhonda's room and check her out. Mercer, too, if you catch my drift." He handed her the flashlight.

Marie nodded and led Tracee away, the flashlight beam playing against the stucco walls.

Yip was still standing helplessly by the pool. "It's Lisa. . . ." he repeated.

"Who'd you think it was?" Zalman probed sharply.

"I'd just come out of the pool house," E.Y. mumbled. "Gonna go get Mercer, have a nightcap, when I heard her splashing around in here. Thought I'd see if she was still mad at me. Then I heard a funny noise, and the lights went out."

"Should we try to . . ." Yip gestured toward Lisa's body, now bonking gently against the ladder at the deep end.

"We shouldn't do a damn thing," Zalman said, shaking his head. "The pool could be hot, and I don't feel like getting fried. Looks like Lisa was electrocuted, and that means she's very dead. It's too late for CPR, or anything else," he added darkly. "The important thing now is not to tamper with evidence. The cops'll go over this place like archeologists, and I don't want anybody to say we messed anything up. Got it? Marie is phoning them right now, and they should be here any minute. . . ."

"Good thinking, Jerry," E.Y. mumbled, still staring at Lisa's lifeless form. "Good thinking," he mumbled again.

"In a little while," Zalman continued, "tell Brunson to get an electrician up here, since I figure your power loss is connected to, uh . . . this unpleasantness." He gestured slightly at the body.

"This is awful," Yip moaned. "Poor Lisa. Dad, shouldn't we call Art Carmichael?"

"Damn good idea, son," E.Y. said, visibly brightening. "I gotta get some togs on, too, before I freeze to death. Jerry, can you and Yip stay here with the . . . uh, Lisa?"

"Of course," Zalman said. E.Y. walked slowly back toward his house, now dark and looming in the shadowy night, a ghostly figure in his white robe.

"Who's Carmichael?" Zalman asked Yip as soon as E.Y. was out of earshot.

"District attorney," Yip answered dully. "Big pal of Dad's. They play gin together most Saturdays. Art's a great guy, great guy. . . . He can help smooth things over."

"Is there anything to smooth over, Yip?" Zalman probed again. "Anything you want to mention before Santa Barbara's finest arrive?" In the distance they could hear the faint, almost comforting shriek of approaching sirens. "I *am* an attorney, remember?"

Yip looked uneasily over at Zalman, then looked away. "I know, Jerry. No, I don't have anything to say. Why should I?"

"Just asking, sport. It's funny the things people suddenly decide to mention after a murder."

"Murder!" Yip yelped in obvious surprise. "Murder? Of course," he said slowly, mental wheels beginning to grind, "this was supposed to be . . . Dad. . . ."

"Does this come as a big surprise to you?" Zalman asked, fishing in his breast pocket for his cigar case. He figured he'd better start on his cigar now, because it was going to be a long, long night.

LIEUTENANT PRIMATIVO ESPINOZA COULDN'T HAVE BEEN nicer. He was very careful not to tread on anyone's toes, was polite to the women and respectful of E.Y. as he listened to the complete account of the body's discovery. Meanwhile, the coroner's men cut the power to de-electrify the pool, photographed the body, and hauled it out of the pool with the help of the leaf skimmer. At first, their job was made doubly difficult by the darkness that still bathed the big house and grounds, courtesy of whomever had shorted the pool filter and exposed a length of copper wire which had electrocuted Lisa Comden. When they were through, Espinoza permitted a sleepy, grumbling electrician, summoned by the ever-efficient Brunson, to restore power, so once again, in macabre contrast to the grim events of the evening, the big house and yard were illuminated with jolly, twinkling electric lights.

Afterwards, Espinoza sat gingerly on the edge of a chair in the Wild West bar and smiled at E.Y., who'd changed from his terrycloth robe into a pair of jeans and another fancy cowboy shirt.

"So you'd just gotten out of the pool, then, Mr. Knotte?" the young lieutenant prompted helpfully, a pad and steel pencil lying on the arm of the chair. He was a handsome man in his mid-thirties, with carefully barbered hair and

78

the long, black lashes of a beauty queen. He was wearing a well-cut suit, regimental striped tie, and an excellent pair of expensive wing tips. Zalman thought he was far too handsome and far too well-dressed to be a local cop, but, Zalman reasoned as he watched the interview progress, Santa Barbara was a small town, and things could still be tough for a guy named Primativo Espinoza, especially when it was Primativo Espinoza, Chicano cop, versus E. Y. Knotte, the Sultan of Shrimp.

"Damn right," E.Y. said, pulling on one of his omnipresent screwdrivers. He looked better now, color restored to his creased face, fire once again smoldering behind his watery eyes. "I go in every night, right before my bedtime. Everybody knows it. Hell, I'm past president of the Santa Barbara chapter of the Midnight Polar Bears. Proud of it, too," he added strongly. "Been doing it for years."

"And Miss Comden?" Espinoza asked innocently. "Did she swim every night as well?" He'd refused a drink but had asked permission to smoke and was now toying with an unlit Winston.

E.Y. shook his head emphatically. "Nah. None of the girls here swim much at night. Just me."

Espinoza nodded thoughtfully. "So why did she swim tonight?"

Zalman watched E.Y. with interest, wondering if he was going to tell the truth or lead Espinoza down the garden path . . . a move that, in Zalman's opinion, would have been a big mistake. Unless he missed his guess by a long chalk, and Zalman rarely missed by even a short chalk, Espinoza was nobody to fool with, despite his understated, carefully correct manners.

Surprisingly, E.Y. readily confessed Ed Robin's hysterical accusations and the subsequent gunplay. "Her damn boyfriend broke in here earlier tonight and stirred up a big damn ruckus. I had to fire a few shots to cool him down. Boy, he hightailed it for tall timber, lemme tell you, officer. . . ."

"It's Lieutenant," Espinoza corrected gently. "And you had to . . . what?"

"Fire a few shots," E.Y. repeated, as if it were the most normal thing in the world. "Just to scare him off, of course. Could've winged him easy if I'd wanted to, but I didn't. Just wanted him to stop the hell pestering me while I was trying to eat my goddamned dinner. See, the young fool thought I was making a play for Lisa, his girl. Not true, though. These girls today, they take things too serious, you ask me. Hated to put holes in Rhonda's ceiling, but there you are. . . ." E.Y. spread his hands wide as if resting his case before the bar of celestial justice.

"I see," Espinoza said uncomfortably.

Zalman thought he'd better jump in, even though criminal law wasn't his usual line of business. Still, E.Y. had asked him to handle his legal affairs earlier in the evening, and it was on that basis that Espinoza had let him sit in on the interrogation.

"E.Y.," Zalman said, "I think you'd better see how Mrs. Knotte is doing. I'm sure the lieutenant has a few questions for her, too, although she wasn't present when we found the body, Lieutenant, as you know."

"Hah!" E.Y. barked. "Tough as nails, is Rhonda. Yeah, I'll go get her." He ambled out of the room, carrying his drink.

Espinoza stared at Zalman. "Are you going to be representing Mr. Knotte from now on, Mr. Zalman?" he inquired coolly, twiddling his unlit Winston.

"Mr. Robin—the gentleman who burst in here earlier this evening—Mr. Robin is Mr. Knotte's attorney. But since it's now unclear whether Mr. Robin will continue to represent Mr. Knotte, let's just say I'm here as a friend of the family." Zalman wondered if he should also mention that he just happened to be Mrs. Knotte Junior's ex-husband and decided he might as well get it over with. "Actually, Miss Thrasher and I are here spending the weekend with Yip and Tracee Knotte. Mrs. Tracee Knotte and I used to be married."

Espinoza looked at him blankly and finally lit his Winston in an apparent act of desperation. "Boy, we don't do it like that down in the barrio, I'll tell you that," he murmured. "Okay, let's get this straight. Miss Comden was Mr. Knotte's secretary, and he was trying to throw a loop on her, so her boyfriend, this guy Robin, comes in here screaming and yelling, and Mr. Knotte takes a couple of potshots at him. Is that right?"

"Not *at* him, Lieutenant. Mr. Knotte fired into the ceiling, just to get his point across. Look, Lieutenant, it's obvious where you're going with this, so I should tell you that Ed Robin did threaten Mr. Knotte's life, and yes, he did say he'd be back. All in front of witnesses. But I should also tell you that he didn't mean it."

"That's your opinion, Mr. Zalman," Espinoza said reasonably. "And you know what an opinion's worth in court. From where I'm standing, Robin threatened Mr. Knotte in an argument over the Comden woman. Knotte scares Robin off. Robin comes back, tampers with the pool motor because he knows Knotte goes for a dip every night. But instead of Mr. Knotte, he gets the girlfriend by mistake. I've known juries to convict on less."

Zalman shrugged expressively. "Lots of guys threaten to kill lots of dames, Lieutenant." Zalman glanced around the room just to be sure there were no women present. "Doesn't mean they run out and do it, though. Robin was just mouthing off, you ask me. He's an excitable guy, and he'd had a nasty shock—namely, Lisa Comden had stupidly told him E.Y. had moved in on her."

"Maybe," Espinoza said noncommittally, exhaling cigarette smoke. "But it's the best I got right now."

They were interrupted by a discreet knock at the door, and Brunson slid in on his soundless feet. "District Attorney Carmichael is here, sir," he addressed Zalman. "Shall I show him in?"

Zalman looked up at him. Brunson was wearing a long red woolen dressing gown and a red woolen nightcap with a long tassel on it. He looked like a Dickensian Father Christmas.

"Pardon my attire," Brunson said unflinchingly, catching Zalman's incredulous look. "I retire directly after dinner."

"I'd like to retire next year myself, but what with the new tax law, I don't think I'm going to make it," Zalman said, then turned serious again. "Yeah, Brunson, show him in. And Brunson," he added, "in the future, try and make a little more noise, please? No offense, but if you wouldn't mind clattering a little more in the hall . . ."

"Very good sir," Brunson said, nodding suavely. He retreated once again, this time flipping the heels of his carpet slippers noisily on the floor.

"Perfect," Zalman called. Seconds later, Brunson reappeared on slapping slippers. "Mr. Carmichael, sir," he announced.

Art Carmichael charged into the room like a panting linebacker but stopped short when he saw Zalman. Obviously, he'd expected his card-playing pal, E. Y. Knotte, or at least Yip. The D.A. was a big man, six feet or more, with the full chest and strong arms of an athlete. He had distinguished salt-and-pepper hair and looked no more than about forty-five, although his face was grooved with the deep lines of a man who had hit the bottle a little harder than he should have. In fact, as he came into the light, Zalman thought Carmichael had a slightly bloated look, as if he'd been blown up with helium and then allowed to leak a little. His pale eyes swept the room and fastened on Espinoza, who was standing very quietly at attention.

"You in on this, Espinoza?" Carmichael said nervously. "What happened? I came as soon as Yip called me," he added, looking around the room for one of the Knottes.

Espinoza settled a professionally blank smile on his face. "There's been a death, Mr. Carmichael," he said helpfully. "The victim is evidently Miss Comden, Mr. Knotte's secretary."

"Yeah, I know who she is," Carmichael snapped. "Go on. . . ."

"Miss Comden evidently went into the pool about an hour and a half ago, and it looks like she was electrocuted. There's a piece of exposed wire in the pool filter motor. It could have been an accident," Espinoza said smoothly, flicking a look at Zalman, "but it's probably murder."

Zalman looked sharply at Espinoza. The police lieutenant was some poker player. His face, smooth as an Aztec carving, didn't give away a thing. Zalman said nothing.

"Poor girl," Carmichael sighed, sinking onto a barstool with the look of a man who badly wanted someone to offer him a drink. "Nasty thing to happen. Little late for swimming, isn't it?" He glanced at his watch, which Zalman immediately spotted for a Rolex knockoff.

"Mr. Knotte swims every night around this time," Espinoza continued in the deadpan Joe Friday delivery he'd adopted when Carmichael had come into the room. "Seems there was some kind of ruckus earlier. Mr. Zalman here can tell you all about it, if you'd like."

Carmichael swung his nervous gaze back to Zalman, acknowledging his presence for the first time. "Zalman, huh?" the big D.A. repeated. "Okay, Mr. Zalman, go ahead then."

Zalman smiled easily. "I'm an attorney, Mr. Carmichael, and I'm just holding the fort for Mr. Knotte."

Carmichael's eyes sharpened, and he smiled thinly. "I see. Go on, Mr. Zalman, fill me in."

"Seems there's some possibility Mr. Knotte was trying to seduce Miss Comden. Probably didn't mean much by it, but the woman's boyfriend, Ed Robin—"

"Ed Robin did this?" Carmichael blurted with genuine amazement. "E.Y.'s lawyer?" Uncertainty and confusion flickered over the big man's red face.

"I'm not suggesting that, Mr. Carmichael," Zalman said

carefully. "All we know for certain is that Robin didn't like Mr. Knotte bothering his girlfriend. So he bursts in tonight at dinner, and then E.Y. fires a few shots through the ceiling—strictly a demonstration, you might say. No harm done."

"But he did threaten Mr. Knotte?"

"He did," Zalman replied.

"The boys are going over the wiring in the pump motor right now," Espinoza put in. "We shouldn't have long to wait. In any case, I'm going to question Robin."

Carmichael nodded agreement. "Good idea, Espinoza," he said energetically, evidently relieved to have a suspect in view. "Got complete faith in you." He reached out from his perch on the barstool and clapped the detective on the back. Zalman thought he saw a faint surge of disgust pass over Espinoza's face, but he wasn't sure.

E.Y. burst into the room. He'd added his cowboy hat to his ensemble, though he'd prudently omitted his guns and hunting knife. "Art! You got Yip's message. . . . Thanks for coming, buddy. Look, Rhonda's in a real state about this. Needs a few minutes to get herself fixed up, makeup and such. You know how she is about her makeup."

Carmichael had replaced his look of crafty cunning with an anxious, placating smile, clearly put on for E.Y.'s benefit. "Of course, E.Y." He smiled sympathetically.

Zalman guessed that Rhonda had passed out. He'd seen her tank up on several screwdrivers at dinner, plus lots of wine, and he guessed she'd had a couple of brandies in her room afterward. When she'd left the dining room earlier, she'd picked her way along with the careful steps of someone who wasn't too sure of what was in front of her.

"I had to wake her up to tell her, of course," E.Y. babbled. "I'm making myself a drink. Anybody else want one? Mercer! Where the hell is he, anyway?"

It was a fair question, Zalman thought. Mercer had been notable for his absence since dinner. Even the power loss and subsequent commotion hadn't brought him out.

E.Y. went behind the bar and whirred some oranges through the blender. "Damn, what a mess," he mused. "Poor little girl. So what do you think, Mr. Detective Espinoza? You think Ed killed her on purpose? Or you think he was trying to kill me and got her instead? Or what?" He fiddled with the juicer but his sharp crow's eyes were riveted on Espinoza. Espinoza in turn looked calmly back at E.Y. and seemed to be considering his reply.

Carmichael stepped in quickly. "Let's just wait and see, why don't we, E.Y.? Espinoza here doesn't want to make wild guesses about something this serious, do you . . . uh . . . it's Primativo, isn't it?"

"That's right, Mr. Carmichael. We'll know more in a little while, Mr. Knotte. I'd like to talk to the other members of the household, sir. Is there a room I can use?"

"What the hell for?" E.Y. snapped. "Oh, hell, I guess you gotta. Mercer, goddammit! Where the hell is that lout?"

Mercer chose that moment to open the door and stick his face in. He wore a pair of baby blue pj's, and his face was bleary with sleep. "Hi, boss!" he said good-naturedly. "What's going on, a party?"

"Please don't, goddammit, call me boss, will you, Merce?" E.Y. said, softening his tone. "We've had a little trouble, and this policeman"—and here E.Y. indicated Espinoza—"needs to talk to everyone. Get Brunson to get the staff together. Rhonda's on her way. Where's Yip, anyway? Where the hell's my damn family? Somebody dies, and where's my damn family? Man who goes and invents the goddamn Shrimpkin expects a little support from his family when things get rough. And Merce, take Espinoza here to the dining room and get him whatever he wants."

"You bet, E.Y.," Mercer said, happy as a dog to have something to do. "This way, Mr. Espinoza."

"I'll sit in with you, uh, Primativo," Carmichael said with false heartiness. "Just as a friend of the family, you know."

Espinoza understood perfectly. "Of course, Mr. Carmichael. This isn't an official investigation of the family, you understand—not yet, anyway." He nodded politely to E.Y. and Zalman and followed Mercer out of the room, Carmichael hard on his heels.

"Now Jerry, I'm glad those two boys are out of here," E.Y. said. "Gives us a chance to talk a minute. You tell me what you think's going on here." E.Y.'s voice was icicle-sharp. "I told you before I want you to handle some of my work. Now I'm sure about it."

"Look, E.Y.," Zalman protested, "I don't take clients away from other lawyers. I'm not an ambulance-chaser."

"That Robin wasn't good for much even before this," E.Y. snorted. "He was around, so I used him to do my busywork, help Lisa out a little. Most of my Shrimpkin business is all out of New York anyway, though it won't be if it looks like you and I can get along together. Robin just handled personal stuff, but I'm damned if I'd let that idiot haul out the Hefty bags now. I don't care if he killed Lisa or not. No man comes into my own damn house and threatens me and gets away with it. You help me out here, Jerry, and I promise it'll do you some good," E.Y. said, his sharp eyes glittering with the promise of cold cash, lots and lots of lovely, ice-cold cash.

Zalman sighed and fixed E.Y. with a sharp stare of his own. "Okay, then let's get one thing straight, E.Y. You're used to giving orders, but I'm not used to taking them. I don't do errands, I don't toe the line, and I don't take out the trash, as you so charmingly put it. I went to law school forever, and I paid a lot of hard dues after I graduated, learning the specific ins and outs of the legal dodge as practiced in our fair and glorious state. As a result of these Herculean labors I now have a very nice practice, and I don't particularly need any more business to stay afloat. I'm not saying I wouldn't like some of your business, but I don't need it to maintain my accustomed standard of living, and I want you to be absolutely clear on that point if we're going to work together. Now, if you're with me so far, a word about the way I work. Like I said, I'm an attorney. You have a legal problem, I tell you what to do about it. I don't tell you what you want to hear, I tell you what you *gotta* hear. So, if we're gonna work together, I won't try to tell you how to make Shrimpkins and you don't tell me how to practice law. Get the picture?" Zalman was careful not to break eye contact with E.Y.

"Man after my own heart," E.Y. rasped, returning Zalman's stare with easy grace. "A straight shooter. So whaddaya think? Think Robin was trying to kill me?"

Zalman saw that E.Y. was pumped up, happy to have something new, exciting, and challenging to sink his fangs into. "Robin?" Zalman said thoughtfully. "I doubt it. But it looks to me like somebody is. First the thing with the car, now this. Hell, Robin bursts in here, he knows you've got Mercer around, he knows the place is loaded with weapons and that you're a crack shot. Guy wasn't even carrying a weapon. What was going to do, whap you with the rib roast? Nah, you ask me, Robin was just a guy crazy for a dame, and it got out of control."

E.Y. nodded sagely. "That's what I think, too, Jerry. Hell, I just gave Lisa a little squeeze or two. Nothing serious, you understand. You stick around for a while, Jerry. You and me're gonna get on fine, and I'll say it again, you won't be sorry on your way down to the bank."

"Man after my own heart," Zalman said with a wolfish grin. "Shall we go into the dining room and watch the wheels of justice grind?"

ESPINOZA QUESTIONED THE STAFF BUT LEARNED NOTHING.
Brunson claimed he'd taken Rhonda a cup of Yipnotic tea
in her room, then retired to his own room and gone to
sleep. The cook and maid had settled down after dinner to
watch a "Route 66" rerun on the kitchen telly. Mercer
claimed he'd done his usual evening workout, then hopped
into the Jacuzzi to relieve some nagging muscle tension
and fallen asleep. Zalman, Marie, Yip, and Tracee had
been together in the dining room. Finally, Espinoza returned to the Wild West room, sighed heavily, and asked
E.Y. if it would be all right if he talked to Rhonda, who
still hadn't put in an appearance.

E.Y. grunted. "Yep. I'll go get her," he said. "But she's a
regular she-bear when you wake her up, I'm warning
you. . . ."

A few moments later Rhonda swept into the room,
wearing a demure little lace negligee that looked as if it
had cost about ten thousand Shrimpkins. Her hair was
flawless, and she was wearing a couple of pounds of
freshly applied eye makeup.

"What a tragedy," she breathed. "Tragic. It's a tragedy."
Her creamy bosom, amply displayed, heaved gently, and
she dabbed very carefully at her perfectly shadowed eyes
with a silk handkerchief. "Lisa was such a dear girl, such a

88

comfort to the family, and Ed was so much in love with her." Rhonda's voice throbbed with matronly fervor. "I'll never understand how he could do such a terrible thing, hurt her like that. . . ."

Zalman tried to look concerned, but he noticed that Rhonda seemed awfully sad about the death of the little chickadee who'd maybe caught her husband's roving eye. Besides which, her performance stank. Rhonda had never been much of a thespian, but even so, her portrayal of the grieving friend of the deceased was about as believable as Reagan's portrayal of a president—*A* for effort, *F* for effect.

"So, Mrs. Knotte," Espinoza said gently, "did you hear anything? Were you aware of the death at all?"

Rhonda shook her burnished mane. "I'd turned out my lights and was lying quietly in bed, reviewing the accomplishments of the day. . . ."

Zalman shot a glance at Espinoza, who looked stunned. "The accomplishments of . . ." the cop repeated, not quite believing his ears.

"Oh, yes," Rhonda said, blinking. "It's a little habit of mine. I find that at the end of each day, if one simply runs over the little tasks, the little accomplishments of the day, it gives one a sense of, well, security? Of having been of some use, do you know what I mean, Lieutenant?" she asked breathily. "I try to make every minute count."

Espinoza nodded wearily. "Right," he managed to say straight-faced. "Of course. Well, so you weren't aware of the, uh, incident?"

"No, not until I heard noises, people calling to one another outside. Even then, well, I didn't think too much about it. My husband swims every night, and there's often quite a bit of noise from the pool area. I don't pay attention. Later, of course, I realized that it must have been just after the accident that I heard the noises, but right then I didn't think too much about it." She motioned to Mercer to bring her another drink, and he happily responded. "Will that be all, Lieutenant?" she asked as her red nails closed around the Waterford glass Mercer handed her. "I find I'm a bit unnerved by this tragic event."

"Of course," Espinoza said smoothly as he got to his feet. "I may have to speak to you again, however, Mrs. Knotte."

"Of course," Rhonda replied as she gave him her hand and lowered her eyes demurely. "Of course." The lace of her negligee swirled around her bare legs as she left the room on a cloud of "Joy."

"I need to look at Miss Comden's room," Espinoza told E.Y. "I won't need much time. Just a quick once-over."

"Merce," E.Y. said tersely with a flick of his head to indicate that Mercer should take Espinoza to Lisa Comden's room.

Five minutes later, Espinoza returned, triumphantly waving a handwritten note. " 'I love you,' " he read aloud. " 'My heart beats as one with yours. How can you think of destroying what we have together? I'll kill you if you leave me for that old geezer.' . . ."

"Geezer!" E.Y. muttered defensively. "Old geezer! The hell I'm a geezer, and besides, I didn't *ask* her to leave him. Just wanted her to fool around a little on the side, that's all. Didn't want to marry the girl!"

"Blah blah blah," Espinoza said, "it goes on. Well, Mr. Carmichael," he said, carefully folding the note and putting it in a polyethlyene envelope, "I'll be getting along to Robin's place now. I think we have grounds to pick him up, unless he can come up with a damn solid alibi, and assuming we can find him. . . ." he added darkly.

Zalman looked over at Marie, who was sitting at the table next to Tracee. Yip was off in the corner of the room, his camcorder by his side. He'd tried to get a few shots in earlier, but once again his father had warned him off. "Lieutenant," Zalman said, "if you don't need us anymore, I think the ladies are getting tired."

Espinoza picked up his cue quickly. "Of course, Mr.

Zalman. But if you wouldn't mind, there might be a few questions tomorrow." Espinoza smiled and let it hang in the air.

"Certainly," Zalman replied, just as smoothly. "Miss Thrasher and I will be at Mr. Knotte's." He indicated Yip, then turned to Marie and Tracee. "Ladies . . ."

A few minutes later Tracee once again wheeled the big Country Squire wagon down the long driveway, away from Knotte Pines. Yip sat silently beside her on the front seat, Marie sagged against Zalman in the back seat.

"I feel like I've spent the evening with Dracula," Marie moaned.

"Me, too," Tracee said softly, her profile flawless in the moonlight. "I'm awfully sorry about this, you guys. I thought E.Y. was in trouble, but this is worse than I dreamed."

Zalman pulled Marie closer and nuzzled her head. "So, gang," he said, "before this charming evening fades into memory, what do you think? Let's have the instant replay."

Marie snorted. "Hah! That Rhonda! What did she say, Tracee? 'Running over the little accomplishments of the day'? She thinks she's Mother Teresa? The most she accomplished today was a new coat of lacquer on her nails. Can you believe it? And if she was asleep through all that, then I'm Godzilla."

"She wasn't asleep," Tracee said with great certainty. "When she floated downstairs her face was perfect, and I know for an absolute concrete fact that it takes her forty-five minutes minimum just to get her eye makeup on straight."

"Her makeup *was* perfect," Marie agreed.

"Hah!" Tracee said cattily. "She had her eyeliner tattooed on! But the eyebrows and the shadow, that's what takes all the time."

"Tatooed?" Zalman said in horror. "That's disgusting. Doesn't it hurt?"

"Of course it hurts!" Marie snapped. "All beauty stuff hurts."

91

"Yeech." Zalman shuddered as Tracee pulled the car up in front of the long, low house and everyone got out. "Tattooed eyes! It's barbaric!"

Tracee and Marie looked at each other and shrugged. "Men aren't very observant," Tracee said to Marie as they went inside. "I've always thought so, but I guess I've been afraid to say it out loud."

"They're observant in their own way," Marie's voice echoed in the hallway. "They just don't see as much as we do."

"Huh?" Zalman said to Yip, who had lingered on the steps to get a quick shot of the women as they went inside. Yip lowered his camcorder and looked at Zalman expectantly.

"So what do we do now?" Yip asked.

Zalman looked at him, with his dream of returning to his office within several days, his Toulouse-Lautrec safely under his arm, evaporating before his eyes. "I don't know about you, pal, but I'm gonna hit the sack. It's been a long night, and I'm beat."

"Yeah, but what do we *do*?" Yip insisted, following him into the big living room and gently tossing his camcorder onto one of the sofas. Beyond the windows the Pacific pounded endlessly at the dark cliffs.

"Talk to me tomorrow," Zalman said, shivering. "I'll tell you in the morning." He yelled good night to Tracee, who'd already disappeared down the hall to her room, then went down the opposite hall to the guest room.

Marie was standing in the middle of the room, an agonized expression on her face. "Oh, God," she moaned. "I never unpacked. Everything's going to be wrinkled! I'll have to iron! I hate ironing!"

Zalman had the horrifying feeling she was about to burst into tears. It was amazing. She'd put up with shooting, general hysterics, and a dinner party spent underneath the table. She'd faced a dead body floating in the swimming pool like a bloated olive in a day-old martini, she'd stood up to a police grilling, and she'd even taken care of his ex-wife. Ironing would be just the ticket to send her spiraling into dementia.

"Lie down on the bed, doll," he commanded in his "Father Knows Best" voice. "I'll get you a nice cold washcloth for your head." Oddly, she obeyed him without her usual protestations, and a minute later she'd relaxed and was allowing him to soothe her. "You don't have to iron," he assured her. "We'll send it all out. Tracee always has somebody for that. . . ."

Marie's voice was muffled by the washcloth. "So what do you think, Jerry? Who's the bad boy in the Knotte family? I don't think Robin did it, do you? Tracee doesn't either, by the way," she said with the air of one who has just solved an irksome problem. "Could it really have been an accident? I don't think so," she continued without waiting for an answer. "I think Tracee is right. I think someone *is* trying to kill E.Y. I think it's all connected—the thing with the brakes, and now this. . . ." Her voice drifted off, and a few moments later Zalman lifted the corner of the washcloth and peeked underneath. Her eyes were closed, and she was well on the happy trail to dreamland.

Zalman's brain was racing, playing and replaying the events of the evening, an endless loop of incidents running in fast-forward. He undid Marie's clothes, slipped off her shoes, covered her with the taffeta comforter, and turned off all the lights except those in the bathroom, which continued to bathe the room in a soft glow. Then he got his cigar case out of his jacket and went out the sliding glass door onto the patio that ran along the back of the house. The roar of the sea hung in the air, a distant but threatening animal on the loose. Zalman regarded the moonlight on the oak-studded hillside, pierced the end of his cigar with his gold piercer, and lit it with his gold Dunhill lighter.

"Jerry?" Tracee's voice swam out of the shadows like a memory of things past, things obscured in the drift of time but not quite forgotten. "That's you, isn't it, Jerry?"

*Oh, boy,* he thought, *there it is again, that little touch of mink.* "Yeah, it's me, Trace," he said easily. "Just having a little smoke before bedtime."

"Old habits die hard," she chuckled as she came toward him down the patio. "You always did like a smoke before bed." She was wearing an ivory satin negligee with delicate insets of lace, and although it was extremely modest, as such things go, the satin clung to her perfect figure as she walked, a shifting outline of voluptuous beauty. "You *are* still going to help me, aren't you, Jerry?" Her voice trembled in the darkness. "You promised you would. . . ."

"Jeez, Trace, don't nag, will you? You got a husband, go nag him," he said, trying to keep things light. His ex-wife's figure made his stomach lurch a little. He loved Marie a lot, and stepping out wasn't his style, but after all, a guy was only human. "You promised me the Lautrec, don't forget that!" He jabbed his glowing cigar tip in the air for emphasis.

Tracee giggled. "Do that again."

"Do what again?"

"Wiggle your cigar in the air."

Zalman obliged.

Tracee giggled again. "Reminds me of the old days, when I used to go to Zuma with that wacky guru. Remember, the guy who only ate fruit? And he used to feed us acid, and we used to dance around waving all these incense sticks? Boy, that was fun! Remember those days, Jerry? And I'd come home and get sand all over your law books, which were all over the floor of the apartment because we didn't have any furniture, and you'd pout."

Zalman shook his head, chasing away the long-buried memories, memories he'd had to bury years ago in order to survive, in order to maintain his sanity, memories he had no intention of digging up now or any other time. "Trace, you're a great girl, but I never thought you were playing with a full deck, and now I remember why. Too much acid in the old Hawaiian Punch."

"It was pure Owsley!" Tracee protested, laughing softly. "Sri Guru Whatsit swore!" Her voice was mock-indignant.

"Let's let the purity of LSD pass for now, not to mention the subject of the whole misbegotten past, okay, Trace? I mean, it's High Reagan out there. I can hardly remember what love beads look like. Besides, doll," Zalman prodded, shifting into gear again, "now's your big chance. Is there anything you want to tell me, in confidence, like? You're my client, it's strictly protected information. Anything special you'd like to say about the memorable events of the evening past?"

Tracee sucked in her breath angrily, but before she could get started Zalman pressed further, one of his favorite techniques. "Yip inherits? Or Rhonda? How's the will work?"

"Jerry Zalman!" Tracee protested, this time with genuine indignation. "You have a mean little mind! How can you ask me a question like that at a time like this! How should I know who inherits? My Yippie has plenty of money! Why, Yip Tea is a very successful enterprise, and now with World O' Yip opening up—"

"Exactly my point," Zalman said smoothly. "Maybe Yip's running short for World O' Yip. All tapped out at the bank, is he?"

"How did you know, Jerry?" Tracee asked, amazed. "Who told you that?"

"Well, strictly speaking, you did. Just now. But I gotta say I'd already wondered about it on my own. So, Yip would profit by his father's death?"

"Jerry!" Again, Tracee was shocked beyond her personal endurance. "Bite your tongue! What a terrible thing to say! Honestly, Jerry Zalman. I hate to say this, but I remember all over again why I divorced you! You're so . . . so . . . nasty-minded!"

"You didn't divorce me!" Zalman shot back. "I let you divorce me, and don't you forget it, because I'm a gentleman, and don't you forget that either! And besides, I don't have a nasty mind! I'm an attorney, remember? I'm supposed to be skeptical."

"Hah! That's all I have to say to you. Just hah!" Even in the moonlight Zalman could see Tracee shaking with indignation. "My Yippie," she said after a moment, her voice carefully controlled, "my Yippie wouldn't ever think of doing anything like that! He's very spiritual! Why, he's practically a vegetarian!"

Zalman knocked the ash off his cigar and watched it float onto the patio flagstones. "All right, Trace, calm down. I was just trying to shake you up a little, see what you'd do. Listen to me, my dear, and let's get one thing perfectly clear, as a beloved ex-president used to say. You're going to be answering lots of nasty questions in the next few days, and so is Yip, so don't blow it. Carmichael would love to sweep all this under the rug, but young Lieutenant Espinoza won't be so easy. Oh, he's tugging his forelock when Carmichael's around, but unless I miss my guess he's a pro, and he's playing for keeps."

"They'll be back?" Tracee asked, hugging herself beneath her substantial bosom.

"Sure they will! Weren't you listening, for Pete's sake? They have to arrest somebody, and young Robin did some pretty dumb things this evening. Looks like he's done some pretty dumb things right along," Zalman added to himself, shaking his head in wonderment. "The yolds they're letting out of law school these days, I tell you . . . But anyway, the kid looks good for the part, and I'd bet you a ten spot he's probably in the clink right now. Just remember one thing, Trace, if Espinoza wants to talk to you, or Carmichael wants to talk to you, or the guy who delivers the groceries wants to talk to you, you tell 'em to talk to me first. And the same goes for Yip. You listening to me?"

"Yes, Jerry, I'm listening," she said softly, all signs of anger gone, her tremulous voice like a pat of hot, thick butter. "I'm so glad I called you. I can't tell you how much it means. . . ."

"Enough with the sentiment," Zalman snapped gruffly, grinding out his cigar in a nearby geranium. "It wasn't exactly the kind of weekend I'd expected, but these days, very little is. See you in the morning, kid. Sleep tight, and don't let the bedbugs bite."

She giggled. Zalman started back to the guest room, and just as he reached the sliding door Tracee said, "But those days were fun, Jerry, all the same. . . ."

He waved without turning back and went through the sheer draperies into the room. Marie was still lying exactly as he'd left her, on the bed, under the taffeta comforter. Zalman brushed his teeth, slipped out of his clothes, crawled in beside her, and kissed her gently on her forehead. He lay a moment in the darkness, listening to a coyote bark in the canyon behind the house, its cry sharp and mournful above the omnipresent thunder of the sea. Then he let his mind relax, banished care, put on his blue velvet sleep mask, and proceeded to enjoy a long, lovely, and uninterrupted night's sleep.

ZALMAN WOKE UP SLOWLY ON SATURDAY MORNING. HE reached out for Marie, and when he couldn't feel the comfortable warmth of her body nestled against his, he lifted up a corner of his sleep mask and blearily looked around. The remorseless California sunlight hit his eyes with megaton force, and he quickly pulled the mask down again. "Marie," he croaked, "are you here?" There was no answer from the bath or dressing rooms, so in a few minutes, when he thought he could bear the cheerful light, he staggered into the shower and let steaming water run full in his face. It helped. Jerry Zalman was not a morning person. He hated to greet the bright new day with a song in his heart and two eggs over easy. The smell of bacon frying first thing in the morning made him gag, and he never really felt right until after he'd showered and shaved and had his first cigar. Now, half an hour after getting up, he was ready to brave the living room.

He found the big room empty, but he could see Yip, Tracee, and Marie outside on the deck, sitting around a glass-topped table. They were busy eating, so he figured maybe they'd take pity on him and give him a decent cup of coffee.

Such was not to be his luck. "Jerry!" Yip said happily. "Have some tea!"

"Coffee, please . . ." Zalman begged, fumbling for his dark glasses.

Yip paled. "We don't drink coffee," he hemmed. "All that caffeine. You know what it does to your blood pressure?"

"You know what *you* do to my blood pressure?" Zalman growled, sinking into a cushioned wrought-iron chair. "Look, you want me to grovel, right? Okay, I'm not proud, I'll grovel." He got out of his chair and got down on his knees. "See? Groveling. You know what groveling does to the knees of your trousers? My tailor's gonna kill me. Tracee, I appeal to you. A cup of coffee, for the love of God." He clasped his hands in supplication.

Tracee and Marie began to howl with laughter. Yip, a day late as usual, finally realized Zalman was kidding and whipped out his camcorder so he could shoot a few feet of Zalman groveling. Zalman got up, dusted off his trousers, and sat down next to Marie.

She leaned over and kissed him good morning. "Jerry, you're some nutty kind of guy."

Tracee got up and went into the house. "Don't worry, Jerry. I've never told Yip, but I've got some beans stashed in the freezer for emergencies."

"Thanks, doll," he called. "Cream and sugar . . ."

"Cream," Yip moaned. "All that fat . . ."

"Yip, old buddy," Zalman said, trying to shield his eyes with his palm. The sunlight sparkling off the blue Pacific beyond the deck and cliffs was brutal. "Yip, old buddy, we're going to have to get a few things straight around here. My pal, Mr. Blood Pressure, is remarkably low, and so is Mr. Cholesterol. Why, you ask? Because although I indulge myself in every way possible, I do so in moderation. Because life without vice isn't worth living. Cream in your coffee, a few good cigars a day, the odd snifter of brandy in the evening—these are the vices in which I have chosen to indulge. So until my personal physician, whom I see for a complete physical once a year, tells me to cut down, I'd appreciate the hell out of it if you'd keep your yap shut about my personal habits. Puts me off my game, you know? You gotta realize, Yip, I'm the kind of guy who's proud to be at the top of the food chain. And for a guy who's only five foot five," he added, lying by the usual half inch, "it's a goddamned accomplishment."

"But Jerry—" Yip whined.

"And in return," Zalman pressed on, "I will graciously refrain from questioning your own personal desire to consume textured vegetable protein or soyburgers or tofu or squid cakes or whatever the hell it is you consider as edible in the so-called health food line. So can we shake on it, Yip, old buddy? Man to man? Whaddaya say?" Zalman lowered his palm from its protective position above his eyes and extended it to Yip just as Tracee returned with a potful of steaming coffee on a silver tray.

"Well, uh, I suppose it's only fair," Yip said grudgingly as they shook hands.

"A good piece of negotiation," Marie said. "Can I have a cup, too?" she asked Tracee hopefully.

"Of course you can," Tracee said soothingly. "I knew you'd want some, so I brought extra cups."

In the background the phone rang. "Oh, Christ," Zalman said, "it's going to start." He glugged half a cup of coffee at a swallow while Tracee went inside and spoke quietly on the phone.

"Relax, Jerry," she said, returning to the deck. "That was E.Y. Ed Robin's been arrested for Lisa's murder."

"Big shock," Zalman muttered, sipping his coffee at a more leisurely pace. "What else is new?"

"Robin called E.Y. begging for help. E.Y. said a few rude things to him, then he softened and said that you were his lawyer now and he'd ask you to go down and talk to Robin, who's in jail downtown, see. . . ."

"E.Y. wants me to get him sprung?" Zalman wondered aloud. "Hmmmm."

"Well, E.Y. didn't say that specifically," Tracee said.

"He just wants you to go down there and talk to Ed and see what you think is going on. He's pretty steamed up about Ed carrying on like that, but Ed *was* his lawyer, and it isn't going to look too good on the six o'clock news."

"Got any Danish?" Zalman asked.

"Homemade apple cake," Tracee said without missing a beat. "It's in the microwave right now, warming up."

"You made cake!" Yip cried. "All that sugar—"

"You made cake?" Zalman said in amazement. "How come you never made cake when you were married to me?" He shook his head and smiled at Yip. "You're a lucky man, pal."

AN HOUR LATER, YIP DROVE ZALMAN TO THE COUNTY jail. Tracee had persuaded Marie to go shopping, though Marie swore she didn't need a thing in this world and wasn't going to buy one teensy, tiny item. Zalman rolled his eyes dramatically at this plaintive lie and wished them both a good time.

"Pretty town, Santa Barbara," he said as Yip maneuvered the aqua Country Squire through the heavy Saturday traffic toward the Santa Barbara County lockup.

"Lots of folks think Santa Barbara always looked like this," Yip said expansively, gesturing at the white adobe buildings, their red-tiled roofs gleaming in the sun. "But most of this Early California stuff went in right after the earthquake."

"Earthquake?" Zalman asked. "I didn't know there was an earthquake here. San Francisco, Long Beach, L.A., but here?"

"You bet there was. In 1925, and it was a pip! Busted the dam at Sheffield Reservoir, completely wrecked State Street. Before that, it mostly looked like a regular Western town, but afterward . . ."

"I get it. They decided to go with the theme-park look?"

"Pretty much," Yip said. "Now Santa Barbara is basically a resort town. Sure, we've got the Biltmore and there's the Oaks over in Ojai, and of course we've had plenty of publicity with the Western White House just around the corner and all, but there's a lot of us who want a full-scale, world-class health spa without the hassle. We want healthy food, we want exercise rooms, long walks on the beach, a stimulating yet relaxed atmosphere where we can, well, go on retreat, as it were."

"As it were," Zalman echoed, staring out the window at an Isla Vista blonde doing wheelies on her skateboard.

"And World O' Yip is going to give it to 'em," Yip said excitedly, pounding on the steering wheel for emphasis. "World O' Yip is going to be the flagship of my new health enterprise. If only my dad would let loose of a little more cash . . ." he added.

"What happened to your financing?" Zalman asked suspiciously. "What's your banker say?"

"Ahhhhh, these guys have no vision!" Yip whined. "I'm talking about New Age splendor! World O' Yip has to be first-class, all the amenities. Crystal workshops in the evening, channeling sessions with today's topflight mediums, the works. So I ran a little over!" he blurted, pounding the steering wheel again.

"How much is a little?"

"Not much." Yip squirmed.

"Not much, huh?" Zalman laughed cynically. He looked sideways at Yip, whose mouth was set in a straight, hard line reminiscent of his father's. "Listen," Zalman said in a reasonable tone. "I used to know this guy who was a doctor on a detox ward for alcoholics? He always said that the first thing he asked 'em when they checked in seeing blue snakes and flying rats and suchlike was 'How much are you drinking?' And you know what the answer always was, invariably? 'Not much,' they'd say as pink elephants whizzed through their skulls. 'Not much.'"

"You're an amazing guy, Jerry," Yip said, softening. "Like, you're so perceptive!"

"Ain't I?" Zalman agreed as Yip pulled up in front of the

jail. "Listen, I can take a cab back to the house. This might take a while."

"Hey, no problem," Yip assured him. "I got my camcorder here. I thought I'd do a little shooting, a little local flavor for my video. I'll meet you in a couple of hours, okay? No problem," he repeated cheerfully as Zalman got out of the car.

TWENTY MINUTES LATER ZALMAN WAS SITTING IN A FACE-less green room, waiting for young Ed Robin to come up from the holding cells. A weary, rumpled sergeant, who fit the part of jailkeeper so perfectly that he looked like he'd come from Central Casting, ushered Robin in, stared at Zalman, and left without speaking.

Robin slumped into a metal chair. "Got a cigarette?" he asked dully. "I quit smoking three years ago, but this looks like a good time to start up again."

Zalman smiled and produced his cigar case. "Try one of these," he said, offering Robin a Macanudo. "It'll get you off cigarettes for life."

Robin accepted the cigar and managed to light it, though his hands were trembling like aspic. He was a thin, slight young man, disheveled after a night in jail, but even so, Zalman noted, Robin's fashionably short hair was combed, and the collar of his gray silk jacket was turned up, denoting a man who hadn't forgotten his sense of style. He'd managed to regain his dignity, despite his ridiculous behavior at E.Y.'s house the previous night, despite his shrieking and yelling, despite the untimely demise of Lisa Comden.

"I need your help, Mr. Zalman," he said simply, exhaling a long stream of cigar smoke and staring off at the blue sky beyond the wire-mesh window. "Somebody's gotta help me, I know that." He suddenly looked very young, completely helpless, and totally pathetic. "I can't believe she's dead . . . that somebody . . . electrocuted her . . . Jesus," he moaned suddenly, shaking his head like a retriever.

Zalman saw that Robin was holding himself together by force of will, and despite his better judgment he felt a twinge of pity for the young man. "Easy does it, kid," he said softly. He sat down across from Robin and lit his own cigar.

"We were going to move in together," Robin said after a minute. "Get married next summer when my folks could come out from Ohio. I guess I went a little off my rocker when she told me about E.Y. Jesus!" he said again. "It really creeped me. E.Y.'s a great guy, but at his age . . ."

"You think he doesn't want a little action now and then, just like anybody else?" Zalman shook his head pityingly. "What are you, Robin? Some kind of moron? What the hell did you bust in there for last night?"

Robin put his head in his hands and moaned. "I don't know, Mr. Zalman. I just went nuts! You gotta help me! I'm a fellow attorney. You can't let them to this to me! For God's sake, we're both members of the bar association! I'll work for you! I'll work it off, I swear it!"

"For Christ's sake, don't whine at me!" Zalman exploded. "I got enough loonies on my hands already without you! Besides," he added, softening at Robin's pathetic expression, "E.Y. sent me over here, so I'm on his tab for now."

"E.Y.! That maniac!"

"Mr. Maniac to you, seeing that he's paying the freight. And besides, where do you get off calling somebody a maniac, for Christ's sake, Mr. Always Rational Robin? Give it a rest, will you and tell me what happened after you left E.Y.'s. Just the facts."

Robin slumped in his chair. "Well, after E.Y. pulled out the gun, I left. . . ."

"First you threatened to kill him."

"I did? *I* threatened to kill him? I don't know what I said. I'd had a couple of drinks . . . more than a couple . . . I guess I sort of blacked out."

"Hmmmmm," Zalman said. "Everybody at the damn dinner table heard you. Everybody under the table, I should say. Most of us were under the table at that point, if you recall," he added pointedly.

"Oh, God," Robin moaned. "What was I thinking of?"

"Probably nothing, but we'll let that pass for now. What about the note in Lisa's room? The one where you threatened to kill her and E.Y.?"

"Oh, God . . ."

"You know, you've got the brain of an eel, Robin," Zalman said disgustedly. "You threatened to kill two people, on paper and within the hearing of several reliable bystanders, all of whom would make swell witnesses for the prosecution."

"Oh, God . . ."

"Love may be blind, pal, but in your case it's also flat stupid. So after E.Y.'s, where did you go? Some place filled with people, I hope? All of whom know you well and can swear to your presence?"

"Oh, God . . ."

"No such luck, huh?"

Robin shook his head sadly. "I went for a walk on the beach."

Zalman looked at the ceiling and shrugged. "Why do they always go for walks on the beach?" he asked the ceiling. "Why don't they run over to the mayor's house for tea?"

"I hadn't been home ten minutes when the police showed up," Robin said miserably. "I fell asleep on the beach and got wet . . . that's what woke me up."

"Charming. Well, at least it's seawater and not pool water. We can prove you weren't in the pool fooling with the damn heater."

"You gotta help me, Mr. Zalman," Robin begged.

"Well, somebody's gotta help you, pal, that's for sure. Otherwise you're gonna spend the next half of your life writing your memoirs—when you're not making license plates, that is. A regular criminal mastermind I got here." Zalman laughed harshly and stood up. "Listen, Robin," he said suddenly, leaning forward over the chipped Formica table, "you kill her or not?"

Robin's head swung up slowly, and he stared at Zalman through a cloud of cigar smoke, a look of incomprehension on his pale face. Slowly he began to tremble. When he finally spoke his voice was hollow through his chattering teeth. "I didn't, I swear," he said brokenly.

Zalman straightened. "Okay, kid, I don't promise anything. But listen up—nothing for nothing, see? If I help you beat this thing, you'll owe me. I'm not a criminal lawyer, so if you go to trial you're on your own. We'll have to send for one of the criminal law guys. But if I do get you out of this, just think of yourself as an indentured servant for the rest of your natural life, maybe longer. Got it?"

Robin nodded miserably. "I'll do anything you say, Mr. Zalman, I swear it. . . ."

"You bet you will, Robin. Trust me." Zalman picked up his cigar case and rang for the weary sergeant.

Primativo Espinoza was waiting for Zalman out in the hall. The young lieutenant was leaning up against the wall, playing with another unlit Winston. He nodded to Zalman. "Carmichael wants to talk to you."

"Oh, yeah? Let him call my secretary and ask for an appointment."

"Gimme a break, Mr. Zalman. He's leaning on my ass hard enough as it is, and I don't have a lot of choices here. You and I know he's a dork, but he thinks he's some kind of Perry Mason or something."

"More like Hamilton Burger, you ask me."

"*Verdad*, amigo. He likes to hang out with the Knottes,

other rich types around here, thinks maybe if he works hard enough they'll forget he comes from the wrong side of the tracks, just like me. I dunno, Mr. Zalman, but it would be a favor to me if you'd come see him."

"Call me Jerry. You really love the guy, I can tell."

"A real twerp. Kinda guy who used to hang around school hoping somebody'd let him bang a few erasers. My name's Primo, by the way," he said.

"And he's your boss."

"He ain't my boss," Espinoza said savagely. "But he *is* the D.A., and he thinks I'm just a cholo punk from the barrio and likes to let me know it."

"So what about Robin?" Zalman asked, jerking a thumb at the room behind him. "Carmichael gonna let him out?"

"Hell, no. Robin's down for murder one. Carmichael thinks he's got a big press case here, wants to go on TV, write a book, get sent to Sacramento as an elected servant of the people." Espinoza shook his head. "Thinks he can squeeze the dough out of E.Y. for his campaign. The guy's in pork heaven."

"You talked me into it, Primo," Zalman said. "Sounds like a fun meeting, as we say in Beverly Hills. Lead the way, pal."

Carmichael was on the phone when Zalman walked into his office. Espinoza had declined to join them, saying he had enough trouble with Carmichael without asking for more. Carmichael waved at Zalman to sit down, and Zalman took a cracked leather chair across from Carmichael's beat-up desk. Zalman looked around at the cheap office furniture and dust-layered, withered plants and decided he didn't blame Carmichael for wanting to move up. His office was enough to depress even the most conscientious public official. Carmichael continued to yammer into the phone, so Zalman, who hated to be kept waiting, got up and began to circle the office, picking up various objects, pretending to inspect them and replacing them in different positions. It was a tactic which drove most guys crazy, and

Carmichael was no exception. He watched Zalman out of the corner of his eye for about thirty seconds, by which time Zalman had worked through the golf trophies and was about to start on the photographs in tarnished silver-plate frames, then Carmichael hung up abruptly.

"Thanks for coming in, Mr. Zalman. Sorry to keep you waiting," the D.A. said genially. In daylight, Carmichael looked no better than he had the previous evening. The dark circles under his red-flecked eyes testified to a long night's drinking.

"Call me Jerry," Zalman said, returning to the chair. "No trouble at all. E.Y. asked me to see Ed Robin, try and figure out what the hell's going on here."

"Murder is a horrible crime," the D.A. said pretentiously.

"Think it's murder, do you?" Zalman asked, settling back into the cracked armchair.

"Of course, of course. Robin threatened the girl, then burst into E.Y.'s in a deranged state of mind. I shouldn't be saying this to you, Jerry," he said, leaning forward conspiratorially, "but I think the boy's insane. Still, the decent, law-abiding citizens of our community deserve to be protected, and I've charged him with murder one. I've got the evidence, the note. He had no alibi. . . ."

"You don't think there's a chance that somebody was after E.Y. and got the girl by mistake?"

"Noooo," Carmichael said after a brief pause. He replaced his nervous smile with a crafty one. "Noooo, I don't. He did threaten E.Y., after all. You yourself were a witness, isn't that right?"

"I myself was a witness. But I wasn't thinking of Ed. I was thinking of somebody else entirely. You heard about the incident with the brakes? How the Sultan of Shrimp went for an accidental dip?"

"Ruined the Cadillac," the D.A. said, trying to suppress a smirk at Zalman's irreverent reference to E.Y. "The car was a dead loss. He kept it in perfect condition, too."

110

"I take it you don't believe the two incidents were connected?" Zalman asked flatly.

"Frankly speaking, Jerry, I honestly don't. I like Ed. He's a young guy, and one way or the other this'll ruin his career. We both know that. But as the chief law enforcement officer of this county, I have no alternative." He spread his big hands, fairly begging for understanding. "Try and understand my position. He threatens his girlfriend. The girlfriend dies. He's got no alibi."

"Well," Zalman sighed as he got up, refraining from brushing dust from the seat of his dark blue silk trousers, "we shall see what we shall see." Carmichael laughed uncertainly. They shook hands, and Zalman left.

He walked thoughtfully through the crowded hall and back outside into the sunlight, where Yip was waiting for him at the curb in the Country Squire.

"How did it go?" Yip asked anxiously. "You see Ed?"

"I saw him," Zalman said, sighing heavily. "I tell you, Yip, the things I do for money . . . Take me for a drive, my friend. I want to find a cheap motel, preferably with a bar attached, someplace where the beach crowd likes to hang out."

"I know just the place, great local joint. Dad goes there all the time." Yip eased the wagon into traffic. "But Jerry, we've got plenty of room. We love having you and Marie with us. We wouldn't think—"

"Not for me! Not for me!" Zalman said. "For my friend McCoy . . ."

Later that afternoon, Zalman went back to Yip and Tracee's house and took a nap. Zalman, a longtime napper, knew that fifteen minutes at the end of the afternoon with your feet up and your eyes closed would lengthen your life span a great deal more than ten tons of tofu. He woke up about five o'clock to the rustle of unfolding tissue paper in the living room accompanied by the murmur of Marie and Tracee's voices.

Zalman reached out for the phone next to his bed and punched Doyle Dean McCoy's number in Newhall.

"Hi dee ho," McCoy answered. There was the sound of whines and barks in the background.

"How's Rutherford?" Zalman asked.

"Hey! Great! No problem! Been asleep all day, but he'll be up for dinner, if I know my old pal Ruth. So what's up, Zally?"

"We're having plenty of fun up here, I can tell you that. Last night a love-starved lawyer runs in, interrupts dinner with a tale of woe, then E. Y. Knotte, a loose cannon if ever I saw one, fires a few shots in the air just to get the kid's attention. The kid runs out, and later on the kid's girlfriend, E.Y.'s secretary, gets fried when she goes for a late-night swim in the pool. The lawyer's now in jail on murder one. Other than that, a real dull evening."

"They arrested a lawyer?" McCoy was incredulous. "It must have been a stunt for the *Guinness Book of Records*."

"McCoy," Zalman warned, "let's not cast any aspersions on the legal profession, okay? So how'd you like to come up here and . . ."

Marie came into the room, laden with packages. "I bought so much stuff I can't believe . . . Oh, sorry," she said when she saw he was on the phone. "Who are you talking to?"

"McCoy," Zalman said.

"Can I talk to Rutherford?" Marie asked promptly.

"In one minute. McCoy, yes or no? You want to come up and check out a few things for me?"

"What's the weather like?" McCoy wanted to know.

"Overcast in the morning, light sun in the afternoon, no chance of rain. What am I, Willard Scott? It's weather. The weather's always great in Santa Barbara. You want to work or what?"

"Can I please talk to Rutherford?" Marie whined. "Please?"

"Oh, Christ, all right. McCoy, put Rutherford on."

Marie grabbed for the phone. "How's my little doggums woggums?" she crooned. "Does ums miss ums mommy?"

"Jesus," Zalman muttered. "I hope this phone isn't tapped."

"Oootsie woootsie loves ums mommy," Marie gushed. Rutherford howled pitifully in the background. "Oh, hi, Dean . . . ummmm, you are? Hold on, I'll put Jerry back on, but I need to talk to you again, so don't hang up, okay?" She tossed the phone on the bed and ran out of the room.

"I take it you're joining us?" Zalman said. "I've got a swell motel lined up for . . . yes, on the damn beach . . . yes, it's got a bar. . . ."

Marie scampered back in and grabbed the phone. "And it's okay to bring Rutherford," she said happily. "Tracee says she'd love to have him as a houseguest."

"Terrific," Zalman said. "Just what I need." He took the phone from Marie. "See you tomorrow, Dean, early afternoon." He gave McCoy the address and hung up. "You sure this is okay with Tracee?" he asked suspiciously.

"Of course! I just asked her! Rutherford's such a good boy, he can sleep here with us."

"Boy, I'm looking forward to that, let me tell you. These long nights just aren't the same without the smell of dog hair in your nostrils."

Marie got into the bed and cuddled up next to him. "Don't you want to see what I got? Tracee took me to this super place where they have sexy underwear."

"Be still my heart," he said, putting his arm around her and nibbling on her earlobe. "So let's go to bed early and play fashion show. . . ."

But after dinner Yip wanted to take Zalman and Marie over to see the World O' Yip construction site, which was in the final frenzied phase of completion. "You're gonna be fascinated, Jerry," Yip promised. "World O' Yip is going to be an important new entrepreneurial venture, a mini–La Costa, except more nutritional, you know?" Yip's by-now familiar spiel was heartwarming in its sincerity.

"How far is it?" Zalman asked. He wasn't in the mood for any three-hour buggy ride with the Knottes just to look at a dusty pile of two-by-fours, especially when he had Marie's frilly purchases on his mind.

"Fifteen minutes! C'mon, Jerry. You're gonna love it," Yip insisted.

Zalman agreed dully, keeping his reservations to himself. A good guest, he reminded himself as they piled into the Country Squire, always acquiesces cheerfully to the entertainment provided by his host.

As promised, World O' Yip was only fifteen minutes

north up U.S. Highway 101, but it was far more elaborate than a pile of boards. Zalman got out of the car and looked thoughtfully at the huge building, looming up out of the darkness like a giant stingray, illuminated by shafts of pale moonlight. It was nearly complete. The walls and roof were in place, the windows and doors were in. And Yip had been right about another thing—the location. World O' Yip occupied perhaps twenty acres of choice land on the cliffs north of Goleta, the dusky Pacific crashing below, the lights of Isla Vista and Santa Barbara twinkling merrily to the south down the coast. All that remained was some interior finishing and exterior landscaping, he heard Yip tell Marie proudly. Plus a few minor details, like the new oxygen tubes for longevity promotion, some carpeting around the big redwood hot tubs strategically placed so the guests could gaze out over the sea while soaking away the myriad cares of modern life. And, of course, the statue still had to be mounted on its pedestal.

"It's a thirty-foot bronze of Tracee, sort of rising out of a bed of clamshells like that Botticelli Venus? Boy, it's swell!" Yip said enthusiastically.

"I bet it is," Zalman agreed honestly. He was sold. It was some place all right, and he began to think that maybe Yip was onto something, that his constant salesman rap was more than just sizzle.

"See, the whole place stems from an ocean motif," Tracee put in. "We believe our guests will feel truly at home with an aquatic theme." She beamed.

Zalman stared up at the building. "Any lights?" he asked. "I'd like to get a better look."

"You bet," Yip said. "I'll go turn on the work lights. Everything's hooked up inside. Boy, I knew you were gonna love this, Jerry!" He disappeared into a corrugated steel work shed, and a moment later World O' Yip lit up like Captain Nemo's submarine.

Zalman had to admit it was spectacular. Two great

winglike galleries curved up and away from a central pillar of glass that leapt out of the sandy ground like a gigantic flying fish. Glass and iridescent tile glittered on every surface and gave the impression of the sea retreating from a pebble-strewn expanse of beach. Tracee was right; the effect was truly aquatic. An oceanic world of fantasy lay before them.

"Wow!" Zalman said. "I'm impressed."

"Holy smoke," Marie breathed. "It's just gorgeous."

"Isn't it something?" Yip said, returning to the little group. "Of course, we have a great architect, but it's all Tracee's concept."

"Some concept," Zalman agreed.

"Yipper did it all," Tracee demurred. "I just motivated him so he could let his true creative potential shine through."

"Can we go inside?" Marie wanted to know.

"Of course." Yip led them inside through the cavelike entrance that served as the front door. The lobby looked more like a large, comfortable living room than a hotel. The ocean motif was continued in every piece of furniture: carved wood end tables inlaid with mother-of-pearl, nubbly sea-foam-white armchairs, frothy green sofas. The golden chandeliers that glowed with hidden fire had graceful sea-plant designs curling their way along the arms like tendrils.

"The living areas, all of them two-room suites, are to the right," Yip said. "They're completely isolated from the gyms, exercise rooms, flotation tanks, saunas, juice bar, meditation chambers. . . . A guest can have total privacy if he or she is on retreat. Why, for them, World O' Yip is totally silent. There's complete room service for any diet, a private path to our adults-only beach. . . . World O' Yip offers every possible comfort." Yip sounded like a commercial for *Architectural Digest*.

He led Zalman and Marie on a complete tour of World O' Yip. But by far the most spectacular room in the joint was the dining room, which was built right on the edge of the cliff. It was extended by a cantilevered deck which hung out over the ocean like a great wooden wave, allowing a Promethean vision of jagged rocks and roiling sea lying far below.

"Ohhhh boy, this is scary!" Marie said as she peered cautiously over the teak railing. "Looks like Godzilla's hideout." She pointed to a rocky crag set in the ocean bed a few hundred yards out. "You don't think anybody's going to fall over, do you?"

"We could have enclosed it, glassed it in," Tracee explained. "But we thought our guests would want to get close to it, smell the sea, feel the spray. . . ."

"Well, you sure can do that," Marie laughed as a wave broke below, casting up a fine mist in the evening air.

"We want World O' Yip to offer as much of the natural environment as possible," Yip said. "Within the context of a world-class resort, of course. So what do you think, Jerry?" Yip's voice trembled with excitement. "Place is great, huh?"

"Let me get this straight," Zalman said. "You want me to go to your dad and try and squeeze . . . what are we talking about here? A hundred grand?"

"Well . . ." Yip hesitated.

"More than a hundred? Yip, Yip, Yip, you're kidding yourself! Your dad ain't coming up with megabucks. He's a tightwad if ever I saw one. Bet he used to give you fifty cents a week when you were a kid and make you account for every nickel of it."

"A dollar," Yip admitted. "It was a dollar."

"You ask my professional advice, your dad ain't gonna pop for the dough. But I gotta admit, I like this place, Yip, and Santa Barbara is just the spot for it. People can fly down from San Francisco, they can come up from L.A., yet it isn't too far from home base. L.A. types get nervous if they're too far from home, especially the studio guys.

117

They think somebody's gonna set their desk on fire. Let me think about it. Maybe I can come up with something."

"You think you can?" Yip asked anxiously. "Aw, that'd be great, Jerry. After all, this is a business venture, not just a weird idea. We offer a world without pressure, a world *away* from the world, even if you're just here for the weekend. We sort of like to think of it like a luxury cruise. . . ."

"I'm sold, Yip," Zalman laughed. "Let me think on it."

McCoy, Rutherford, and Chester showed up at noon on Sunday. McCoy had driven his rattletrap Chevy pickup up to Santa Barbara, and he had Rutherford and Chester in the back along with empty beer cans, dusty old dog rugs, and the rest of the strange assortment of equipment he always carried in the truck in case of emergencies —hanks of frayed rope, a couple of chipped bricks, rusty tools, a pair of old boots, and a galvanized pail that looked like it had last done service in the Spanish-American War. McCoy had his own slant on preparedness.

Zalman was relaxing on the deck. He'd slept till noon and was now lingering over a cigar and a second cup of coffee from Tracee's secret stash of mocha java, admiring the view through his dark glasses. He heard the doorbell ring and looked in through the sliding glass door to see McCoy greeting Tracee and Marie, Rutherford and Chester at his heels. Zalman finished his coffee and went inside.

Tracee was giving McCoy a sisterly kiss on the cheek. "Dean, you look the same," she said, smiling.

McCoy cocked his eyebrow and grinned evilly. "Yeah, you can't keep a remittance man down. You look gorgeous, as always, Trace. And you, Miss Thrasher, don't I rate a kiss for bringing this meatsack all this way up here to see you?"

Marie was crouched on the floor, scratching Rutherford's belly. "How's ums little woojie baby," she crooned. She began to get up, but McCoy, who was a good foot taller than Marie, reached down and picked her up bodily. "Put me down, Dean!" She laughed, kicking her feet in the air. Rutherford whimpered and jumped up on McCoy's legs while Chester lifted his lip and growled faintly.

"All right, all right, let's cut the byplay," Zalman said as he joined them in the foyer.

McCoy, still holding Marie, stuck out his hand for a shake.

"Dean!" Marie squealed. "Put me down!"

"Okay, okay." He laughed. "You're such a munchkin I can't resist. . . . Got a cup of coffee for a tired old man, Trace?" he said easily as he let Marie slide to the ground.

"You two go back outside and I'll bring out a tray," Tracee said.

McCoy followed Zalman out onto the deck while Marie returned her attention to her beloved doggums-woggums. McCoy glanced around the plush living room as he went. "Some setup," he observed, settling into a deck chair and gazing at the view through wraparound sunglasses. "A guy could get used to this. You weren't kidding, bucko. Our Tracee has done all right for herself. So where's the husband?"

Zalman shrugged and waved airily. "Off to work, I suppose?"

McCoy shook his head and grinned. "I don't know how you do it, pal. You got the wife and you got the girlfriend, and they're both in the same house. . . ."

"I'm a great guy, Dean, that's how I do it. Besides, Tracee is my *ex*-wife, and don't you forget it. Believe me, I haven't. Divorce is a great equalizer if you know how to handle it. Besides, a weekend setup like this, it's kinda like polygamy without the pain. But enough of this psychological yimmy-yammy. Let's run over to the Blue Fin Inn, where you'll be staying."

Tracee pulled open the glass door, came out onto the deck, and set a tray down on the table. Chester followed her, stared belligerently around, then, satisfied there was nothing to kill, lay down on McCoy's booted feet.

"We're going to have facials now, so if there's anything else you want, you'll probably find it in the kitchen," Tracee said as she left.

"So where's the Toulouse-Lautrec?" McCoy asked as he sipped his coffee.

"I'll get it, I'll get it."

"You sure?" McCoy needled.

"Sure I'm sure." Zalman blew a double smoke ring and watched it drift out over the Santa Barbara coastline. "It's in the bag."

"Unless Tracee double-crosses you," McCoy laughed.

Zalman shook his head knowingly. "Not a chance. Take a look inside, Dean, and tell me what you see."

Obligingly, McCoy shifted his bulk around and stared into the Knotte living room. He did a double take and turned back to Zalman. "What the hell are they doing in there?" he asked. Tracee and Marie, both with a green substance on their faces which made them look like a pair of dissatisfied Trobriand Islanders, were sitting on the living room floor. Both were very serious, and Marie had a yellow pencil stuck behind her ear and was totting up numbers on a pocket calculator.

"Plain to see you're not a marital vet, Dean old buddy," Zalman said, leaning back in his candy-striped deck chair. "They have masks on their faces. They've been in the kitchen with their heads stuck over a pot of steaming water, sweating. Then they put on this green muddy gunk and wait till it hardens. Then they wash it off, spritz themselves with Evian water, and go out and buy something expensive to compensate themselves for all that suffering. But what you really see in there are two women who've become bosom buddies. Tracee won't double-cross me. It'd be just like double-crossing Marie, and she'll never, never do that. Besides, she needs my legal expertise."

McCoy nudged Chester off his feet and stretched out his long blue-jeaned legs. He helped himself to a piece of cake. "Pretty good cake," he said after a minute, munching contentedly.

"Tracee made it."

"Tracee?" McCoy was incredulous. "She didn't make cake when we knew her."

"Lay off, Dean, I'm warning you. So, you ready to go play detective?"

"You bet, pal. Who do we have to kill to get out of here?"

Zalman shivered and looked around. "Dean, I wish you wouldn't say stuff like that. Somebody might hear you and misunderstand."

"Bang bang bang," McCoy said, firing a finger gun in the air. "What're we after, local gossip?"

"Yeah. E.Y. Knotte was after the secretary, and I'd like to know what else is going on at Knotte Pines. Rumor, innuendo, trash, slander, that's what I'm after. I thought you and I might go undercover and check out the local watering hole."

"Sounds like a fun afternoon." McCoy grinned, daintily cleaning himself up with a linen napkin. "Chester, into the truck. I'll drive, Zally. The Mercedes is the wrong image for this expedition."

THE BLUE FIN INN WAS A SLEEPY LITTLE JOINT NEAR THE bay in an unfashionable part of Santa Barbara just begging for gentrification. The joint consisted of twenty or so motel units strung out in back beneath red tile roofs and a couple of massive eucalyptus trees. The bar was out front where nobody could miss it. In the afternoon it catered to the RV crowd, to Mom and Pop out spending the kids' inheritance on the dusty retirement trail that led from Arizona to the Oregon coast and back again. Along with the seniors, sports fishermen made up a substantial part of the clientele, as well as a few peroxide dames with poodles, a little insurance money, and too much time on their hands. There were some longhair hardhats with paychecks burning holes in their wallets. And of course, the place was also a favorite for the semipro hookers from Isla Vista, working their way through college. That was Happy Hour at the Blue Fin bar. Zalman had gotten this information from Yip, who'd also given him an idea of what the joint was like after dark. Then it was flush with Surf City sinners, with long-haired guys of all ages who'd never fallen out of love with Annette Funicello, with women who thought *Where the Boys Are* was high art, with aristocrats from the hills and plebes from the flats, with the hitters and the shell-shocked and everything in between. Yip said that after dark the Blue Fin was the hottest cantina on the beach.

"Looks right, Zally," McCoy said as he pulled the pickup into the big blacktopped parking lot. "How'd you find it?"

"Yip took me for a drive. It's a night scene, he says." Zalman dusted off the seat of his gray flannel summer-weight trousers as he got out of the truck. He looked disapprovingly at Chester, who was sleeping in the pickup bed on a dusty rug, surrounded by crushed Coors cans. "Why don't you get this thing washed, Dean?" he said. "You could get a disease here."

McCoy shook his head. "Kinda girls I go for, *they* go for a guy with a truck like this. I'm manly, see, but I'm sensitive." He grinned. "Most of 'em read too many magazines, you ask me. Now Zally, you just follow my lead here, okay? Put your watch in your pocket, leave that snazzy blazer in the truck and pull out your shirttails. Try and look a little distressed, got it? Like a guy having a hard time at home. Chester, you stay here and lemme know if anybody fools with the truck, okay?" Chester opened an evil eye and bared his two-inch fangs.

"Chester isn't as friendly as my pal Rutherford," Zalman observed as he pulled out his shirttails.

"Nah," McCoy said as they walked toward a set of plank doors set in the low adobe building that housed the Blue Fin bar. "Chester's a real villain, is what he is. That's why he stays in the truck. Don't need no locks if you got Chester. . . . Say, this place looks all right!" he said as he pulled open the battered doors and peered into the gloom.

Zalman looked around. The Blue Fin bar was dark and comforting, the way a bar should be at two o'clock on a Sunday afternoon. There were a lot of little tables scattered around a dance floor and a long curved bar with glittering mirrors and glasses and Christmas lights strung all up and down the shelves, although Christmas wasn't around the corner by a long shot. There was a big, battered Sebring jukebox playing what was probably Art Tatum, and a chubby blue swordfish that must have been eight feet long over the back bar, right under a brightly painted Day-Glo surfboard. It was quiet, and there were only a few midafternoon patrons at the tables, mostly tanned sports-fishermen types getting an early start on the day's drinking, plus a couple of poodle ladies. A big, good-looking blonde looked up from behind the bar where she was busy polishing glasses.

"Hello, boys," she said throatily. "What'll it be?"

Zalman felt McCoy stiffen up beside him. When he looked over at his pal, he had the feeling that McCoy had died and gone to heaven. He was gazing at the woman with the expression of a stunned salmon on his big face, his mouth hanging open slightly, his eyes glazed. Zalman had the distinct impression that all one hundred of the World's Most Beloved Melodies were playing inside McCoy's fevered noggin.

The woman was a full-blown but firm blonde with her long hair braided and coiled on top of her head like the crown of a Wagnerian heroine, minus the hat with the horns. She looked about thirty, and it was obvious that her pale, creamy skin had never seen the inside of a tanning bed, a fact of some note in a beach community like Santa Barbara. She was clearly a woman who worshipped the Great Indoors.

"Seven and seven," McCoy said dreamily as he took a stool next to the service well. "Zally?"

"Seven and seven, huh? It's a little early for me."

"The hell you say," McCoy said heartily. "My buddy here's having a bad time," he told the blonde. "His wife . . ."

"Awwww, that's too bad, hon," she said, delicately removing a wad of gum and wrapping it in a paper coaster. "Well, a little drink's just the thing to cheer you up, isn't it?" she said as she expertly mixed McCoy's drink and slid it across the bar, leaning over slightly as she did so. She had quite a chest on her, a fact not lost on Doyle Dean McCoy.

Zalman slipped into his role of the beaten divorce victim. "Some women," he said with the crestfallen air of a man done wrong, "Some women just don't know when they've got a good thing. I bought her a microwave! I bought her one of those food deals that whizzes stuff up into little bits! I bought her a Corvette. Sure, it was pre-owned, but it was low miles, and it had a ground-glass paint job on it, plus tuck-and-roll straight from T.J. I tried to be a good husband. . . . I'll have Black Label and a Perrier back."

"We got regular club soda, that okay?" the bartendress said. "By the way, my name's Molly." She pushed a dish of beer nuts across the bar and poured Zalman's drink. "Don't let it get to you, hon," she advised. "Marriage don't mean what it used to. I been married twice so far, and I'm only thirty."

"You're thirty!" McCoy said with an air of amazement. "I don't believe it. You believe she's thirty, Zally?"

Zalman squinted at Molly and shook his head in disbelief. "No way," he pronounced emphatically. "Never would take you for thirty. Twenty-six, tops."

Molly preened under their scrutiny and adjusted her off-the-shoulder Mexican lace blouse. "Well, you boys are sweet." She laughed skeptically. "I'll say that! Another round?" She leaned forward conversationally. "I'd like to make it on the house, but my boss is as tight as a gnat's ass!"

"No problem!" Zalman said expansively, pretending he was already a little tight. He hauled a wad of cash out of his wallet and smacked it on the bar. "Set 'em up and have one yourself, Molly! Now I'm gonna get divorced, I only got myself to blow my dough on. No more microwaves," he brooded.

Molly shot him a sympathetic glance, set up another

round, and drew herself a Lite Beer. "What happened? Was it another guy?"

Zalman nodded sadly. "This rich geezer, lives around here? He started to put the moves on her, and, well, sure, he was a lot older'n her, but when a guy has so much dough . . ." He buried his head in his hands, and McCoy patted him on the back, man-to-man.

Molly sucked in her breath. "Oh, no!" she squealed. "Not you, *too!* This guy, was this guy E. Y. Knotte?"

Zalman stared at McCoy. McCoy stared back at Zalman. "How did you know?" Zalman asked in feigned astonishment. "You psychic or what?"

Molly was hopping up and down behind the bar, her considerable chest rippling. McCoy leaned forward to get a better look. "I just can't be-leeeve it!" she said. "That Mr. Knotte is the absolute end! He just can't keep his hands off the girls," she said conspiratorially. "He's caused *more* trouble in here. And the thing of it is," she said, sipping her beer with ladylike gentility, "he always comes down to the beach bars to do it! With that ritzy wife of his and that big house you'd think he'd stay home nights, but noooo! He's always slippin' round. You poor thing." She patted Zalman's arm. "How about another shooter, on the house?" she said slyly.

Zalman had a long pull on his Canada Dry. The jukebox slid into Linda Ronstadt's "Lush Life." The afternoon stretched soddenly ahead for divorced guys with payments on Corvettes they'd never see again.

"Married to some rich dame, huh? Figures . . ."

Molly leaned up against the bar. "You bet he is. A movie star, Rhonda Warwick. Remember her? And do you know, with all his money, with all his big fancy stuff, that wife of his steals?"

"Steals!" McCoy said. "I'm shocked."

"Well, you know, pinches stuff, from expensive stores. Nobody knows why, but everybody up and down the beach thinks it's a regular hoot!" Molly was indignant. "The thing is, she drinks. First she drinks, then she steals. Now, a girl like me, working as a bartender, well, I guess you boys know I've got nothing against a little recreational liquor, if a person can handle it. But I never would serve nobody who's drunk, and that's a straight fact!" she said proudly. "She came in here once, loaded up to the eyeballs, and I just plain wouldn't serve her. 'Mrs. Knotte,' I said, 'you go home now and put your feet up, 'cause you aren't getting a drink from Molly McCafferty!'"

McCoy reached out and took her hand. "Baby," he said, "this sure as poop must be kismet on a stick. My name's Doyle Dean McCoy. What say you and me get married? You won't even have to change the monogram on your lingerie."

Molly shrieked with laughter. "You just never mind about my lingerie, Doyle Dean McCoy!"

"How come she doesn't get arrested?" Zalman asked, not wanting Molly to lose her ability at ratiocination.

"Oh, I think she does," Molly said vaguely, gazing into McCoy's baby-blue eyes. "But rich people know how to get away with things, don't they? And that district attorney, whatshisname, Carmichael, he's a big friend of theirs, and they just call him up, is what I think. Another one, hon?"

Inwardly, Zalman digested this newest piece of information on the nutty Knottes. Outwardly, he moaned, enmeshed in the emotion generated by his character of the husband wronged. "How could she do this to me? I loved her! I gave her everything!" he exclaimed fervently.

"Awwww," Molly said. "You poor thing. It always amazes me, the power of true love, and that's a straight fact."

"There any rooms in this motel?" McCoy asked innocently. "I came up from L.A. to help out my pal here, and now it looks like I'm gonna need me a motel room for a few days. Maybe longer," he said, leaning forward on the bar and gazing hopefully at Molly McCafferty.

"Well, I think so," Molly said coyly. "Just go straight

out the back door and up the path and talk to Art, the desk man. Can't miss it."

"Be right back, Zally," McCoy said as he slid off the bar stool. "Now Molly, what time do you get off work anyway?"

"My, my, my, Mr. Doyle Dean McCoy, aren't we fast? Well, we'll just see about that when you come back. I'll have to ask your friend here all about your character. I don't go out with just anybody. I have very high standards."

"Gimme a good ref, Zally," McCoy said as he started for the back door. "I got a feeling Miss Molly is one in a zillion."

"Don't worry," Zalman called. "I won't say anything about your six kids. . . ."

McCoy laughed hollowly. Zalman turned back to Molly, who regarded him quizzically. He moaned pathetically and buried his head in his hands. "I can't believe this is happening to me." The statement held more than a grain of truth. "You sure this is the same guy, this Knotte guy?"

"Sounds like it to me," Molly said as she resumed polishing glasses on the mirrored back bar. A look of horror crossed her face, and her eyes widened dramatically. "Saaaay, your wife isn't that Lisa that got killed up there last night, is she?"

Zalman shook his head and ran his hands through his hair, getting into his part. "Tiffany," he said wretchedly. "My wife's name is Tiffany. Somebody got killed?"

Molly nodded, polishing more vigorously. "You damn betcha. It's all over the beach. Heard about it first thing when I came in! Mr. Knotte's secretary got sizzled in the swimming pool, just like a french fried potato! Can you believe it? Goes in for a swim and *zzzzzzzz!* I heard Mr. Knotte was trying to play whoop-dee-doo with her, and her boyfriend found out and put the plug from the whatsit into the thingbat, and zipitty zip goes the girlfriend, is what I heard." She shook her head sadly, got out a feather duster, and tickled the bottle tops along the back bar. "You ask me, it's all pretty darn fishy. Now, Zally—that really your name? Tell me the truth—your friend, he isn't married, is he?"

"No way," Zalman said with complete honesty. "No kids either. I was just joking. Never been married at all, as a matter of fact."

"Not at all?" Molly queried. "Well, what do you know. Just a baby, huh? What kinda car's he drive?"

"See for yourself. Pickup with a big ugly dog in it, right outside," Zalman said, gesturing toward the parking lot.

Molly came around the bar and took a look out the front door. "Just as I thought," she said, returning to her station. "Well, I'll probably go out with him, but he's gonna have to clean out the front of that truck before I get in it, and that's a straight fact."

"I'm always telling him the same thing," Zalman agreed.

McCoy came back inside and sat down at the bar. "Well, I got a room," he informed them happily. "You tell Molly that I'm an upstanding citizen?"

Zalman nodded. "I had to tell her everything, Dean," he said lugubriously. "She'll never go out with you now, fella!"

Molly put her hands on her hips and surveyed Zalman and McCoy shrewdly. "I bet you two've known each other a long time, am I right?"

Zalman and McCoy nodded like a pair of puppets.

"I thought so. Well, loyalty's a good quality. Okay, Dean, I get off work at eight, and I'll let you take me to dinner—if you clean out the front of your truck so it's fit for a girl to ride in."

McCoy grinned. "You got a deal, Miss Molly. I'll even run it through the car wash for you, return the empties and everything."

"Well, don't go too far now," she laughed. "I don't believe in changing a man, just trying to take a tuck in his behavior."

Zalman got the check and left Molly a good tip. "See you later, Molly," he said as he and McCoy went out into the crashing brightness of the parking lot. He blinked and fumbled desperately for his dark glasses.

"Boy!" McCoy said with fervor, "that's some attractive-type lady." Chester leapt out of the truck as they approached, barking merrily.

Zalman reached down absently to pat him on the head, but the dog snarled and laid his ears back. Zalman jerked his hand away as if from a hot stone.

"Cute, huh?" McCoy grinned. "It's a trick, see? Every time you reach out to pat him, he does that. Scares the pants off people. Good boy, Chester," he said, tossing the dog an empty beer can to play with. Chester caught it on the fly and threw it up into the air. "Now what, Zally?" McCoy asked as they got back in the truck.

"Now you take me back to Tracee's and I take a shower to remove some of this dog slobber. Then I go have a little chat with Mrs. Knotte, see if I can worm my way into her confidence."

"Sure, anything you want," McCoy said, staring longingly at the door of the Blue Fin bar as he eased the Chevy's motor to life and let it idle gently in the soft ocean wind. Chester leapt back into the bed, pressed his wet snout against the rear window, and eyed Zalman's ear hungrily.

"What are you going to do?" Zalman asked, trying to ignore the dog.

"Hell." McCoy grinned broadly. "You saw Molly. I'm gonna go get this sucker washed."

MARIE AND TRACEE WERE IN THE LIVING ROOM WATCHING "Moneyline" when Zalman came in. Marie, who usually wore her auburn hair loose around her shoulders, had it piled on top of her head in a cascade of ringlets fastened with a pair of ebony chopsticks.

"So," she was saying seriously to Tracee, "the higher the interest rate, the higher the risk, see?"

"Ohhhh, I get it!" Tracee said knowingly. "That's why you get so little if you go to a bank! Banks are supposed to be safe!"

"Exactly," Marie said. "But you've gotta figure the ratio of risk to return. It's just the same as Vegas, *I* think, though my broker swears it's not."

"Nice hair," Zalman said as he kissed Marie on the cheek. "We get fortune cookies with this?"

She bopped him on the arm and flicked off Lou Dobbs. "A girl likes to try something new every once in a while."

"Gee, I hope not!" Zalman said.

"Besides, I thought you'd like to get a good look at the nape of my neck before this relationship goes any further."

Zalman bent over, inspected her nape, and gave her a playful nibble. "Soy sauce, my favorite. It's obvious you ladies have been to the beauty parlor. Do they still call them beauty parlors, now that everybody's so trendy and modern and sincere?"

"Salons," Tracee said. "But I just say I'm going to see Ruby. Ruby does my hair, Betsy does my nails." She held out her hands for inspection. "Pretty, huh?"

Tracee's nails were dragon-lady long and colored an iridescent pink that rippled off to a light blue when she moved them in the light. "We thought you might want to find out about E.Y.'s various girlfriends, and Ruby Toucan's is the place to do it," she said smugly. "That's my hairdresser's, Ruby Toucan's."

Zalman stared at his ex-wife. "What?" he asked. "What girlfriends?"

"E.Y.'s girlfriends," Marie repeated. "He's a positive love weasel!"

"Did you know this all along?" Zalman asked Tracee in exasperation.

"Of course," she answered innocently. "Didn't you?"

"Other than Lisa Comden?"

"Of course other than Lisa! Everybody knows it! You can't help but know it, he's positively awful. Do you know," she said, turning to Marie, "one time I'd just hired this new woman to come in and cook three times a week? I love to cook, but you *do* want a break once in a while. . . . So I'd just hired this new lady, and she was from Thailand and did all this simply wonderful stuff in peanut sauce and mint leaves? Well, here she was, she'd just done her first dinner, and was it good! E.Y. and Rhonda were here, and let me tell you, Rhonda was skunked!

"But anyway," Tracee went on, "I turned my back for a minute, and there's this terrible squeaking coming from the kitchen! Positive *squeak*ing, like a very big mouse. So I rush in there, and there's E.Y., he's got poor Miss Tung or whatever her name is backed up against the counter, and she's going *Eeeeee! Eeeeee!* like a gigantic mouse! Was I embarrassed!"

133

Marie was fascinated. "Were they actually doing it?"

"Well, that's the thing. I couldn't really tell! I mean, I didn't really peer at their private parts or anything, and of course they had their clothes on, and I just whipped right out of there, let me tell you!" Tracee giggled. "He's just awful! Don't ever let him get you alone, that's all I have to say."

"Well, I told you I had to poke him with my fork last night," Marie said. "I just didn't know what else to do!"

Zalman slipped off his loafers and put his feet on the coffee table and his head in his hands. "Why is this happening to me?" he moaned. "Tracee, couldn't you have mentioned this before? I bring Dean all the way up here— at great personal expense, I point out—so he can play detective—"

"Dean isn't a detective," Tracee said with great certainty. "Dean is a darling, but he's no detective."

"Don't let him hear you say that," Zalman muttered. "What am I saying? Don't let *me* hear that, either. Be that as it may, I'm paying him to romp around Santa Barbara and pry into the personal lives of the various members of the Knotte family—"

"Jerry, that isn't nice," Tracee said seriously. "You shouldn't do that."

Zalman took a deep, calming breath and glanced over at Marie, who was innocently staring off at Andy Warhol's "Endangered Species" panda, pretending to study it intently. "Tracee," he said with tremendous forbearance, "can you remember what happened last night, hmmmm? Remember how we went outside and there was a formerly living person floating in the swimming pool? And how maybe that person could have been your father-in-law? You asked me to come here because you were worried about him, because *you* thought he might be in danger. Is that image etched on your memory, dear?"

"Well, yes," Tracee said, "but I don't—"

"And you *do* remember," Zalman continued patiently,

134

"that there is a young man in jail now because of last night's events, a nice but very stupid young man who claims that he is not the killer of said young lady? Do you?"

Tracee nodded, her blond hair catching the light like mica in a star embedded in a Hollywood Boulevard sidewalk.

"Well, let me tell you, as your attorney, I can promise you that before this thing is over, Lieutenant Primativo Espinoza is going to know more about the entire Knotte clan than the *National Enquirer* could dig up in ten years of trying. So if there's anything else you'd like to tell me, feel free. I don't want Espinoza creeping up on me with some nasty bit of trivia from your past, got it? And until such time as I'm satisfied that I've got the full picture of what's going on here, I intend to keep McCoy poking around. He may not be much of a detective, as you note, but he has a curious way of running across things accidentally, and believe me, I'll take all the help I can get. Earth to Tracee, are you receiving me?"

"Well, of course." Tracee fidgeted. "But, like, what do you want to know?"

"How the hell should I know?" Zalman exploded. "For one thing, you might have told me about E.Y.'s penchant for pulchritude."

"Huh?"

"Girls, Tracee! You could have told me about E.Y.'s girlfriends!"

"Well, I didn't know what you wanted to know!" Tracee whined. "If I'd known what you wanted to know I would have told you, for heaven's sake! It's just that I didn't know it, okay? Honestly, Jerry, it's just like looking words up in the dictionary! How can you look something up so you can spell it when you don't know how to spell it so you can look it up?"

Zalman stared blankly at her.

"You just tell me what you want to know and I'll tell you

135

everything I know about it, okay?" Tracee reached out and patted Zalman on the hand like he was a disgruntled four-year-old who'd gone too long between naps. "Good, I'm glad we settled that!" she said.

"Marie, if I sniveled and begged, do you think you could rub my back?" he asked weakly.

"Of course, sweetheart." Marie smiled. "Just don't mess with my chop suey."

A FEW MINUTES LATER ZALMAN WAS LYING FACEDOWN ON the bed and Marie was rubbing his back with a firm, practiced hand. "So tell me everything," she said. "Are we going to have high jinx in high society? Love nest raided? Society swell snuffed? Tell all, Jerry," she said as she wrenched his shoulder blade. "Gee, you're awful tight!"

"Errrrrgh," Zalman groaned. "I spent the afternoon riding around in McCoy's filthy truck, which smells like a toxic waste dump, and sitting in dark bars listening to zaftig blondes."

"Blondes, hmmmm," she said, twisting his arm playfully.

"Errrrrgh!" he said again. "Please, Marie, light of my life, there's no cause for alarm! McCoy's got a date with her later tonight, and I think he's hoping he'll get lucky. He actually went off to get the truck washed."

Marie stopped rubbing. "You're kidding! He washed the truck? It must be true love!"

"For God's sake, don't stop. Higher."

Marie resumed her ministrations. "Jerry, darling, you could forget the whole thing. After all, Tracee didn't know there'd be a murder when she asked you for help, and besides, the police are investigating, and for God's sake, you don't actually need the Toulouse-Lautrec. Tracee would probably give it to you, at this point. You *have* helped her."

Zalman sat up on the bed and put his arm around her. "Let me tell you something, doll. You're probably right. Tracee would give me the litho at this point. It does belong to me, and she's basically honest. Not too bright, but honest."

Marie rose to her friend's defense. "You shouldn't say that, Jerry. Tracee is every bit as smart as she needs to be."

Zalman laughed. "Dead right, doll. Tracee is exactly as smart as she needs to be. And she's smarter than that empty-jumpsuit husband of hers, that's for damned sure."

Marie opened her mouth to protest but realized she couldn't. She giggled. "Yip is very sweet," she said helpfully. "Nice-looking, too."

"Sure, sure. He's a face man, know what I mean? The guy you put out front 'cause it fits the image. Hell, he gives great commercial, I'll say that for him. But cuteness is not the issue here, my darling. Both Yip and Tracee are exceedingly cute. Very cute, very modern, and they have good taste. My ex-wife also makes a helluva apple cake, something she did not do when she was my wife, I point out, more's the pity. You want to know the truth? I'm not staying here because of my Toulouse-Lautrec, although I fully and completely intend to have it hanging on my office wall inside a week."

"So why are you staying, Jerry?" Marie asked, turning over on her tummy. "Now you do my back."

"Delighted." He reached up under her flowered sweatshirt and began to rub. "I am staying because the milk of human kindness flows through my veins. . . ."

"Now Jerry . . ." She laughed warningly.

"It's true! It's true! Listen, you and Tracee and Yip and Rhonda and E.Y. don't seem to realize it, but there's a young guy sitting in jail right now, and if I don't help him, who's going to? Not E. Y. Knotte, and certainly not Arthur Carmichael. Maybe Espinoza, if I work on him a little. But

138

Robin's got the brain of a turnip, and I'll tell you, Marie, I feel sorry for him. The poor kid looks like a fox with the hounds on his heels."

"How would you know what a fox looked like? You ever been fox hunting?"

"Me? Perish the thought. A guy named Jerry Zalman doesn't ride to hounds. You think I'm crazy? But guys named Zalman know what the fox feels like, know what I mean?"

Marie rolled over and looked at him with a questioning, half-serious expression. "Yeah, I get it. Go on."

Zalman pulled up her shirt and began to kiss her on the stomach. "So," he said between kisses. "I'm going to get this poor fool out of jail because I think somebody framed him. I have three very good reasons for doing this. One, the aforementioned milk of human kindness flows in my veins. Two, if I can get this guy off, I'll have some much-needed free legal work done around the office for the rest of my life. I need a guy to run errands for me, and Robin looks like a good candidate, especially if I don't have to shell out for him. And three, and most important, I'm on E.Y.'s payroll, so what the hey?"

"I knew it!" Marie cried. "I knew we'd get to the money part of the deal. Do you mean that you're going to take money from E.Y. for getting Robin off *and* you're going to sock the poor dolt with a fee? Jerry, you're impossible!"

Zalman looked up at her and grinned. "And I'm gonna get my litho back, don't forget that. Hey, the milk of human kindness doesn't run cheap, doll."

"And all this time I thought it was Dom Perignon you had in your veins."

"It's hot Hungarian blood in my veins, and don't you forget it," he said as he rolled toward her on the big, wide bed. "And now," he grinned, "the defense rests. . . ."

AN HOUR AND A HALF LATER ZALMAN LEFT TRACEE'S
house, got into his Mercedes, and drove up the crushed-
rock road to the Knotte mansion above. It was a beautiful
late afternoon with warm, buttery sunlight filtering through
the eucalyptus trees and a cool wind off the sea, which
sparkled in the distance. There wasn't much smog, and far
below the roofs of Santa Barbara dozed beneath the light
haze. Zalman puffed on a Macanudo and felt exceedingly
satisfied with his station in life, which now included some
of E. Y. Knotte's legal business. Zalman drummed happily
on his walnut steering wheel. Things were definitely
breaking his way.

Just for the hell of it, he gave Esther Wong a buzz on the
way. She wasn't in the office, of course, but he left some
instructions on the answering machine and told her to can-
cel his appointments for the next few days. A few moments
later he pulled up in front of Knotte Pines, which looked as
gloomy as a Charles Addams cartoon despite the warm
sun.

Brunson opened the front door and didn't look exactly
overjoyed to see him. "Good evening," he intoned. "Are
we expected?"

"Nope," Zalman said as he pushed past the butler and
marched into the entrance hall. "We ain't. But why don't

you just scamper upstairs and tell Mrs. Knotte I'd like a word with her, Brunson. Won't take long." He smiled engagingly. Brunson folded his lip over his long teeth and humpffed slightly as he turned away.

Zalman hung around for a few minutes, admiring the tin soldiers, until Brunson oiled noiselessly into the room. "Mrs. Knotte asks if you'd care to join her in her sitting room," the butler said.

"Sure, Brunson, lead the way."

Brunson gave his mocking half bow and ushered Zalman past the row of armored men and up the broad staircase to Rhonda's sitting room on the second floor.

Rhonda opened the door herself, a shaft of light from within illuminating her red hair with angelic highlights. "Thank you, Brunson," she said huskily.

Brunson inclined his head slightly. "Very good, madam." He turned and minced down the stairs.

Zalman stepped in. "Where'd you get that guy, the Screen Extras Guild?"

Rhonda twittered a light little laugh. "Actually, I did. He played a butler in one of my last pictures, and after I married E.Y. I looked him up. He was out of work. . . . He makes a perfect butler, don't you think?"

"Too perfect by half," Zalman replied. "Shades of Erich von Stroheim. I don't think Brunson approves of the cut of my jib. Or maybe it's my lapels."

"He *is* very strict about style," Rhonda sighed. "And he's murder on my table settings."

"The guy can butle, I'll give him that," Zalman muttered, surprised by the room, which was completely different from the rest of Knotte Pines. Rhonda's sitting room was large and airy, with French doors opening onto a balcony at the back which overlooked the rear lawn. Rhonda's taste, as one might expect, ran to the exquisitely feminine. The room was packed with spindly-legged white and gold tables and chairs, a powder-blue satin chaise longue, and an entire wall of beveled, gilt-framed mirrors. A large pair of grinning golden cupids flanked the white marble fireplace, and there was a row of elaborately inlaid music boxes lined up on the mantel. "Very baroque," he said.

Rhonda was posed theatrically against the closed door, her arms behind her, shielding the handle. "You like my little hideaway, Jerry?" she breathed. "I think a woman needs a place to herself, especially in the midst of my husband's rampant masculinity, n'est-ce pas? A little island of calm, as it were."

She smiled at Zalman, and he had the uncomfortable feeling she was going to poke him like a bon-bon, just to see if he had a nougat center. She drifted away from the door and sank down on a blue chaise, crossing her dainty little ankles. She was wearing a long white chiffon gown which was deeply décolleté, and she wasn't wearing any jewelry. With a figure like Rhonda Warwick Knotte's, jewelry was redundant.

Zalman perched on one of the lacy white and gold chairs, feeling overwhelmed by the excessive femininity. "Thanks for meeting with me, Rhonda," he said.

"I think we ought to get to know each other, don't you?" she said, arching her little foot in its cunningly strapped gold sandal. She wasn't wearing stockings either, and her toenails showed a deep ruby red as the white chiffon swirled around her long legs like incoming sea foam.

Zalman smiled with professional ease. "Rhonda, I hope you don't mind my asking personal questions, especially when I haven't known you very long . . . but under the circumstances . . ."

"Of course, Jerry! Anything! Ask me anything you want!" Her movie-star smile flooded the room like a klieg light.

"Tell me about E.Y. and Art Carmichael. What's the nature of their relationship?"

"That social climber!" she shrilled in a voice that could have shattered a TV tube. "He's always hanging around E.Y., and now he wants E.Y. to back him for the state

senate, which he might be able to handle, though I have
my doubts. He's just after our money, but he can be useful.
I thought he was quite helpful the other night, didn't you?"
she asked, indicating that Carmichael might come in handy
if ever there were a worldwide shortage of Twenty Mule
Team Borax.

"Oh, very helpful," Zalman agreed. "Very helpful indeed. But that's what started me wondering, Rhonda.
D.A.'s don't usually come running that fast, even in a
small town like Santa Barbara."

Rhonda shrugged. "He's E.Y.'s friend, so I put up with
it. Just like that horrible Mercer! Oh, he just makes my
skin crawl!" She shivered. "Did you see Art when you
came in? I think he's here now, playing gin rummy or
something with E.Y. Mercer, of course, isn't bright enough
for that. *He* can barely manage Go Fish. The things I put
up with! But if you tell my husband I'm out to get rid of
Mercer, I'll deny it," she said with a flirtatious toss of her
head.

"I won't tell him. Why should I?"

"Oh, you men are always sticking up for each other."
She frowned. "You think I'm a bored woman who's got
sawdust where her brains should be. Well, I am bored."
She smiled disarmingly. "Movie acting is an awfully silly
profession, but the pay is good, and at least it isn't dull.
But being a rich wife does have its dull aspects, even if
you're a rich wife who loves her rich husband. And I do
love E.Y. He has his little peculiarities, but he's very, very
sweet. And besides," she said with sudden candor, "I
wasn't a very good actress."

Zalman laughed. "Rhonda, that's not true. You play the
wealthy wife to perfection."

"Thank you," she said graciously. "God knows I try. It's
the best role I've ever landed, but it does get away from me
once in a while. The boredom creeps up on me, and then I
do something silly. I'm only a woman, Jerry," she said,
which was sort of like saying that the Taj Mahal was only a

summer cottage. She rose gracefully from the chaise, went over to the lace-skirted dressing table, and misted herself from a flacon of "Joy." Almost as an afterthought she reached into a small gold filigree casket, took out a dinner ring with a ruby on it the size of a golf ball, and slipped it on her finger.

"Shall we go downstairs and join the boys for a little drinkie?" she said as she took Zalman's arm.

"Why not?" Zalman said agreeably.

They went downstairs and found E.Y., Art Carmichael, and Mercer in the Wild West bar. E.Y. and Carmichael were sitting at a small oak game table playing gin rummy. Mercer was sitting at the bar watching "Mr. Ed" on TV. Mr. Ed, who was wearing a visor, was shooting pool with a sweating Thomas Gomez, who couldn't understand how a horse could beat him so badly.

"Oh, hi, Mr. Zalman," Mercer drawled. "I remember you. Say, do you know who does Mr. Ed's voice?"

"I'm sorry, Mercer," Zalman admitted. "But I don't. Doesn't it say on the credits?"

"Uh-uh," Mercer said unhappily. "Darn, I been trying to find out forever."

Rhonda poked Zalman in the ribs. "See?" she whispered. "Mercer," she called coolly, "would you make me a screwdriver?" She took a stool at the bar.

"Well, Jerry," E.Y. said, not looking up from his cards, "Art says you two had a good meeting. Art says that cluck Robin's up for murder one. Don't know how that's gonna look in the papers, don't know at all. . . ."

"He says he didn't kill Lisa," Zalman observed.

"I liked Miss Lisa," Mercer chimed in from behind the bar. He slid a tall, frothy screwdriver over to Rhonda, dribbling some orange juice down the side. "She was very nice to me. Gave me a tie once, even showed me the way to knot it. Say, that's a good one. 'Knot!' 'Knotte!' Get it? They sound just the same, get it?" Mercer scratched his head and thought about the wonder of the English language while Rhonda rolled her eyes.

"Jerry, I know you feel sorry for poor Ed," Carmichael said sententiously as he drew a card and rearranged his hand. "And I agree with you one thousand percent. But like I said earlier, I think we have a solid case against him."

"You gotta case against Mr. Ed?" Mercer said, doubly amazed. Clearly the strain of linguistics coupled with this latest astonishing piece of information was too much for his limited cranial capacity. "What'd he do?" Mercer asked plaintively.

Carmichael looked at Mercer openmouthed.

Zalman ignored Mercer completely. "You're probably right," he told Carmichael, wondering why the D.A. had agreed with him. Zalman didn't trust any guy who agreed with him readily. Carmichael looked up sharply at Zalman, who smiled back at him like the open, friendly guy he was.

"Coming to the contest tomorrow?" E.Y. demanded, his icy blue eyes on Carmichael's discard. He picked it up.

"Contest?" Zalman asked.

"Damn!" Carmichael muttered. "You wanted that?"

"Gin!" E.Y. exclaimed. "Hah! I win! Yeah, the contest. I told you about it. My quick-draw contest. Just me and a few of my pals. Have a little fun."

"Of course," Zalman said dubiously. "Be delighted. Sounds just great."

"You come along with Yip," E.Y. said, shuffling the cards. "Bring that pretty little girlfriend of yours. We'll show you some real shooting."

"Miss Thrasher!" Mercer said, demonstrating an astounding mental wattage. "She's real nice, too."

"Usually I hold it a little later on in the month," E.Y. explained expansively, dealing another hand. "But I didn't want to make any trouble for Yip, what with that damned-fool health deal of his. He's gonna have a big opening for it in a few days, y'know, and I wanted to give him his head."

"Very considerate of you," Zalman said. "I took a look at it the other night and I like it. Very upscale."

"Upscale, my Aunt Fanny! Damn thing's gonna send my boy into bankruptcy, and I told him I ain't going along for the ride! Nobody wants to have fun anymore," he muttered moodily. "All of 'em are too busy eating that goddamn health junk and exercising!"

"Now dear, don't upset yourself," Rhonda said lightly.

"You sure you don't want to kick in a little more dough?" Zalman asked. "You'll hate yourself if it's a big success, and look, your son's got a damn good track record with Yip Tea."

E.Y. puffed up like Dizzy Gillespie on a high note. "I told him, not another nickel!" he screeched. "He wants to put some big naked statue of his wife right out in front of the place for God and everybody to see—well, that's his own damn lookout! I ain't exactly a schmo from Shamokin, PA, you know! Not another dime! He's my son and I love him and all that, but the kid's gone crazy! You want a drink, Jerry? I'll make you one myself soon as I beat the pants off Art here," he rasped. Carmichael laughed heartily.

"No, thanks, I've got to get going," Zalman said quickly. "Just wanted to let you know about Robin."

"The stupid cluck!" E.Y. harumphed. "Poor little Lisa. How could he do it to her? See you tomorrow, Jerry. We'll have plenty of fun."

"I can't wait," Zalman said as he left the room.

"I HATE BEING NONCOMMITTAL," ZALMAN SAID MOODILY. "How do politicians stand it? It's so boring!" Zalman and Marie were in bed, listening to the surf roar in the background. The only light came from the big color TV in the corner. Marie, who liked to watch TV with the sound off, flicked through the channels in her usual random manner. Rutherford slept on the floor, snoring softly. Zalman stared at the ceiling and considered the way of the world.

"I'd like to make a statement," he announced.

"Should we hold the front page?" Marie asked.

Zalman ignored her. "The quality of intelligence in America is below that of the average squid."

Marie resumed her channel zapping. "Yesterday's news, toots."

"Every one of the Knottes lacks the brains that God gave geese. Ed Robin, a member of my own highly technical profession, is lucky if he can direct his fork from his plate to his mouth. Art Carmichael is merely a toadying fool." He rolled off the bed in disgust, waking up Rutherford, who crossed his paws in the "dog at prayer" position.

Marie laughed at him. "Jerry, I'm crazy about you. I've had more damn fun since I've known you than at any time in the previous ten years of my life, but I have to tell you, you're an arrogant son of a bitch!"

147

"Mrs. Zalman's little lad Jerry? Surely you're joking. The milk of human kind—"

Marie shook her head vigorously, her curls bouncing from side to side. "No go. You did this speech earlier."

"I did? The one about how I grew up in Boyle Heights and worked my way through elementary school running errands down at the nunnery . . ."

Marie made a time-out sign with her hands. "Jerry, you grew up in Mar Vista and haven't been in Boyle Heights in your life, except maybe on the Harbor Freeway. Gimme something new or I'm going to watch *Fright Night*."

"Not that! Anything but that! I can't sleep to *Fright Night!* Isn't there a Carson rerun? I can only sleep to Johnny Carson. I'm used to sleeping to Johnny Carson. I've been doing it since I was a nipper."

Marie was adamant. "Tell me about Ed Robin, then. Tickle my mental fancy. Drive my deductive powers wild with your strong Socratic reasoning. Cerebrate me, baby!"

"I love it when you talk intellectual. . . . Okay, Ed Robin. Ed Robin is non compos gesundheit, as my sainted father used to say. Here's a young guy who's hacked his way through law school, managed to pass the bar exam, h.. a big client, is making all the right moves. And what does he do? He rushes into the dining room and starts raving about his girlfriend, and is the big, rich client playing pat-the-bunny with said girlfriend?"

"Jerry Zalman, I'm ashamed of you! Men give me a big pain, and that's the truth! There's no romance left in this wacky world of ours!" Marie bounced up and down on the bed in a fever pitch of excitement. Rutherford made nervous grunts and got up on the bed to lick her face.

"Not on the lips!" Zalman implored. "Don't let him lick you on the lips."

"You're looking at it wrong!" Marie said, pushing Rutherford down onto her lap. "See, here's this guy, and he's in such a frenzy of love that even though his whole future hangs in the balance, he's determined to protect his true love when he thinks she's been threatened." Marie ran down like an alarm clock. "I think it's so romantic, and all you're thinking about is the guy's freaking job! There's no chivalry left; it's all careerism!"

"I love a dame with ideals." Zalman grinned. "Okay, okay, so he's been bitten by the love bug, he's still a yold. He should've finessed the thing. That way he gets what he wants, plus he hangs on to his client. But I feel sorry for him anyway."

"The old milk of human kindness again?" Marie giggled. "You want to turn on Johnny Carson?"

"I thought you'd never ask."

RUTHERFORD WOKE ZALMAN THE FOLLOWING MORNING AT some appalling hour, well before ten o'clock. Zalman's foot was hanging out of the covers, and Rutherford began to wrap his long, pink Doberman tongue around it, evidently in the mistaken belief that it was something good to eat, perhaps a cocktail weenie, a treat which Rutherford liked very, very much.

"Ecccccccccch!" Zalman moaned, clawing desperately at his blue velvet sleep mask. "Quit it, Rutherford, please. . . ."

"Wuh wuh wuh?" Marie said, pulling the covers up over her head. "Whuszit?"

Zalman glared at the grinning canine. "God, I can't stand it, Rutherford," he mumbled. "Why do you do this to me?" He looked at his Dunhill travel clock ticking merrily on the nightstand. It read 8:30. Rutherford put his two front paws on the end of the bed and drooled. Zalman moaned again and slid down under the covers, cuddling Marie's warm body against his own.

"Nargh," she said.

"That foul beast woke me up," Zalman told her. "And if I'm up as a result of wretched Rutherford, you're up. C'mon, today's the big day. We're gonna have plenty of fun today, boy. . . ."

"Narg," Marie whined pitifully.

"You've forgotten? Let me refresh your memory, my little cabbage. Today is E. Y. Knotte's rootie-tootie cowboy quick-draw contest. Doesn't that sound like something you just can't wait to miss?"

Marie pulled the covers off her head and stuck out her tongue. "You've no heart, Jerry Zalman. C'mere, ootsie boy," she addressed Rutherford, "and give ums momma a nice kiss."

"Boy, dogs knock the poop out of your sex life," Zalman observed. "Please *don't* let him kiss you on the lips! That's all I ask, Marie! I have my standards, after all. C'mon, doesn't the very thought of today's fun and frolic put a song in your heart?"

"Wait till you see my costume," she said, brightening.

"Costumes? Not me, doll. I don't wear costumes."

"Well, I'm going to. You'll like it."

"Boy, I hope it's a dance-hall outfit," Zalman said dreamily. "Fishnet stockings, lots of sequins, a feather boa . . ."

"Pervert! How about the schoolmarm? Grace Kelly in *High Noon?*"

"Much too pure for me, doll, unless the schoolmarm wears the fishnet stockings underneath her calico dress. . . ."

Marie rapped him with her pillow as she bounced out of bed and headed for the shower. "Make yourself useful," she called, "and rustle up some java."

Sure enough, at noon everybody piled into the Aqua Country Squire and took the short ride up to Knotte Pines. Both Tracee and Marie were wearing short-skirted cowgirl outfits that made them look like depraved versions of Dale Evans. Marie's, a red skirt with black high-heeled boots, had a sequined vest and jaunty little hat, while Tracee had opted for a beige suede affair with more fringe than Sly Stone wore at Woodstock.

True to his word, Zalman had refused Yip's plaintive offers of a ten-gallon hat and cowboy shirt and was wearing his usual three-piece suit. Yip wore a complete John Wayne Red River outfit, and even Rutherford sported a red bandanna neckerchief.

The big circular driveway in front of Knotte Pines was filled with expensive cars, mostly Mercedes, a few Rolls, the odd Ferrari and Excalibur, all of which were ignored by their bored chauffeurs, who were crowded around the back end of a Bentley, shooting craps. Tracee wheeled the Country Squire up to the entrance and handed the keys to one of E.Y.'s housemen. "Try to put it somewhere it won't be blocked, Sammy," she said. "Just in case we want to leave before it's all over."

"You bet, Miss Tracee," the young man said happily as she slipped him a five. "No problem."

Looking uncomfortable in a riverboat gambler's frock coat, fawn trousers, and Congress gaiters, Brunson stood on the front steps, meeting and greeting the arriving guests, then directing them to the rear of the house. "Good day, Mr. Knotte," he addressed Yip in a pained voice.

Yip nodded and whirred his camera in Brunson's direction, then panned it around the parking lot.

"Why did I think this was just a family barbecue?" Zalman mumbled. "Why didn't I realize this was a full-dress loon gathering?"

"C'mon," Tracee laughed, her fringe quivering. "Let's go around back. You'll hate it, Jerry."

The four of them wound their way around the side of the big house, Rutherford frisking at their heels, pausing to lift his leg on a few shrubs just to set the local dogs straight. As they rounded the corner and got a good look at the back lawn, Zalman stopped and stared blankly. The scene was one of incomparable chaos and total insanity.

The entire back lawn of Knotte Pines, from the house to the oak-covered hillside above, had been turned into a Western campground. There was a full-sized chuckwagon doling out chili, a gigantic hole in the ground where a pair of young men in cowboy cook gear were tending to rotating slabs of beef impaled on spits, while a shooting gallery stretched out at the rear of the lawn. A gang of E.Y.'s pals, in cowboy hats and furry chaps, were back there, happily blasting away at targets set up on a wall of hay bales, while another group, togged out as Indians, were twanging off arrows at paper targets of General George Custer. Some of the ladies were indeed in dance-hall outfits, but the great majority favored the cowgirl look, accented with plenty of diamonds . . . just to show they knew how to play dress-up.

"Hello, darlings," Rhonda called gaily. She'd opted for the sexy cowgirl, with a rose-red skirt and matching rhinestoned blouse that set off her creamy skin to perfection. Her ruby earrings and big ruby ring sparkled in the warm

153

Santa Barbara sunlight, and her hands, of course, were wrapped tightly around one of E.Y.'s screwdrivers. "E.Y.'s at the bar," she said as she came up to them. "Over there . . ."

Zalman followed her glance to where E.Y. and Mercer, both in Old West drag, were tending bar, along with a crew of cowboy bartenders, pouring red-eye for the thirsty guests who were bellied up to the long plank bar set on whiskey barrels. Behind them, on a raised platform, a six-piece cowboy swing band belted out Bob Wills's greatest hits with a jaunty beat. Right now they were blatting their way through "Yellow Rose of Texas," and Zalman had the bad feeling he'd be hearing plenty more of it before the end of what promised to be a long day. There were at least a hundred milling guests, and more people seemed to be arriving all the time, but the grounds behind Knotte Pines were large enough to accommodate everyone in comfort.

Zalman looked over at Yip, who was panning his camcorder over the happy throng. "I'm showing this video at the opening of World O' Yip, you know," he told Zalman for the umpteenth time. "Usually my dad has his annual shindig later on, but since I'm opening World O' Yip then he moved it up so we wouldn't conflict. Lotta his friends are staying through the week, just so they can come to World O' Yip," he said proudly. "I've known most of these folks since I was a kid, and I thought it would be nice for 'em to see how I've done." His own pride in his undertaking was evident.

Zalman punched him lightly on the shoulder. "It's going to be great, Yip. World O' Yip is going to be a big success." He thought the guy needed some encouragement. Besides, the World O' Yip building was beautiful, and the whole scheme was so screwy, so completely Southern California, that it just might work.

"Say, Jerry, I don't mean to bug you or anything, but have you had a chance to see if I can get any more money?" Yip was embarrassed and his eyes were down-cast.

Zalman felt bad. In all the excitement he'd sort of for-gotten about Yip's financial problems. "Jeez, Yip, I'm sorry," he confessed. "I talked to E.Y., and I don't think he's gonna go for it, Yip, old buddy. The timing's wrong, know what I mean? This whole problem with Lisa, I think it's put him off his feed. Besides, he doesn't like that naked statue of Tracee, and that's a fact. Never talk him into it. But I've got other sources. I'll make some calls, I promise."

Marie, who'd been off with Tracee admiring the roses, came over and took Zalman's hand. "Let's circulate, Jerry," she suggested. "I don't want to miss a thing. Be-sides, I think one of E.Y.'s screwdrivers would be just the ticket right now."

"Get along, little dogie!" Zalman said. "What the hell is a dogie, anyway?"

"Hey, look," Marie said, pointing at the dance floor. "There's McCoy! What's he doing here?" Rutherford yipped happily at the sound of his former master's name.

Zalman peered over the dance floor where McCoy, look-ing completely at home in his ratty jeans and silver-toed cowboy boots, was dosey-doing with Molly McCafferty, who was clad in a low-cut, blood-red satin dance-hall-girl dress with a generously spangled skirt, four-inch heels, fishnet stockings, and ostrich feathers in her Valkyrie hair.

Zalman burst out laughing. "McCoy's found his spiritual home," he told Marie. "Let's go give 'em some gas." They ambled over the grass to the side of the dance floor and waited till the number was through.

McCoy kissed Marie on the cheek and introduced Molly. "Ah hah!" Molly said. "I've got news for you, Jerry Zal-man, you big fibber!"

"What'd I do, what'd I do?" Zalman grinned as she glared at him, her hands planted on her generous hips.

"You told me a big fib about your wife and how you

155

were so sad she left you, and you not even married! I told Dean, Dean, I said, you two better not try any more funny stuff with me, is all!" Her eyes flashed from man to man, then fastened on Zalman.

He laughed and tried his engaging grin on her. "I admit that I didn't tell you the whole truth and nothing but the truth the other day, but hey, you'll forgive me, right?"

"Welllll," she said.

"Anything new, Zally?" McCoy asked, out of breath from his unaccustomed sashaying.

"Nah. Love your stockings, by the way," Zalman told Molly.

"Aren't they sleazy?" She laughed, evidently forgiving him. "My girlfriend down at the beach told me they were totally trendo."

"So who invited you, McCoy?" Zalman needled. "I thought this was an exclusive bash just for us society swells."

"Oh, E.Y. invites lots of beach folks," Molly put in. "One big happy family and all like that. Well, aren't you a cute little puppy," she said to Rutherford, who was snouting her about the thighs. "You look just like Chester. Say, where is Chester, Dean?"

"Dirty mutt took off after some big standard poodle he fancied."

"I think that's Rhonda's dog," Marie said.

"Don't ask me, I ain't a hound lover," Zalman muttered. He pulled McCoy aside. "Say, Dean, see if you can get the feel of the place, okay? Some polite eavesdropping, maybe a quick run through the joint when that skeleton Brunson isn't around . . ."

McCoy nodded. "You bet. Molly knows everybody, too. Like who's what and when."

"Great!" Zalman nodded. "Talk to me later."

Zalman and Marie ambled over to the target range where Yip, his camcorder untended on the grass at his feet, was blasting away at the bull's-eye with a Colt .45. "Jerry!" he called over the noise of the gunfire. "Have a go, man." He grinned and offered Zalman his smoking pistol.

"No, thanks," Zalman said, regarding the shooting iron as W. C. Fields might have regarded a glass of water. "I'm a peace-loving city slicker."

"Whatsamatter, Jerry?" E. Y. Knotte demanded over Zalman's shoulder. "'Fraid of guns, are ya? Don't like guns?"

"Like I said before, E.Y., they make me nervous. Actually, though, it isn't the guns, it's the fools behind them that scare the stuffing out of me."

E.Y. rasped a dry laugh. "You ain't half kidding, either, boy. Some of the fools pick up a gun, why, they oughta be shot!"

"With any luck maybe they will be," Zalman said quietly.

E.Y. reached into his tooled leather Bianchi holster with a practiced gesture and pulled out a long-barreled single-action Colt .45. In one easy motion he squeezed off four rounds, all of which thudded into the target in a tight little grouping the diameter of a quarter. "Your turn, Yip," he said proudly.

Yip smiled, lifted his own pistol, and followed his father's lead. His grouping was even tighter than his father's.

E.Y. patted his son on the back. "All that herb tea ain't ruined your aim, son. Nice shooting. Well, gotta circulate. Rhonda's always after me to circulate, you know. Circulate, circulate! See you kids later on." E.Y. blew theatrically on the barrel of his Colt and melted into the crowd.

"Yip, I'm impressed!" Marie said.

"Ahhh," he said deprecatingly, "my dad drove me crazy when I was a kid. We had to go shooting most weekdays, so I got pretty good at it. Tell you the truth, though, Jerry, these things make me nervous, too." Yip put down his pistol and picked up his camcorder. "Think I'll go find Tracee, see if she wants to eat. See you later!" he said as he disappeared.

"Son of a gun," Zalman said. "Do I detect a soupçon of father-son rivalry?"

"Son of a gun is right," Marie said thoughtfully. "Yip's a funny guy, isn't he? Here he comes on with all this New Age, let's-meditate-and-levitate stuff, but . . . I don't think he's as wimpy as he appears."

"Right you are, doll," Zalman agreed as he watched Yip talking with a small group of people. "Shall we chat up the rest of the Knotte nutties? I'd like to grill Mercer a little bit."

"Poor thing," Marie said, looking around. "He's a little dim, I think."

"About fifty watts short," Zalman muttered. "Ahhhh, there's our target now." He pointed over at the bar where Mercer Lamont, a blank expression on his face, was standing and staring dreamily off into space.

Zalman steered Marie over to Mercer's post by the bar. "Hi, Mercer," he said, smiling a nice, open, sincere smile.

"Oh, hi, Mr. Zalman. Hi, Miss Thrasher. Some nice party, huh?" Mercer's blank expression was replaced by his other expression, a blank smile. "Plenty of good food over at the barbecue pit. I always like plenty of good food." He was happy to have somebody to talk to.

"How long have you been with Mr. Knotte, Mercer?" Zalman asked jovially.

Mercer thought on it. Then he thought some more. It took him a minute, but he came up with an answer. "I think about a month. Maybe two. No. A month. Maybe more. I really like it here. Me and Mr. Knotte, we have a lot of good fun! You know," he said, his eyes downcast, "I was in prison before this."

"No!" Zalman said.

"Why, you poor thing!" Marie said, patting Mercer's bulging biceps.

"Yeah." Mercer hung his head. "It was a bum rap, though. I was framed! You know, lots of guys in prison, they were framed!"

"No!" Zalman said again. "That's amazing. I didn't know that, did you, Marie?"

Marie jabbed him with her elbow. "That's sad, Mercer."

"Yeah, but when I told that to Mr. Knotte, he said he didn't care. He gave me the job anyway, on account of my character," Mercer said proudly. "Lotsa guys, they get out of prison and even though they was framed, they can't find a job, so then they go back to prison. It's called . . . it's called . . ." Mercer screwed up his face, trying to think. "Something with an *R*. Restavision. Yeah, restavision. When you get out and then you have to go back to prison."

"I've heard of it," Zalman said. "Restavision."

"But I got me a job!" Mercer said again, happy as a kid with a pocketful of night-crawlers, "so I don't have to go back. Welll"—he smiled—"I'm gonna go get me some of that barbecue. I love ribs. In prison, you know," he said thoughtfully, "the food's pretty bad. We hardly ever got any ribs. Maybe once, twice in all the time I was up there."

Marie reached out and patted him again. "You're a nice guy, Mercer," she said sincerely. "You really are."

"Gee, Miss Thrasher. Thanks a lot." Mercer beamed like he'd gone supernova and ambled off in search of his dinner.

Zalman and Marie enjoyed themselves for the next forty-five minutes, watching Santa Barbara's wackies at play. They danced to "Yellow Rose of Texas." Marie did a little target shooting and proved herself a surprisingly sure shot, while Zalman, just to prove he was a regular guy, took a turn with the bow and arrow.

"Seems like we used to do this at summer camp." He grinned. "Me and my sister went to Arizona one year, after my dad hit the Daily Double at Santa Anita. Lucille's hair was real long, and just before we went home I cut it for her. She looked sort of like Grace Jones when I was through. We thought it was great, but my mom had a conniption fit." He twanged an arrow into General Custer's left kneecap and laughed. "A debilitating wound if ever I saw one. Let's mosey over to the trough, ma'am. All this shootin' gives a man a powerful hungry feeling." Marie took his proffered arm, and as they started across the lawn they heard a loud voice coming from the bar.

"Mercer, you varmint!" E.Y.'s voice thundered. "You're a four-flushing cardsharp!"

An uncomfortable silence descended over the crowd, then swelled into a low wave of mumblings. If there's one thing a high-class audience hates, it's a scene, and it was obvious E. Y. Knotte did not consider it necessary to spare his guests any unpleasantness.

"Say, Mr. Knotte," Mercer exclaimed with slow deliberation, "them's fighting words!"

"You're a damn tinhorn," E.Y. rasped. "I caught you red-handed. Think you can deal off the bottom of the deck, you got another think coming!"

"Saaaaay . . ." Marie began, half turning to Zalman, "what's going on?"

He shushed her impatiently. "Quiet," he said. "This is going to be good."

Mercer drew himself up to his full height, straightening his broad, muscular back until it seemed the buttons on his white satin cowboy shirt were going to pop off his chest. "I won't take that from any man!" he trumpeted.

"Wanta face off, you weasel?" E.Y. yelled. "You've got it coming, and you're gonna get it!"

"Jerry," Marie whispered, "do some—"

Zalman waved her down. "Quiet! It's only a gag."

The crowd in Mercer's vicinity parted like the Red Sea in front of Charlton Heston. E.Y. settled his ten-gallon hat low across his forehead, and the two men took active gunfighting stances, face-to-face at about twenty yards, then began to advance on each other.

Suddenly, Zalman felt a glacial chill of premonition run down his spine, but before he could act Mercer Lamont and E. Y. Knotte drew their revolvers and blasted each other with the speed of Roy Rogers. The crowd gasped in horror, a woman with blue hair and a red fox jacket fainted, and Mercer, in obvious disbelief, clutched at a great nasty red hole in his chest. Slowly, he bent his head, looked at the wound uncomprehendingly, then sank to his knees.

"But boss . . ." he said wonderingly. "Boss . . ." He sprawled onto the ground, his hands still clawing feebly at the terrible hole from which bright red blood pumped over his beautiful white satin shirt.

"Jesus," Zalman growled as he leapt forward to Mercer's side. Marie was close behind him, and she knelt down and pressed her pink bandanna to the hole in his chest in a futile effort to stanch the spouting blood.

"Boss . . . boss," Mercer gurgled.

E. Y. Knotte squatted down next to his stricken cohort.

"Merce, what the hell?" E.Y. said, dazed. "It was just a joke. That's all, just a joke. It was blanks, supposed to be blanks. Merce, Mercer! Somebody get a doctor!" he bellowed.

Mercer was already blue-white, and flecks of blood appeared when he spoke in a soft, whispering voice. "Won't do no good, boss," he said. "I'm done for. Sorry things didn't work out the way you wanted. . . ." Mercer coughed gutturally, and an amazed expression of shock and terror swept over his face. His neck loosened, his head dropped limply to one side, and he was dead.

"Merce!" E.Y. said with a strangled cry. "What happened? It was just a joke, Jerry! We didn't have real bullets! Just blanks!"

Zalman looked up from Mercer's contorted face as Marie cradled the dead man's head in her lap. "I think you'd better call Espinoza," Zalman told E.Y. "Unless I miss my guess by a country mile, somebody reloaded your guns with live cartridges." Zalman reached out and took his revolver. E.Y. didn't resist.

"Merce never was any good with shooting irons," he muttered. A thought seemed to darken his features. "Yip and I were gonna do this trick," he said to himself. "If we had, we'd both be dead instead of poor Merce. . . ." He shook his head and stood up quickly, rubbing his shoulder.

"You guys at the bar!" he shouted angrily. "Get one of them damn tablecloths to cover this boy with! And where the hell's my wife when I need her? Rhonda! And where's that son of mine?" He stared pugnaciously at the gawking crowd. "Yip, goddammit! Rhonda!"

Rhonda Warwick Knotte appeared behind Zalman, her hands twisting nervously at her great ruby ring. "My God, darling!" she said as she saw her furious husband. Her eyes widened further when she saw Mercer, still lying in Marie's lap. "What happ—"

"Never mind that crap!" E.Y. shouted, his bright eyes sparking like flint on stone. "Get aholda Art Carmichael! And get that cop, whatshisname, Espinoza! Get 'em on the damn horn and tell 'em . . . no," he reconsidered, "don't tell 'em anything. Just get 'em up here, pronto. You lot!" he snapped at the blanched onlookers. "Cops're gonna want to talk to all of you, so don't anybody try to beat it outta here! Got it? Brunson, goddammit!"

Rhonda scurried off to do her master's bidding as Brunson minced gingerly over the grass. He looked very uncomfortable, and it was clear he didn't like the idea of picking his way over nasty old dirt and grass when he could be back inside, gliding over a nice deep-pile carpet. "Sir?" the butler said smoothly, as if a stiff on the lawn were an everyday occurrence for the rich and famous.

E. Y. opened his mouth to bellow further instructions, but the effort was too much for him. His leathery face drained of color, and he turned an ugly, ashen gray. He grabbed at his chest with one clawlike hand and sank down onto the ground next to his former companion-in-arms. "Ack, ack, ack," he croaked. His hand clawed at his throat. "Ack, ack, ack," he croaked again.

"Holy smoke!" Zalman said, leaping forward with the practiced step of a man well versed in fancy dancing. He handed E.Y.'s gun to Marie. "Get Rhonda!" he yelled as he undid E.Y.'s neckerchief. "Maybe he's got some pills!"

"I'll get them!" It was Tracee, stepping into the fray. "I know where they are!" She knelt down next to Marie and began to rummage around in Mercer's pockets. Triumphantly, she pulled out a pill vial, shook a pair of tablets into her palm, and then put them into E.Y.'s mouth. She stroked his head like he was a pet cat on its way to the vet. "He'll be better in a minute," she said as she took a glass of water from a waiter and helped E.Y. to swallow a few drops. "It's happened before, when he gets overexcited," she said calmly.

Sure enough, in a minute E.Y. opened his eyes and looked blearily around. "Damn!" he said weakly. "That was a nasty one! Thanks, folks," he told Tracee and Zalman. "Almost popped off there," he said matter-of-factly. "Always see this long tunnel of light, you know? Long, long tunnel of light . . ." With that, E. Y. Knotte smiled like a peaceful cherub, pulled his ten-gallon hat down over his face, and passed out blissfully.

Seconds later the shrill squeal of a police siren echoed over the long green lawn, with the harsh nasal edge of a stuck pig. E. Y. lay stretched out on the ground, his head on somebody's balled jacket which had been pressed into service as a makeshift pillow, but his guests had retreated into small muttering groups, gnawing voraciously on the remains of their barbecue. The murder had enhanced everyone's appetite. Even Zalman had taken advantage of the brief respite to fortify himself with a sandwich and a bottle of beer.

"It's going to be another long session," he told Marie between bites. "Never face the cops on an empty stomach if you can possibly avoid it." Marie sniffled, still in shock over Mercer's death. Zalman put his arm around her shoulders and gave her a buck-up squeeze. She smiled bravely, then tossed a beef bone for Rutherford to catch, but both Rutherford and his brother Chester were more interested in Rhonda's fluffy white standard poodle, who was coyly frisking about the now-empty dance floor, tossing her poufy, beribboned head.

"The girl can't help it," Zalman said wryly, gesturing with the remains of the sandwich at the three happy dogs.

Moments later, Brunson led Espinoza around the corner of the house, and Zalman saw the nattily dressed cop freeze in horror at the daffy yet tragic scene before him. The costumed guests were still clustered in little groups around the fast-disappearing food, and E.Y. was still stretched out next to his dead sidekick, who was now covered with a gaily checked red and white tablecloth. Only the lizardskin toes of Mercer's Tony Lama boots were visible as they reached poignantly for the sky one final time.

Espinoza made his way slowly across the lawn toward Zalman and the others, Brunson picking along in front of him. "What's going on?" Espinoza asked tightly, looking around. He looked down at Mercer's body, pulled back the tablecloth, knelt down, and checked for a pulse rate. Not finding one, he sighed and gently replaced Mercer's arm across his chest.

"Nasty wound," Espinoza said, straightening. "Any ideas about how he came by it?" he addressed Zalman.

"It's a long story, Primo," Zalman said, finishing the last of his sandwich and putting his paper plate aside.

"Suppose you just start at the beginning," Espinoza suggested.

"Mercer Lamont has taken a ride on that chuckwagon to the sky," Zalman said, polishing off his beer. "Mr. Knotte," he added, gesturing at the recumbent E.Y., "was overcome by the full hideousness of the, uh, incident and had an attack. Mrs. Knotte has called for his doctor, and he's on his way, no doubt."

Espinoza walked over to where E.Y. lay on the ground, attended by Tracee. "He okay?" he asked. She nodded weakly and stroked E.Y.'s head. Espinoza turned to one of his uniformed men. "Get the medics up here, fast!" The officer barked into his transceiver. Espinoza returned to Zalman. "What the hell's going on here, Jerry?" he whispered, his shoulders sagging under his impeccable gray summer-weight suit.

Zalman glanced around and sighed. E.Y. was out cold. Rhonda and Yip were nowhere to be seen. Tracee was busy with E.Y., and even Marie was looking absently at the sky, whistling tunelessly under her breath. He, Zalman, was clearly the man in charge. He took Espinoza's arm and gently guided him away from Mercer's body.

"Lieutenant," he said, "tell you what. Have your boys take their pictures and make their little chalk outlines. . . . Can you *make* little chalk outlines on grass? Never mind," he sighed. "Get names and addresses from the guests, do whatever routine stuff you guys do, and meanwhile, why don't you and I go inside, have a nice cold bottle of beer, and talk things over in private?" He gave what he hoped was a sincere smile and rocked back and forth on his heels. Espinoza hesitated.

"I think I know as much about this tragic event as anyone," Zalman continued, "and since it won't be possible for you to question Mr. Knotte until he recovers . . ." He gestured meaningfully at the behatted figure on the lawn. "Bottle of beer?" he inquired hopefully.

Espinoza looked around, then hesitation vanished and he seized on Zalman's suggestion as a drowning man might seize on a rubber ducky. "Okay." He shrugged. "I'll have Foster do the legwork. No point in getting my bottomside in a sling over whatever the hell we have here, since I figure Mr. D.A. Carmichael will want to run this show, too. Give me a minute to get the show on the road, then I'll take you up on that beer, even if I am on duty." With that, Espinoza walked off and gave brief instructions to a plainclothesman. Just then, Yip came running across the lawn, towing a florid man with big ears and a loud sports coat. Yip breathlessly introduced the man as Dr. Troup.

"Oh, my, my, my," Dr. Troup said mildly, kneeling

down by E.Y. and checking his pulse, chattering as he worked. "It's just that he won't listen! He could avoid these little spells if he'd just take it easy, as I've prescribed time and time again! Learn to enjoy life! But no! He has to throw big wingdings, have these silly shooting matches! Carry on! Really, it's very frustrating!" Troup shook his head as he prepared an injection. "After all, I'm only a doctor," he said portentously. "I'm not God!"

"First time I've ever heard a physician admit that," Zalman whispered to Marie as Troup jabbed E.Y. in the arm with the hypo. "Now, doll, while I'm busy with Espinoza, go talk to Rhonda. Tracee, too. See where they were when the shooting started, okay? I don't remember seeing any of them in the immediate vicinity, including Yip. And where the hell's McCoy? What am I paying him for, I'd like to know?"

"Calm down, Jerry, will you? I'll chat up the Knottes. And no, Yip wasn't around until the doctor showed up, I'll put money on it. After all, his father just shot a man, for Pete's sake. You'd think he'd want to help!" Marie was indignant.

Zalman nodded. "That's what I mean. All right, I'll see what I can do with Espinoza. Jeez, the poor guy looks like he's gonna cry. And babe," Zalman added, giving Marie's little paw a squeeze, "you did a real good job back there. Hang in a little longer." Marie gave him a wink and a smile and went off on her scouting mission.

As a pair of white-suited medics ran across the lawn toward E.Y. and Dr. Troup, Zalman collected Espinoza. They went inside and settled down in a pair of leather chairs in the Wild West bar. Zalman found some cold Beck's in the bar fridge and let Espinoza, who was clearly shaken by this latest Knotte idiocy and the prospect of having to take further guff from Art Carmichael, tell him the story of his life.

"I'm a cop," Espinoza moaned. "But I got ambitions. A guy named Espinoza in this town's gotta keep moving, otherwise the suckers'll roll right over you. So I'm going to law school nights at the university so I can get out of here, maybe join the FBI or the Secret Service," he said, his dark eyes misting over with bureaucratic pride. "I could guard the president! Me! Primativo Espinoza! But Carmichael's out to get me," he muttered morosely. "He thinks I'm some kind of wetback. Hell, my family's been here since the 1800s, since all this was *our* land!" He gazed out the window, a strange fervor lighting his eyes. "And it will be our land again!"

"Please, please, enough with the separatism!" Zalman pled. "You can't join the Secret Service until we solve this case, and we can't solve this case till we figure out what the hell's going on here. Then, after we solve the case, *then* you can guard the president, secede from the union, whatever you want."

Espinoza looked disheartened. "What happened, Jerry?" he asked quietly. "I figure if anybody knows, it's you. Looks like E.Y. plugged Mercer, but I can't believe it!"

Zalman sipped his bottle of Beck's. "Near as I can see, Mercer and E.Y. had cooked up this elaborate practical joke, a big argument and shoot-out, and Mercer is supposed to slap some ketchup on his chest and die in agony. Then he gets up, big joke, everybody laughs. Only one problem."

"He didn't get up."

"He didn't get up, since it wasn't ketchup, it was real live blood. Tell you what I think," Zalman said, leaning forward in his chair. "I think somebody reloaded both guns with live ammo. That way, it doesn't matter who's got what gun. So both E.Y. and Mercer get killed, no problem for the killer. Doesn't matter to him. The only hang-up was Mercer was a bad shot and E.Y. is a good shot. That's why E.Y.'s alive and Mercer's gone west. . . ." Zalman was suddenly aware that Espinoza was regarding him curiously.

"I can't see you and Tracee Knotte being married," Espinoza mused. "You seem so different. . . ."

"We are different, we were different, and it was a world long ago and far away," Zalman said with exasperation. "Now look, Primo, let's talk suspects. Rhonda is the kind of dame who always needs more money than she's got, right? Yip needs money for World O' Yip. And Tracee loves Yip, and she wants him to have the money, since it's what *he* wants. On the surface, Mercer looks good for the part of crazed killer, but I think we can dispense with him, unless we try to believe that he loaded both guns by mistake."

Espinoza snorted and rolled his eyes. "That's just the kind of dumb-ass thing Carmichael would go for," he said, picking at the label on his bottle of Beck's. "That way, he could still send Ed Robin to the chair, kicking and screaming. He'd love that. Lots of headlines."

"Carmichael ain't got squat!" Zalman snarled. "We both know that! Besides, how's Carmichael gonna pin this one on Robin? Teleportation?"

"I know Carmichael," Espinoza insisted. "He'll say this is a tragic accident and it doesn't have anything to do with the other murder. Wait and see."

Zalman shook his head in disgust. "I'll tell you, Primo, it won't wash. You know it and I know it, so what do we care what *he* thinks? Carmichael's a lame if ever I saw one, and believe me, in Beverly Hills you see plenty. He's so eager to keep E.Y. happy that he's headed for quicksand, you mark my words. Not that anybody has asked me, but since it looks like I'm representing E.Y., temporarily at least, I'm gonna have a talk with old Art before any serious damage gets done."

"Lame, huh?" Espinoza chuckled. "More like a cockroach, you wanna know my opinion. But like I say, Jerry, I know Art, and he's gonna hang on to Robin 'cause Robin's his big ticket to the legislature. Besides, he thinks Ed's a weak sister. He even told me so."

"Well, Robin's a jerk, it's true. But he's a member of my own sanctified profession, and I'm not letting the guy's career go down the pipes just for some egomaniac D.A. with a whim on." Zalman smiled happily. "Also, Robin's my slave for life if I get him off, and I can use some free help around the office. After all, we're all busy men or we wouldn't be here, right?"

"You'll help me with Carmichael, won't you, Jerry?" Espinoza asked pitifully. "I'll never get into the Secret Service if that idiot . . . oh, hi, Art!" He beamed quickly as Brunson ushered a frantic, sweating Art Carmichael into the room.

"Mr. Carmichael," the butler announced.

"Thank you, Brunson," Zalman said. "Art, good of you to get here so quickly. I knew that as a friend of the family you'd want to keep posted."

"Yes, yes," Carmichael muttered, his eyes fixed hopefully on the bar. He wiped his hands with his handkerchief and sank onto a barstool. He looked like a man who'd gone to the medicine chest for Di-Gel and found the bottle empty. "I spoke briefly with Mrs. Knotte," he said, his hands clutching his stomach. "She told me Mr. Knotte accidentally killed Mercer. Is this true?" he asked, astounded.

"I'm afraid so," Zalman said. "Let's trot out back and you can see for yourself," he suggested. "By the way, Art, I thought we'd see you at today's shindig. Funny you weren't invited."

"I was invited," Carmichael said with a wounded air. "Of course I was invited. Unfortunately, it was my day with the kids. My ex-wife dropped them off early this morning. I was going to come over later on," he explained as the three men left the Wild West bar and headed for the back lawn. "I don't have to tell you that E.Y.'s parties are important social events here in Santa Barbara, and as district attorney they give me a valuable opportunity to mingle with the electorate. But a caring, sharing father doesn't let his kids down."

"Right, so where'd you take 'em?" Zalman asked, trying

not to break up at Espinoza, who was behind Carmichael grimacing and making silly faces.

"Pony rides, the mall for new Reeboks, McDonaldland for burgers. Where the hell does every divorced father take his kids?" Carmichael snapped. "Anything else you want to know?"

"Hey, Art, just trying to maintain a close personal relationship." Zalman smiled, pleased to have found Carmichael's weak spot. "Shall we inspect the remains of the late Mercer Lamont?"

Carmichael shivered as the three men went outside. "I hate dead bodies," he said gloomily as they rounded the corner of the house and started across the lawn toward several uniformed officers who were standing guard over Mercer's inert form. "I always get this overwhelming sense of the fierce temporal beauty of life. . . ."

Zalman and Espinoza looked at each other and shrugged. "Very philosophical, Art," Zalman said dryly, "but enough word-meistering. Let's pull together and see what we can do for E.Y., right, Art?"

"Of course, of course, Jerry," Carmichael said with an air of completely false enthusiasm.

E.Y. WAS STILL LYING STRETCHED OUT ON THE LAWN, AL-
though now his head was cradled in Rhonda's lap. "She
won't let me get up," he announced proudly. "Damn grass
is gonna stain my shirt, but Rhonda here won't let me get
up, will you, Buttercup?"

Rhonda smiled down at her husband, her creamy skin set
off to perfection by the mauve cashmere shawl she'd
wrapped around her shoulders and partly draped over
E.Y.'s body. Zalman observed that her many years spent on
movie sets hadn't been wasted; John Huston couldn't have
composed a better scene. Tenderly, she nestled the shawl a
bit closer around her husband's chin. "Dr. Troup said you
should rest before you get up," she said softly, her eyes
drifting vacantly over the littered lawn.

Espinoza's minions finished their ritual Polaroiding of
the late Mercer Lamont. The coroner, a large black man
with a jaunty Vandyke beard, announced he was finished
also and the stiff could be bagged and hauled away anytime
Espinoza was ready.

Espinoza grimaced at his colleague's turn of phrase, then
took Carmichael a few steps away to inspect the body. Although Espinoza walked carefully around Mercer and
peered at him with studious interest, Zalman noticed that
Carmichael made only the most perfunctory survey of the

body, hardly looking at all. Carmichael really didn't like to look at dead bodies, Zalman thought. It was a curious quirk for a D.A. On the other hand, Zalman reflected, he wasn't exactly nuts about stiffs himself.

"I loved that boy," E.Y. said sentimentally. "Why, I woulda rather plugged myself!"

"Now, honey," Rhonda soothed. "Don't get excited again."

Despite his wife's fluttering protests, E.Y. struggled to his knees. "Man can't talk business with his head in a lady's lap," he said gruffly. "He either looks like a mama's boy or a lily-livered coward, and I'm neither!" He waved away Rhonda's assistance. "It's okay, Buttercup, I'm over my fit!"

Carmichael looked blank. "Fit?" he called.

"E.Y. had a little attack after the shooting," Zalman explained quietly. "The doctor's come and gone. . . . E.Y., don't you think it's about time to go inside? It's getting chilly, and besides, there's nothing more we can do out here now that the district attorney's had his look around."

"Damn good idea!" E.Y. agreed brusquely. "I'm hungry as a bull elephant, I'll tell you." Slowly and a bit unsteadily he got to his feet, balanced himself on the heels of his cowboy boots, then retrieved his Stetson from Rhonda. He flourished the hat over his heart. "Adios, Mercer, my old saddle pal," he said simply, his voice choking up audibly. "No man e'er had a truer companion. . . ."

Everyone was silent as they watched the coroner's men load the last of Mercer Lamont onto a gurney and cart it off across the lawn.

Rhonda took E.Y.'s arm, but he shook her away irritably. "I'm not dead yet, woman!" he snapped. "I can walk on my lonesome!" Then, with a surprisingly sure step, he hustled off toward the house, leaving the rest of the party to straggle along behind.

Marie, Yip, and Tracee were waiting in the Wild West room, and Zalman saw that, faithful to his instructions,

Marie was head to head with Tracee, her bright curls bouncing up and down as she nodded agreement with Tracee's hushed jabbering. McCoy, however, was nowhere to be seen.

"Brunson!" E.Y. shouted. "Rustle up some chow, pardner! We got a hungry gang of cowpokes out here!" E.Y. was still deep in his role of King of the Cowboys. "Give a holler when cookie's got some grub on the table."

"We don't eat grubs," Yip hazarded in a mild attempt at humor, but his father fixed him with a glare that would have withered cactus, and Yip piped right down again.

"Everybody up to the bar!" E.Y. ordered. "Now who the hell's gonna play with me?" he asked, his trembling lower lip revealing that he'd suddenly felt the full effect of Mercer's death. "Who's gonna help me in the bar, Buttercup?" he asked plaintively, turning to his wife.

Rhonda made faint clucking noises designed to soothe him and stroked his arm tenderly. "Yip will help, won't you, Yip?" she asked, looking to her stepson for assistance.

"You bet, Dad!" Yip beamed enthusiastically, and before his father could wave him off, Yip jumped up and went behind the bar. Swiftly, he began to toss oranges into the blender to prepare a batch of screwdrivers.

Zalman watched out of the corner of his eye. It was probably the first time in years his father had needed Yip for anything. Ahhh, the old father-son conflict, Zalman thought. And women bitch about their mothers!

Morosely, everyone settled down at the bar, and Yip began to pass a large silver tray of drinks around. Zalman glanced over at E.Y., who watched his son with a baleful stare. E.Y. looked tired, but it was obvious that it would take more than a shooting and a mild attack of the willies to keep him down. Marie and Tracee had settled in on the couch and continued to talk in low voices. Espinoza and Carmichael were at the bar, looking glum. Espinoza looked especially glum, since he was still on duty and, in Carmichael's presence, had settled for a Coke. Carmichael, of course, had no such compunction and was working on a screwdriver.

"Tell me, E.Y.," Zalman asked loudly, "who loaded the guns today?"

E.Y. accepted a screwdriver from Yip, sipped it judiciously, and nodded his approval. "Why . . . Mercer did," he said thoughtfully.

"You saw him do it?"

E.Y. shook his head. "Nope. Trusted him about things like that. I know old Merce was a coupla cards short, but when you gave him instructions . . . like, 'Load the guns with blanks' or 'Get a sack of oranges' . . . why, he could handle that stuff just fine."

"And obviously you didn't check the guns before," Zalman pressed.

"Like I said, Merce was okay on stuff like that. Never thought to check the guns. Wish to hell I had," E.Y. muttered fiercely.

"Jerry?" Marie interrupted. "Remember when you and I were talking to Mercer? He didn't have any guns on then."

"Had 'em outside," E.Y. piped up. "Keep most of my good stuff in here, locked in the cabinets." He gestured toward the glass-fronted cases along the walls. "But those guns we were shooting today, they're just old things we keep around for parties. They were out on the tables up at the shooting range."

"Anybody could have tampered with them, then, is that what you're saying?" Carmichael asked in an astonishing display of district attorneyish acumen.

"Hurry up Brunson with those eats," E.Y. muttered to Rhonda. "I'm starved. Yeah, Art, we had 'em out there for anyone who wanted to shoot, so I guess anyone coulda taken the blanks outta those two guns Merce and I used for our stunt and reloaded 'em with live ammo."

Rhonda rang Brunson on the house phone, spoke into it,

then patted her husband's arm. "We'll have food in just a few moments. Brunson's on his way."

"Thank God," E.Y. said.

"So the next question is, who knew what you and Mercer were up to?" Zalman asked.

E.Y. drained his screwdriver, poured himself another slug from the icy pitcher Yip had placed on the bar, and waved his gnarled hand around the room. "I suppose you're referring to my nearest and dearest? Everybody here, if that's why you're asking, Jerry."

There was a little murmur of protest from Rhonda, Yip, and Tracee, who looked at one another openmouthed.

"Why, I think that's . . . that's . . ." Carmichael sputtered.

"Yip?" Zalman called, ignoring Carmichael.

"Sure, Jerry," Yip said forthrightly. "I knew what they were up to. Didn't Dad tell you that he and I were going to do the skit ourselves? I backed out," he said softly. "Even as a game, I didn't think it was a good karmic move."

"Huh?" Espinoza said. He shook his dark head as if an invisible tennis ball had just whizzed by his ear.

"Mercer picked up the guns himself," E.Y. said thoughtfully. "Got 'em from Porter the other day."

"Who the hell is Porter?" Zalman demanded.

"Gunsmith!" E.Y. barked. "Damn good one, too, even if he does have a filthy parrot! Had the firing pins adjusted, the actions oiled up. I told you, they were just junk guns. Porter's an old pal of Mercer's, so I haven't been using him long, but he does good work, I'll tell you that. You think he had something to do with this? Him and Mercer? But it was Mercer got killed, not me. . . ."

"But if you and Yip had done the shooting, as planned," Carmichael said quickly, "you'd both be dead."

E.Y. was apparently unfazed by this possibility. "Yep, sure would be. Yip's a damn good shot, I'll say that for him. Taught him myself. . . ."

"Or," Carmichael suggested, "perhaps it wasn't an attempt on your life at all. Perhaps it was just a horrible, tragic accident."

Zalman could hear Espinoza clenching his teeth.

"Perhaps the two events aren't connected at all," Carmichael went on.

"Three events," Tracee put in. "You're forgetting about how E.Y.'s car went backwards instead of forwards and into the swimming pool."

At this moment, Brunson entered with a big platter of hot hors d'oeuvres and began to pass them around. E.Y. and Art Carmichael loaded up gigantic plates and began to chow down. The others picked desultorily at their food.

"Well, of course, taken all together it does look a bit suspicious, but when viewed separately—as separate events, that is—it's clearly possible that all three incidents are unconnected," Carmichael said with his mouth full. "They're separate, see?"

"Who would want to kill me?" E.Y. wondered. "I can't believe anyone would want to kill me. Bad publicity for my Shrimpkins, too," he added, gnawing on a chicken wing. "Bad for business all around. Bad for the old image. People don't like a place connected with murder. Makes 'em shiver and shake, it does."

Carmichael nodded his assent. "That's right, E.Y. Bad for business. The first episode, a mechanical accident. The second, a cruel and heartless murder committed by a cruel and heartless young man. The third . . . well, we'll certainly have to question this man Porter, right, Lieutenant? We'll certainly want to go over the guns with all the sophisticated lab equipment available to a modern, up-to-date police department such as ours. Lieutenant, I want you to get on it first thing!" he said with an air of authority mitigated by the butter dripping down his chin.

"I'd been planning on it," Espinoza said tightly. He looked to Zalman for help.

Zalman shook his head. "I've already given my opinion. Both guns were reloaded with live ammo. Somebody wanted to kill both men. The only question is, which two was the killer after? E.Y. and Yip? After all, Yip was supposed to be the second gunman. Or E.Y. and Mercer? Or doesn't our cutthroat care? But whomever else the killer was after, he *was* after E.Y., and that's a dead certainty, you should pardon the phrase."

He looked around at the faces in the room, all staring at him like crème fraîche wouldn't melt in their mouths. Rhonda, backlit as usual, looked stupefied, but Zalman figured she thought she was being seductive. Yip and Tracee were doing their imitation of intertwined turtledoves, sitting so close to each other it was tough to tell where Yip left off and Tracee began. Carmichael, red in the face from a surfeit of bluster, looked like he could use another drink, and Espinoza just looked nervous and tired.

E.Y. drained his glass and plunked it down on the table. "Well, I'm going to bed," he told his wife. "Unless you have any more questions for me, young man," he told Espinoza.

"Nothing that can't wait, sir," Espinoza said smoothly. "Of course, there'll be an inquest. Another inquest, you understand."

"Yep, sure do. The law's the law. That's what made this country great, the law," E.Y. said grandiloquently, then shook his head sadly. "Two people killed in my own house. A terrible day for the Knottes. Buttercup, ask Brunson to bring me some scrambled eggs and bacon up to my room, will ya?"

"I'll bring it up myself, dear," Rhonda replied. "Well, Lieutenant, I think I'll say good night now, if that's all right." She floated over to Espinoza and gave him her hand, then smiled thinly at Carmichael. "Arthur, good night." She nodded to the others and followed her husband out of the room.

"I think we've all had enough for today, Lieutenant," Zalman said. "Let's be in touch tomorrow."

Espinoza looked glumly around the room at the assembled company, all of whom looked weary and drained after the bizarre events of the day. He put his untouched bottle of Coke on the bar, nodded, and went out wordlessly.

"Well," Carmichael pronounced, "I've seen all I need to see here. First thing tomorrow, Espinoza," he called after the cop with an air of incredible self-importance. Still, he showed no signs of leaving. He just sipped his drink and tried to look thoughtful.

Tracee clearly wasn't going to stick around and play hostess. "I'm going to go get the car," she announced. "You guys meet me in front."

"Where's your pal McCoy?" Yip asked innocently as Tracee left the room.

Carmichael looked away, pretending he wasn't interested.

Zalman shrugged easily. "He's around somewhere, I imagine. He had a date, so perhaps he left before the shooting started. As it were," he added, making sure Carmichael was listening, just in case Carmichael got hold of McCoy before he, Zalman, had a chance to talk to him. Zalman knew damn well McCoy hadn't left early, and he had high hopes that McCoy and Molly had picked up plenty of intelligence during the party. With any luck McCoy had also searched the house, but that would be an added bonus.

Luckily, Marie distracted the D.A.'s limited attention. "Yikes!" she cried. "I forgot all about Rutherford! Where is that big baby?" She ran out of the room. Zalman could hear her voice echoing off the armor in the entryway as she called wistfully for the Doberman.

Zalman herded Yip and Carmichael out to the front door just as Marie returned with Rutherford in tow. "He was out on the lawn," she said breathlessly as Rutherford frisked happily around her feet. "What a bad little woojums you are," she cooed, rumpling the dog's pointy ears. "He was fooling around with the poodle," she whispered to Zalman. "I hope Rhonda isn't planning to breed show dogs. . . ."

Zalman rolled his eyes. "That's all we need," he muttered. "For God's sake don't tell her about it. . . ."

Tracee pulled up in front, and they got into the aqua wagon, leaving Carmichael standing forlornly on the steps. "Well . . . bye, everyone," he said lamely, waving as they drove off.

"WHAT'S WITH THAT GUY?" ZALMAN WONDERED ALOUD AS the car wound its way down the road toward Yip and Tracee's house. "How come nobody wants to play with him?"

Tracee laughed. "He's such a jerk, and he's so purse proud about it, too." She shook her blond head. "I mean, he isn't exactly a Nobel Prize winner, after all. What's he got to be so almighty snooty about? And he's always sucking up to E.Y.! It gives me the creepie-crawlies! It's just sickening! He—"

"Fawns," Marie interjected. "You don't see much fawning these days, and it's kind of interesting, actually, because very few people know how to do it anymore. I thought it went out in the Edwardian era myself. But Carmichael definitely fawns."

"Yeah, that's it," Yip said. "Bowing and scraping all the time, hanging around in case Dad wants the trash taken out. Fawns, that's it."

Tracee stopped the car in the driveway, and everyone went inside and flopped down in the living room, too tired to talk but too tired to go to bed.

"I'm frightened," Tracee announced miserably. "Jerry, this is so icky! Real murder isn't at all like TV, like on 'Murder, She Wrote.' I always watch that show. It's my favorite, especially when they just stay in Cabot Cove and don't make Jessica go to the Kentucky Derby or something dumb like that. But now I think I'm kinda off TV for a while."

"Death *is* icky, Trace," Zalman said simply. "Icky blood, icky killers . . ." He sighed and glanced around the room. Andy Warhol's animals leered down at him from the walls, and the surf pounded like a migraine. He realized again that he hated the country, hated fresh air, hated sports clothes, hated golf, tennis, and relaxation.

"Ladies," he said, "I'm going outside to smoke a cigar. Yip, perhaps you'd care to join me?"

"Sure, Jerry," Yip said, happy to be asked.

"Tell me a little more about Mercer," Zalman said as they stepped out on the deck. He got his gold clipper and trimmed the end of his Macanudo. "What kind of relationship did he have with your father?"

Yip leaned up against the railing and stared across the lawn into the dark. "He wasn't a bad guy, Jerry. In a lot of ways I think my dad woulda rather had him for a son than me. I love my dad, and I want to make him happy, but I gotta go my own way, have my own business, my own life." Yip gave a broad grin, and even in the murky gloom his teeth shone dazzling white. "I guess my dad and me, we're a lot alike. . . ."

"That's true," Tracee said, as she and Marie came out onto the deck. "You've done very well with your own ideas, and World O' Yip is going to be a big hit, you wait and see."

"Rah rah Yip!" Marie said.

Zalman laughed. "They're right, pal. Go get some sleep, and we can rehash all this in the morning. Then we'll take a run downtown and see this Porter, okay?"

"You bet, Jerry," Yip agreed. "Porter is a funny guy, but you'll like him once you get used to it."

"Get used to what?" Zalman asked warily.

"I'll tell you in the morning." Yip laughed. "If I tell you now, you'll never get to sleep. Night, you guys."

"PORTER'S NOT A BAD GUY," YIP SAID EARNESTLY THE next morning. "He's a little weird on the surface, but once you get to know him it's no problem. You forget."

Zalman was sitting at the glass-topped table on the deck, looking out at the horizon and enjoying an after-breakfast cigar. "Forget what?" he asked cautiously.

"Weeeelllll," Yip said, "Porter looks pretty ostentatious. See, he used to be an Angel. Kind of an Angel. Not a real bad Hell's Angel–type Angel, just an Angel type of guy. But the thing is," Yip said with a conspiratorial giggle, "he wasn't very good at it, so one day when he was kick-starting his Harley it fell over on him, and they had to amputate his leg."

Zalman shivered. "Yeeeecccch. That's terrible."

"Yeah, I know. But the thing was, after he lost his leg he wouldn't get a regular artificial limb. Porter had to go and get a peg leg. Had it hand-carved by this ex-hippie, back-to-the-lander over in Ojai, and this guy put veins running up and down it and a little squirrel peeking out right at the kneecap. Or where the kneecap would be if there was a kneecap. It's a beautiful job," Yip concluded. "I'm putting some of this guy's carvings in my gift shop at World O' Yip. Rich agents and producers from L.A., they lap up that stuff like it was cream. Makes 'em feel they're plugged into nature."

Zalman felt slightly relieved. "Okay, so Porter's a little eccentric, but he doesn't sound so bad."

Yip was warming to his subject. "Yeah, but listen to this. Once he had the peg leg, he kinda got a case of pirate-itis. Next thing he did, he started wearing a big gold hoop earring. Then a red bandanna over his head, you know how pirates do?"

"Sure, I saw *Peter Pan,* for Christ's sake!" Zalman said irritably. Things were piling up again.

"Well, then"—Yip chuckled—"of course he had to go and get a parrot."

"A parrot. Sure," Zalman agreed. "Why not? You gotta have a parrot if you're a pirate. So, Yip, what you're telling me is that we're about to go see a one-legged ex–Hell's Angel who likes to dress up like a pirate and wear a parrot on his shoulder? Hey, no problem. All in a day's work!" Zalman had the sensation that he and Marie, clearly the only rational beings in a thirty-mile radius of Knotte Pines, were in a little rubber dinghy drifting ever closer to a dark and nasty whirlpool where they would be forced to choose between certain doom and inevitable death. Either way, things were looking down. "I'll go change," he told Yip tonelessly.

He came back fifteen minutes later and found McCoy sitting on the deck, smoking a Lucky and wolfing down a chunk of Tracee's cake. "I thought we finished the apple cake," Zalman said mildly.

"This's banana," McCoy said with his mouth full. "From a freezer." He swallowed and chased the cake with a cup of coffee. "Just gave it a quick blast in the microwave. Nice and warm. Have some," he offered generously.

Zalman took a piece. "Where're the girls?"

"Shouldn't call 'em girls, Jerry. You know they don't like it."

"I only do it when they're not around." Zalman grinned. "You think I'm crazy?"

"Marie said to tell you her and Tracee went to get their nails done. You ask me, they're up to something. The two of 'em were deep into some heavy conversation when I showed up. Heavy air, know what I mean? Yip's in the shower. He can't wait to play Mike Hammer."

"Yeah. Lots of fun. So Dean, old buddy, tell me what you found out yesterday. I noticed you beat it out of there pretty fast."

"Jeez, Jerry," McCoy said, sounding aggrieved. "You told me to check out the house. Me and Molly were having the old look-see."

"So? So? Let's have it."

McCoy grinned. "Nothing you can take to the bank, buddy. Rhonda's got a lot of loose cash stashed all over the place in her room, mostly in books and dried flower arrangements and stuffed into Estée Lauder giveaways. Brunson's got a tasty collection of Victorian erotica—you know, pictures of fat dames with their heels in the air. E.Y.'s room's like a monk's cell or something. World's hardest mattress, hospital corners, barbells—no smoking gun, though. Soon as I saw there was trouble I beat it out the back way with Molly. Guys like me that have been your long-term guests of the state, we like to avoid your casual shootings." He grinned.

"Can't blame you. Yip tell you about this guy Porter the jolly pirate?"

"I think maybe I know this guy from San Q.," McCoy said thoughtfully. "Seems like there was this guy in there same time as me, and Mercer for that matter, that used to be a biker, only he dropped his bike on his leg and like, adios leg. It was a big joke. 'Course, he wasn't a pirate then, if it's the same goofball. Anyway, I heard all about him from Molly," McCoy added, placing his hand reverently over his heart.

"Nice lady," Zalman observed.

"You ain't kidding," McCoy said dreamily. "We got another date tonight when she gets off work. She's gonna teach me to rhumba."

"Rhumba!" Zalman said with some surprise. He couldn't picture McCoy scuttling around the dance floor, twitching his hips.

"Well, she'll rhumba. I'll kinda hang out," McCoy said around a fresh mouthful of cake.

"Say, guys, ready to go?" It was Yip and his camcorder. He was wearing a pair of white pants that looked like they'd last been worn by Ali Baba, blue espadrilles with rope soles, and a white Oingo Boingo T-shirt with squiggly red lizards hopping all over the chest. His blond hair was freshly washed, and as he sat down, sipping a steaming cup of Yip Tea, Zalman thought once again that the guy was straight out of *Esquire*. "We gonna go question Porter?" Yip asked hopefully. "Is it okay if I take my camcorder? Maybe I can get his confession on tape. Kinda like the Zapruder film."

"Right, Yip, it'll be just like the Zapruder film," Zalman said, his brain reeling. "Sure, take your camera. . . ."

"Gee, great, swell, Jerry!" Yip said ingenuously. "I always wanted to be in on something like this!" His clean-cut, freshly scrubbed face beamed with boyish enthusiasm.

"Terrific," Zalman mumbled. "I gotta go call Primo, then we're outta here." He went into the house. "Primo!" he said heartily when the young cop came on the line. "How's the wacky world of crime and punishment?"

"Terrible!" Espinoza moaned. "Carmichael's been chewing me out all morning. Guy's really got it in for me. What'd I do?"

"You've got better suits," Zalman told him. "Try dressing down a little. Listen, I'm headed over to Porter's place, and I thought you might want to come along. Yip's the point man, and my legman Dean McCoy's gonna be there, too. McCoy's an ex-con who was in the joint same time as Mercer and knew him up there. He also thinks maybe he knows this Porter. I thought you might want to know about McCoy's pedigree before you made a commitment."

"What the hell." Espinoza said despondently. "I might as well get busted for consorting with known felons as anything else. How could it get any worse?"

Zalman laughed. "You'd be surprised, pal. Meet you at Porter's place in half an hour."

PORTER'S SMALL GUN EMPORIUM WAS TUCKED IN THE REAR of a light industrial storage building next to a 7-Eleven. Most of the other cubicles were vacant and had weeds poking up through the blacktop in front, but despite the absence of a sign or any advertising denoting his establishment, Porter's place was unmistakable. A big Harley with a jolly red sidecar was parked in front of a rolled steel door, and next to that there was a battered wooden door with a crude spray-painted skull and crossbones. As they climbed out of the aqua wagon, Yip panned his camcorder over the tableau.

"So much macho around these days," Zalman sighed, adjusting his three-piece suit. "So few brains."

At that moment, Espinoza's gray Plymouth sedan appeared behind them, and Espinoza, looking distinctly disgruntled, got out and joined them. Zalman introduced the two, and McCoy and Espinoza nodded coolly.

Before McCoy had time to get up in Espinoza's face, Zalman jumped in. "Okay, guys, here's the drill. Yip, you and I go knock on the door. Primo and McCoy, you two stay here and lurk. If everything goes okay, then Yip fades back to the car and Primo comes in. Got it?"

McCoy laughed as he sucked on the Lucky he held between nicotine-stained fingers. "Yowsah, Mr. Zalman," he said.

"I'm the cop," Espinoza said dispiritedly. "I'm supposed to be in charge here."

"Cops!" McCoy laughed harshly, shaking his head. "You don't know a good deal when you're looking it in the face." McCoy unexpectedly reached over, grabbed Espinoza by his shoulder pads, and gave him a rough massage. "Loosen up, dude. You'll last longer!" Espinoza looked like he was trying to decide if he should shoot McCoy on the spot or wait till later when there weren't any witnesses.

"Cut it out, you two!" Zalman said. "We got business here!" He squinted dubiously at Porter's so-called place of business. "What a dump!"

Zalman and Yip went up to the wooden door and knocked. As soon as they did the door jerked open so quickly that it was clear they'd been watched as they'd stood around in the parking lot. A wave of stale cigarette smoke and WD-40 spray lubricant wafted out into Zalman's face. Despite his careful plan, he jumped slightly.

"Yeah?" Porter growled ominously as he took in the foursome with a quick flick of his unpatched eye. Just as Yip had said, Porter had a heavy dose of Long John Silver going for him. He was wearing a red bandanna pulled low on his Neanderthal brow, and his good eye had four San Quentin teardrops dripping from its corner, a tattoo for every year he'd served in the slammer. A large gold hoop earring dangled from his right ear, and he wore a white shirt and black pants, rolled up on one leg to reveal the highly polished, elaborately carved peg leg. He did not look happy, and one of his ham-sized arms was ominously tucked out of sight behind the door.

Yip stepped forward without hesitation, a sincere smile lighting his face. "Hey, Porter, how you doin', man? We came about Mercer. . . ."

Porter looked past Zalman and Yip at the two men waiting by the station wagon. "He's a cop," he said flatly, pointing at Espinoza. "And him"—here Porter squinted at McCoy—"him I think I remember from the joint. What is this?"

Yip nodded smoothly. "Hey, there's no problem, Porter, man! We just want to talk . . . about Mercer."

"Mercer was my pal," Porter stated, his one eye scowling. "We did a jolt together, so what?" His singular gaze shifted to Zalman. "You're not a cop!" he said decisively.

"I'm an attorney," Zalman said suavely, wondering if this was the moment to whip out his card.

"A mouthpiece, huh?" Porter said belligerently. "You guys're bloodsuckers!"

"Hey, Porter, don't get steamed," Yip said softly. "Mr. Zalman here is trying to help my dad. You know my dad's all right."

Porter considered this, then nodded slowly. "E.Y.'s cool."

"My dad shot Mercer by accident," Yip went on. "We think somebody loaded the guns with live ammo, that they were after my dad but Mercer got killed by mistake. Can Mr. Zalman and the lieutenant just ask you a few questions? It would be a real favor to my dad, honest."

Porter looked suspiciously from man to man. "Your dad wants me to?" he asked Yip.

"It'd be a real favor, man," Yip said again.

"I never talked to a cop in my life, leastwise not willingly, but if your dad says it's okay . . ." Porter folded back his eye patch to reveal a second, perfectly good eye and stood in the doorway, staring at Espinoza and McCoy. "All right," he agreed, "tell 'em to come ahead."

McCoy and Espinoza walked up to the door, and Porter threw it open. He lumbered off down a short hallway toward his tiny office, and Zalman saw that he was carrying a stainless steel Ruger Mini-14 with a pair of banana clips taped end to end in the breech.

"Nice piece of hardware," McCoy observed laconically.

"Hey, McCoy, right?" Porter said, sinking into a wooden swivel office chair behind his junky desk. He laid the rifle carefully on the desktop. "If you can't stop it with this, it can't be stopped." He grinned evilly. "What you been doing with yourself?" he asked McCoy, ignoring Espinoza.

"Keeping out of trouble"—McCoy grinned—"most days." He offered Porter a Lucky, and the two men lit up.

Porter's desk was littered with tools and firearms in various states of disassembly, and more broken-down firearms covered a second worktable. An electric lathe and drill press stood to the side. But by far the most notable thing in the shop was a large green parrot with a red head and nasty eyes who perched on a chrome stand next to Porter's creaking chair. Porter reached out and gave the bird a sunflower seed from a tin can on his desk. The bird craned his head to one side, took the seed, ate it, and looked darkly at its master. "Quack quack quack," the parrot remarked.

"Cute," Zalman said, studying a large travel poster tacked to an unfinished drywall partition. A green Bahamian sea gave the room a bilious look that, combined with the smell of oil and cigarette smoke, made Zalman slightly queasy.

"Well?" Porter demanded, tapping his peg leg on the floor.

"Unlax, Doc," Espinoza said, echoing McCoy's earlier injunction. He leaned against the drywall partition. "This ain't official," he added.

Zalman decided to take charge. It was easier than sitting around. "You were working on E.Y.'s guns? The ones he used yesterday?"

Porter nodded. "Firing pins needed adjusting on some of 'em. A little oil here and there. Otherwise he just wanted me to check 'em out. No big deal. I fixed up the blanks for him, too. I done quite a bit of work for Mr. Knotte. He's good people."

190

"So when the guns went out of here they were loaded with blanks?" Zalman asked.

"Two of 'em, those two four-inch Colts Mr. Knotte was gonna use in his shoot-out deal. I fixed up twelve blank rounds, six in each gun. The other guns, they was unloaded. Old Merce, he was here when I did it, too. Looking over my shoulder the whole time, poor dude. Then I give him the guns in a cardboard box, and he takes it up to Mr. Knotte's place in the hills. That's the way it went down."

"Why was Mercer here?"

Porter shrugged and stroked the parrot's head with an oil-stained forefinger. "Hanging out, is all. Him and me, hey, we go way back. So we like to keep in touch. He comes over with the hardware, we hoist a couple, no big deal." Porter looked at the men in the room. "These guys make me nervous," he sighed, as if he'd just seen something disturbing in his horoscope. "I can't talk to a cop. Goes against the grain, know what I mean?"

Zalman looked at the others. "Why don't you fellas wait outside?"

Espinoza opened his mouth to protest, but a look from McCoy closed it for him. "C'mon, guys," Yip said enthusiastically. "I've got a great idea. . . ." The three men left Zalman alone with Porter and his parrot.

Zalman looked at the piratical gunsmith and shook his head. "Porter," he said quietly, "we're talking murder here. If you know anything about anything, you'd better spill it fast, before that junior G-man outside gets outta control. You already did one stretch. C'mon pal, I'm an attorney, you can tell me. . . ." he wheedled.

"You ain't my lawyer," Porter said.

"Gimme me five bucks," Zalman said. "C'mon, c'mon, no yimmy-yammy. Just fork over a five and I'll save your worthless life."

Porter reached grudgingly into his pocket for his wallet,

extracted a raggedy bill, and handed it to Zalman. "Blood-suckers," he mumbled.

Zalman pocketed the dirty bill with distaste and handed Porter a card. "Now I'm *your* bloodsucker," he announced, "official-like."

"Do I get a receipt?"

"What is this, K-Mart?" Zalman shook his head in dis-belief. He looked at the parrot, who rotated its head and belched loudly. "Nothing but class," he observed.

"So there was this girl . . ."

"Ahhhh, now we're getting somewhere." Zalman was delighted. "Tell me all about it."

Porter tapped his peg leg impatiently on the floor. "Hey! I dunno nothing! Merce used to meet her here sometimes. I think she was thick with old man Knotte, so big deal! So she was slipping Mercer a little on the Q.T. Happens all the time," the gunsmith said with an air of worldly-wise ennui. "They used to go outside, have real serious talks."

"Her name?" Zalman prompted. "What'd she look like?"

"Jeez, nice-looking chick. Surfer doll, know what I mean? Blond, blue eyes, got a pair of strong legs on her, which is how come I figure she surfs. I figured she had something going with Mr. Knotte but wanted a taste on the side, you catch my drift?"

"Perfectly. Her name?" Zalman said again.

"I dunno. We was never like formally introduced."

Zalman stared at the parrot and thought back to the af-ternoon in the bar of the Blue Fin Inn and the conversation he'd had with Tracee afterward about E.Y.'s various girl-friends. He sighed. He hadn't been paying sufficient atten-tion, a fatal flaw for a high-priced mouthpiece. These days a guy had to have a computer for a brain.

"Okay, pal," he told Porter. "You think of anything, you can get me up at Yip's place. Talk to me later." As he shut the door to Porter's grimy office he heard the parrot say,

"Open, sez me!" in a perfect rendition of Popeye the Sailor Man.

Zalman strolled thoughtfully out to the station wagon, and as he opened the door he heard McCoy say, "Okay, John Wayne for my dad, of course. Doris Day for my mom, 'cause of how she's kind to animals. Maybe Victor McLaglen for my uncle . . ."

"What the hell are you guys talking about?" Zalman asked curiously as he got into the back seat.

The three men in the car looked abashed, as if they'd just been nailed by the boys' vice-principal for smoking under the bleachers. Finally, in a meek, innocent tone, Yip said, "We're playing Fantasy Family. It's a game I made up. It's real psychological, see? You pick out the movie stars you want for your family, and when you do, you kinda get in touch with yourself, like get down to the core experience. Know where I'm coming from?"

"Jesus," Zalman muttered. He stared from one man to another as they fidgeted under his scrutiny. They were so clearly embarrassed that he couldn't help laughing. "Okay." He grinned at Yip. "So who'd you pick?"

"Well, I always wanted Spencer Tracy for my dad."

"Good choice," Espinoza approved. "All I can come up with is Pedro Armendariz," he said glumly.

"And Jane Wyman for my mom, though I think she'd be pretty strict, and Katharine Hepburn for my sister. She's so intelligent. I bet she could give me a lot of good advice. And maybe John Lund for my older brother, 'cause he'd set a good example, but like wouldn't be too uptight if I made a mistake, and—"

"God, you guys are so wholesome!" Zalman laughed. "How come nobody picks Zachary Scott or Gloria Grahame? John Carroll, maybe. Or Linda Darnell?"

"See!" Yip cried with delight. "It's revelatory, huh? C'mon, Jerry, who'd you pick?"

Zalman considered the proposition. If you could have a

family composed of movie stars, who would you choose? "Okay, okay, I wouldn't take Zachary Scott for my dad. I'd rather have him for my black-sheep cousin. I'd have Ronald Colman for my father and Marlene Dietrich for my mother."

"Hotsy totsy." McCoy grinned.

"I figure she'd always smell good when she came in to kiss you good night. And I'd have Bogart for my uncle—"

"Duncan Renaldo!" Espinoza mused. "See the trouble. You guys have lots of choices. . . ."

"Nothing wrong with Cesar Romero or Delores Del Rio or Katy Jurado!" Zalman snapped. "Be creative, Primo! You got Martin Sheen, you got his kids, you got Gilbert Roland, for Pete's sake. You got Tony Quinn, you got Lupe Velez!"

"Say, you're right!" Espinoza said, cheering up. "I gotta think on this," he said thoughtfully as he got out of the car. "Where're you guys headed now?"

"Blue Fin bar," Zalman said.

"Anything I should know about?" Espinoza asked.

"Don't ask," Zalman told him. "Thanks for coming along today, Primo. Let's talk later on."

Espinoza waved and walked off toward his car as Yip started the wagon and headed for the Blue Fin bar.

"We looking for somebody?" Yip wanted to know. He was almost bouncing up and down with the sheer thrill of the chase.

"Yeah, some girl," Zalman said. "I got a feeling Miss Molly McCafferty is gonna be a big help to us."

McCoy looked at his watch. "She's just coming on shift," he said. "Boy, what a woman!"

A few minutes later, Yip pulled the wagon into the parking lot in front of the Blue Fin Inn. The beer signs blinked a cheery good-morning greeting as the three men got out of the car and walked toward the door.

"Oh, by the way," Yip said offhandedly, "I came up with

the money I needed for World O' Yip, Jer. I just wanted you to know."

"That's great, Yip, glad to hear it," Zalman said with false heartiness, once again feeling bad that he hadn't done more about Yip's financial problems. "Your dad decided to let loose of some cash after all?" he asked as he opened the door and peered into the welcoming gloom. "Hey, we'll talk later, okay?"

"Howdy, boys!" Molly smiled, fixing McCoy with a frank look. "What'll it be?"

"Corona." McCoy grinned.

"Perrier," Yip said, smiling.

"Information," Zalman muttered.

"What sort of information?" Molly asked as she rustled around the back bar and got McCoy and Yip's orders, handing the latter a club soda.

"You gotta tell me who E.Y. was seeing. Blond girl, surfer maybe? It's important."

"Well, for heaven's sake!" Molly said. "Is that all? Why don't you ask his wife?" She pointed at Yip, who instantly looked guilty, although he hadn't done anything.

"His wife?" Zalman and McCoy said in unison.

"Why, sure," Molly said indulgently. "Why, I saw her just this morning! I had my hair appointment," she said, modestly patting her flaxen locks. "I have a standing appointment at Ruby's once a week, regular as can be, and so I was just finishing off with my nails when your wife comes in with this other girl—pretty, too, brunette, short. Jerry, you introduced us at the contest, remember?"

*Marie*, Zalman thought. *I'll throttle her.*

"Why, sure," Molly rattled on. "Your wife and the brunette girl were over in the corner, next to the stand-up bonnet dryers. 'Course, nobody uses them much anymore, most of the girls have it blow-dried or a nice finger wave . . . and your girlfriend asked me about E.Y.'s latest. So I told her to talk to Carole and ask her about the baby—"

"BABY!" Zalman exploded. "Carole who? What *baby* are we talking about here?"

"Why, sure! Carole's going to have a baby, so she doesn't come in to work at Ruby's every day like she used to—"

"Arrrrgh!" Zalman howled. "Women! Yip, back to your place, pronto!"

TRACEE AND MARIE WERE IN THE LIVING ROOM WATCHING Oprah Winfrey. Tracee was doing needlepoint, and Marie was lying on the floor, flexing a brand new pair of little pink dumbbells. Rutherford was by her side, watching her raise and lower her forearm.

"Oh, Marie," Zalman purred as he stormed through the front door, Yip at his heels. McCoy remained outside to give Chester a run in the driveway.

"Oh, Tracee," Yip echoed.

Tracee looked up from her needlepoint, a bouquet of pink and purple flowers, and smiled at her former and present husbands. She was wearing an absurd pair of gold Ben Franklin specs and a flowing purple caftan with gold threat shot through it. She looked, as always, divine. "Hi," she said absently, her eyes on the TV screen.

"Hi, honey," Marie said as she continued counting under her breath. "Twenty-one, twenty-two, twen—"

"Never mind that Jane Fonda crapola! What have you two dames been up to?" Zalman barked.

"Don't you just love it when they're masterful?" Marie asked Tracee.

"I think it's cunning," Tracee agreed. "Now, darn it, Jerry! You've made me lose count."

"Me, too," Marie said. "Was I on twenty-four or twenty-five?"

"Twenty-three," Zalman snapped, exasperated. "What's with this Carole person?"

Tracee smiled soothingly. "Jerry, why don't you sit down, and Yippie can make us all a nice cup of Yip's Comfort. Wouldn't that be nice? Carole isn't going anywhere, and I'm sure she'd be happy to talk to you, poor girl. But in her condition, you ought to be gentle."

"Gentle! I'm gentle as hell!" Zalman yelled. "This is murder one we're talking here! People are getting killed left and right! This isn't the time to listen to our goddamn Leo Buscaglia tapes!" Zalman flung himself moodily onto the couch. "I'm a busy man. McCoy's a busy man—"

"I'm a busy man, too!" Yip put in hopefully.

"We're all busy men or we wouldn't be here!" Zalman said. *"Now.* What about Carole?"

"Well, she's pregnant, of course," Tracee said, peering at her needlepoint distractedly. "It's not due for a while, so she doesn't show at all yet. After all, if she'd been showing, those dirty old men wouldn't have let her be Miss Kelp of the Coast."

Zalman didn't say a word. He stared at Andy Warhol's panda, which stared back at him, forever munching a bamboo shoot. "Why is this happening to me?" he asked the panda. "What'd I do? Was I a Republican in a previous life?"

"You see, Jerry," Tracee continued, "Marie and I went in for facials after we'd been to the antique shop. I got the cutest little jade elephant, Yippie, to go with the Warhols. So anyway, we went in for facials, and Carole was there, and Molly pointed Carole out to us, and she looked so unhappy, and Marie, who is so clever . . . honestly, Jerry, you two make a fabulous couple, that's all I can say . . . so Marie started asking her why she felt bad, so Carole told us all about E.Y. And the baby and how she'd just won the

Miss Kelp of the Coast contest and was planning on going to Hawaii with the money."

"I wish *we* were going to Hawaii," Marie added pointedly.

"Wait a minute, wait a minute," Zalman said. "How did you know she knew E.Y.?"

"Molly, of course," Marie said. "Tracee *told* you. Molly was there getting her hair done, and she told me to talk to Carole, who was over in the corner crying her eyes out. Carole's awfully sweet but not too bright, in my estimation, and it turns out she was all broken up about Mercer! She hadn't known about it until she got to Ruby Toucan's and—"

"Wait a minute, wait a minute! She's broken up about Mercer's death? She says she's pregnant by E.Y. and she's broken up about Mercer? Porter, the gunsmith, he says there was a girl always hanging around Mercer, and I figure it's this selfsame Carole. Perhaps a light through yonder window breaks here, boys and girls."

Tracee and Marie looked at each other. "What do you think, Marie?" Tracee asked.

"It's up for grabs, as the girl said to the sailor," Marie said thoughtfully. "Jerry's right. Carole's sweet, and I hate to cast aspersions, but I don't know if I really believe her about E.Y. and the baby and all. What do you think?"

Tracee was unsure. "Beats me. You know what I'd do, Jerry? I'd run right over there and talk to her, that's what. She lives in an apartment complex near the beach—I have the address right here in my purse. But I'd be nice. I wouldn't start barking the way you do. Just give her a nice shoulder to cry on. That's the ticket."

Zalman felt like he had steam coming out of his ears. "I don't bark! I'm the goddamn soul of gentility, I am!"

Tracee and Marie looked at each other wordlessly. "Of course you are, Jerry," Marie said. "Nobody said you weren't. And I wouldn't take all the boys with you.

McCoy can give the dogs a run on the beach, and Yip can help with dinner."

"Boy, that'd be great!" Yip enthused. "I'll fix a Caesar salad, we can grill Jerry a steak on the barbie, shrimp cocktail, all my favorite stuff. . . ."

"So you run along, Jerry, okay?" Tracee said with the placid Donna Reed air of the best darn mom in the world, "and we'll see you about dinner time, all right?"

Zalman looked at the two women. He looked at Yip. Clearly, he was outnumbered, outflanked, and outclassed. But despite what Tracee and Marie said, he wasn't about to undertake this particular mission on his own. Prudence dictated that he take a witness. He sighed, dialed Espinoza's number, and drummed his fingers on the end table. "Primo, long time no see, buddy!" he said when Espinoza picked up the phone. "Hey, how'd you like to make another home visit?"

THE GIRL NAMED CAROLE LIVED IN A GLITTER STUCCO
apartment building in Isla Vista where life clearly moved in
an orbit between the liquor store across the street and the
green slice of pool in the center of the courtyard. Every
apartment in the building fronted on the pool, and Zalman
figured that most of the tenants spent their time relaxing on
the plastic lounge chairs scattered everywhere, soaking up
sun and suds. It was an example of California cliché at its
finest.

Zalman and Espinoza, with their hot, tired faces, three-
piece suits, and shiny shoes, clearly didn't fit in at the El
Rancho Adobe Apartments, and several stoned characters
sprawled around the pool gave them the once-over as the
two men climbed the stairs to Carole's second-floor apartment.

Espinoza rapped briskly on the peeling orange door, and
a moment later the dusty bamboo blinds on the front window parted slightly and a thin, girlish voice asked, "Yes?"

Espinoza flashed his shield at the window. "Police," he
said quietly. "May I speak to you, please?" It wasn't a
question.

The door opened a crack, and a pretty, pale blonde in
cutoff jeans and a man's grubby white shirt looked around
the jamb at the two men. "What is it?" she said miserably.

She was obviously frightened. Her eyes were wide, and her voice shook like the eucalyptus trees in the field beyond the apartment complex.

"May we come in?" Espinoza said. He was still holding his badge. "I need to ask you a few questions."

She opened the door wider. "Might as well," she said dully, backpedaling on tanned bare feet. "I don't care."

Espinoza stepped inside. Zalman followed him. The room was one of a million; the living room had a cottage-cheese ceiling with flakes of glitter embedded in it, there was an L-shaped counter that served as a dining area and an avocado-green carpet. Carole didn't go in much for furniture. There was a plaid Salvation Army couch with two old wooden milk crates holding up a slab of planking that looked like it had been harvested on the beach. There were two plush gold velour beanbag chairs, one of them with a calico cat upon it having a bath in a ray of sunshine. The walls held two posters of the beach off Hawaii, with giant tubular waves and some bronzed fools coasting right down their centers. Zalman figured Carole for a girl with a waterbed.

"I'm Lieutenant Espinoza, this is Jerry Zalman. Mr. Zalman is an attorney."

"Do I need an attorney? I didn't ask for an attorney!" Her voice was shrill with fear. "I didn't do anything," she moaned. "Honest!"

"Sit down, miss . . ." Espinoza smiled professionally.

"Fields. Carole Fields," she said, sinking onto one of the beanbag chairs, which was covered with a thick mat of cat fur. Espinoza moved the cat and sat down in the other chair, and Zalman perched on the arm of the couch, hoping he could keep cat fur off his slacks. At least Rutherford had short hair, his single saving grace.

Espinoza leaned forward expectantly. "I'd like to know about your relationship with Mercer Lamont," he said smoothly. "And with E. Y. Knotte. Are you aware that Mr.

Knotte accidently killed Mercer Lamont yesterday? Do you know that, Miss Fields?"

Carole looked from Zalman to Espinoza and back again, then twisted a blond curl around her forefinger. "I know," she said flatly. "I just found out this morning when I went to get my hair done." She pulled at her bangs, fluffing them gently on her forehead. "I was so happy," she said tearfully. "Like I thought everything was going to be so much fun. I won this contest, you know? Like I'm going to be Miss Kelp of the Coast, and I was going to be at Yip Knotte's big opening and get to hang out a lot and go to Hawaii and everything. Like the surf's dynamite in Hawaii," she said brokenly, "and now everything is wrecked. Totally wrecked."

"Hey, you can still do it," Zalman said easily. He figured if Espinoza was going to be the nice cop he'd have to pick up the slack and play the tough cop in the duo. "But hey," he said, more harshly, "you gotta help us out here. What was Mercer to you, hmmmmm?" He hated himself because Carole was obviously miserable, but he continued to bore in on her. "You know there's a rumor going around that you're pregnant? A lot of people think E. Y. Knotte's the proud papa, but I think maybe Mercer was the father. Maybe you told E.Y. he was the father, but maybe that wasn't quite true?"

Espinoza pressed the advantage. "Now Porter—E.Y.'s gunsmith—Porter says you and Mercer were pretty tight. When Mercer was running errands for E.Y. you'd come over to Porter's shop and hang out. Were you there the other day? When Mercer picked up the guns for the contest?"

"Oh, God," she said quietly, a crystalline teardrop coursing its weary way down her tawny cheek. "This is *soooo* awful. . . ."

"Were you or Mercer going to kill Mr. Knotte? Are we in the ballpark, Miss Fields?" Espinoza asked.

Unaccountably, Carole started to laugh shrilly, although

she was still crying. "Honey," she said, "you're not even on the planet! God, men are so stupid! You guys think Mercer and I were going to kill E.Y.?" She got up angrily, went over to the counter, picked up a pack of Kools and lit one with a Bic lighter in a silver scabbard studded with fake turquoise.

"First of all," she said, sharply exhaling menthol smoke, "I'm not pregnant, okay? I told Mr. Knotte I was because I knew he wants a baby. Well, really he wants his son to have a baby, but Tracee hasn't foaled yet, so he's all shook up. So I lied, like really big deal. I had this idea maybe he'd dump Rhonda and marry me and everything would be really dynamite. Like I said, I know it was dumb, okay? Even Mercer thought it was dumb—I mean, dumb as dear old Mercer was, he was smart enough to know that—but I was supposed to be the brains of our outfit—Mercer's and mine—so Merce went along with it. I didn't really think E.Y.'d marry me. I think I really thought he'd lay some cash on me, like five thousand maybe?" she said hopefully. "I'm not greedy. . . ."

Zalman cocked an eyebrow. "You're not pregnant . . . so what was with you and Mercer?"

"So I'm not pregnant, and so Mercer was my brother, and so there!"

"Your brother!" Espinoza moaned in astonishment. "Why didn't you say that before?"

Carole ground out her cigarette in a plastic ashtray, coughing slightly. "I hate cigarettes, knock the poop out of your wind. Because Mercer fixed me up with E.Y., bird-brain, that's why. And because we were gonna try and get a little dough outta the old man and like split for Hawaii, get it? Real simple. Two nickel-dime-quarter beach bums with nothing on the ball trying to cheat a dirty old man outta a couple of bucks. God, I feel terrible," she whined, sinking back onto the beanbag chair and hugging her knees.

"*You* feel terrible! I had a helluva theory there!" Espinoza said, getting up disgustedly and pacing. "Brother and sister!"

"Sure," she said. "Nobody knew about it, so we used to get together at Porter's and talk and stuff. We were just being stupid, I guess." She paused and looked around the half-furnished apartment. "E.Y. liked to come down here because he said it was simple. But it's really me that's simple," she said with a bitter laugh. "Simpleminded. Damn it, damn it, damn it! Why did Merce have to go and get killed? Even though he wasn't too bright, he always kinda took care of me, ever since we were kids. . . ." She trailed off and looked at the two men.

"Time to learn to take care of yourself, dear," Zalman said, not unkindly. "After all, you're still Miss Kelp of the Coast, right? So you'll still get the trip to Hawaii, right?"

Carole brightened. "Yeah. I'd like to settle down over there. I've always wanted to open a bikini shop, you know?"

"Why don't you ask Mr. Knotte to help you?" Zalman suggested in the same voice he'd have used on a not-too-bright twelve-year-old. Carole obviously didn't have the brains of a flatworm, and he figured she needed all the help she could get. "You might even try being honest with him. Mr. Knotte likes honesty. Try it. Believe me, it's a great ploy. Forget all this *French Lieutenant's Woman* jive. Just go for your straight business deal. He gives you some dough, you get out of town and promise to keep your mouth shut about your . . . relationship. Then, when you get to Hawaii, scout around a little first. Don't tell anyone you've got any money. Sort of see if you can find a good location for your shop. Find out about rent. That sort of thing, get it?"

"Gee, Mr. Zalman, that's a wonderful idea," Carole said, tremendously impressed. "How did you think of it?"

"Like I'm a genius," Zalman said modestly.

"Is this how a lawyer in Beverly Hills operates?" Espinoza asked when they were back in his gray Plymouth and driving.

"One of the ways." Zalman laughed, stretching back in the big police car. "Most of the time people want a little parenting. I just tell them what they'd be able to figure out for themselves if they stopped spinning their wheels and thought about things rationally for twelve seconds. Then I charge them a lot of money for it, so they think they're getting something worthwhile."

"What do you mean?" Espinoza asked, fighting his way through traffic.

"Like the psychiatrists say, if you don't pay, you don't get better." Zalman chuckled, gazing out the window at the puffy white clouds hanging over Santa Barbara. "Usually, somebody's ex-wife comes into my office because we've met a few times at parties and I'm a sympathetic guy and always compliment women on their outfits. So they remember me after the divorce when they need somebody to talk to. She tells me she can't live on what she's getting from the old man, so what should she do? I take her out to lunch, listen to her sob story, and in the course of it she waxes sentimental and tells me she's always wanted to do catering or decorating or have a flower shop."

"Like Eliza Doolittle," Espinoza put in.

"Exactly, Primo. So a few days later I call her up and tell her what she ought to do is open a flower shop or whatever. Then I help her arrange a little financing, run over the papers, make sure she'd got a good accountant, and presto change-o, she thinks I'm a genius. I charge her a whopping fee for all of this, of course, but I take it a little at a time so it doesn't hurt her too much. Then, every so often, regular as clockwork, I check out how she's doing, take her to an expensive lunch, listen to her problems, and in return she recommends me to all her friends. It's a cinch." Zalman grinned wolfishly.

"Amazing," Primo said, obviously impressed. "I always wanted to know what you guys did, but I've never seen you in action before. You just tell them what they already know. Even a child could do it."

"Not your child, Primo."

Espinoza laughed ruefully. "I'm afraid you're right about that. But it looks like I'll never be able to afford children anyway, since Carmichael's going to get me fired. Farewell to the Secret Service," the young cop sighed.

"Hey, trust me," Zalman said. "Maybe I can work something out. Just because Carmichael's trying to cast Ed Robin in the killer part doesn't mean that's the way it's going to be. Right now I'm more worried about the next time."

"What next time?"

"C'mon, Primo." Zalman said with exasperation. "Think about it for ten seconds, will you? There's always a next time, and now that the killer's offed poor old Mercer Lamont all he has to do is wait for his big chance, right? After all, Mercer was sort of a bodyguard, or at least he was the only guy who stuck close to E.Y., and now he's one of the late lamented. Look at it this way. If you were planning on killing E.Y. within the near future, say within the next week or so, when would you do it?"

"Wellll . . ." Espinoza said slowly, figuring. "Since I've already tried twice at his house—"

"And failed."

"And failed, I think I'd try somewhere else."

"And where do we know E.Y. will be in the near future, in a nice big public-type gathering, with lots and lots and lots of people around?"

"Ohhhh," Espinoza said, with a slow grin, nodding his glossy head sagely. "*I* get it. World O' Yip!"

"Give the cop a cigar." Zalman grinned, whipping out his case of Macanudos.

AN HOUR LATER, ZALMAN PARKED HIS MERCEDES AND walked slowly into Yip and Tracee's big house, mulling over the events of the afternoon. Something was evading him, something simple, something elemental. Perhaps that was the trouble—life in Beverly Hills was anything but elemental. He'd actually known a vice-president at MGM who'd fled to a hotel in panic when the refrigerator light burned out. Another guy he knew had ground up the motor on a brand-new Jag because it had never occurred to him to have the oil checked. In Beverly Hills, things like refrigerators and cars were regarded as natural objects, similar to air or water. The problem was a world like that could skew your vision if you happened to be dealing with the grittier aspects of life, like hunting a killer who was either terribly inept or terribly cold-blooded. And that's what kept nagging at the back of Zalman's mind. What was he missing?

He went into the kitchen, where Marie was positioning strips of anchovies across the top of a huge mound of Caesar salad.

"Hi, honey," she said, kissing him on the cheek. "You look beat. Dinner's about a half hour off, so why don't you take a nap? You'll feel better."

"Good idea," Zalman said. "I think I'll just stretch out on the couch for a few minutes. I'm starved, by the way."

He went into the living room, kicked off his shoes, and conked out for twenty minutes. When the telephone woke him up, he felt a lot better.

It was Espinoza. "Guess what?" he asked brightly.

"I hate guessing," Zalman snapped. "You shouldn't watch so many game shows, Primo. Just tell me, will you?"

"Carmichael says he has to let Ed Robin out on bail," Espinoza announced, "but Robin can't get the dough up."

"So?" Zalman stared balefully out the sliding glass door at Yip, who was sliding a Mothra-sized shrimp onto a skewer. Zalman's stomach growled ferociously. "I'm not putting up the dough, why tell me?" Yip poured some sauce over the shrimp, sending up a geyser of steam and fragrant odors which wafted into the house through the open windows.

"So Robin would like you to call him," Espinoza concluded.

"I'm not putting up the bail," Zalman repeated. "Believe it."

"I believe it," Espinoza said. "Just talk to Robin, will you? I told the cop on the desk it's okay. Just phone him? Guy's practically in tears."

"Why me?" Zalman asked as he slammed the phone down. "Why me? What did I do to deserve this?"

"Deserve what, honey?" Marie asked, coming into the dining room and putting a large platter of crusty rolls on the table. "This dinner is going to be good, I promise."

Zalman sat and glowered at his sock feet. "I'm *not* putting up the dough," he told her. "I ain't doing it."

"What dough? What ain't you doing?" she asked, slathering a tad of roll with a great glob of butter, then nibbling it delicately.

"Carmichael's letting Ed Robin out on bail, but Robin can't go the dough, and I ain't doing it for him," he said flatly, "and that's the truth. Give me a piece of roll, will you, doll? I'm starved."

Marie ignored him. "That worm Carmichael's gonna let Ed out but he can't get the money? Oh Jerry, we have to help him, poor thing! We absolutely have to! Tracee! Traceeeee!" she called, running back into the kitchen without giving Zalman his bite of roll.

Zalman heard her chattering away and then heard Tracee's excited voice chattering back. Tracee came running into the room.

"Jerry? Honey, do jails take American Express?"

Zalman regarded his ex-wife with a stupefied expression. "If jails took American Express, they'd never keep anybody inside!" he said with fervor. "Now look, Tracee—"

Yip came in through the sliding glass door, a large shrimp speared on a barbecue fork. "What's going on?" he asked mildly, licking sauce off his fingers. "Darn, that's good," he said. "My own blend," he told Zalman.

Tracee explained the situation. "We have to help the poor thing!" she said. "Imagine being in jail but not being able to pay the fine to get out! It's so . . . tacky!"

"It's not a fine, Tracee," Zalman explained. "It's bail! There's a big difference! If that schmuck skips, takes it on the lam, beats it the hell out of here, as they say, whoever puts up the dough is stuck for it! Get it? And I say the little weasel isn't trustworthy, even if he is a lawyer!"

Marie, Tracee, and Yip stared momentarily at Zalman, then continued to talk as if he hadn't said a thing. At that moment, McCoy, Chester, and Rutherford came bounding in through the front door, both dogs with Day-Glo Frisbees in their slobbery mouths. "What's going on?" McCoy asked innocently, helping himself to a couple of rolls off the table and flipping them to the dogs.

"We have to get poor Ed out of jail," Tracee said. "Jerry's going to give us the money. How much is it, anyway?"

"Pass me the rolls, for the love of God," Zalman moaned. "I don't know how much money it is. Espinoza didn't say, but it's got to be a hundred grand minimum on a murder suspect."

"A hundred thousand dollars!" Tracee squealed. "That's too much! I'm going to call Art and talk to him about that right now! Honestly, that's too much money!"

Zalman didn't even begin to try to explain how bail worked. "Aren't those shrimps getting burned?" he asked worriedly. His stomach was rumbling, and it seemed like a century or two since he'd eaten. "They look perfect to me, Yip, and I'm starved. Marie, honey, make me a plate, will you?" he wheedled.

Marie nodded absently and turned to Yip. "You ought to get a bail bondsman," she said.

"Okay. What do you do?" he asked. "Look one up in the Yellow Pages?"

"Hey, Zally," McCoy interrupted. "We know a guy here, don't we? Know who I'm talking about? Guy we used to know on campus? Moved up here right after the Isla Vista riots and went into the bail biz, didn't he? What's that guy's . . . ?"

"Jimmy Federal Never Sleeps," Zalman sighed as he stared longingly at the sizzling shrimps on the barbecue outside.

"That's the guy!" McCoy said. "Split L.A. right after the kids torched off the Bank of America here. When was that, Zally?" he asked sentimentally, his old radical's blood stirring. "Sixty-nine, wasn't it?"

"Nineteen-seventy," Zalman said, kissing his shrimp goodbye. "It was nineteen-seventy. Dean, why don't you see if he's listed?"

"So how come his name's 'Jimmy Federal Never Sleeps'?" Marie laughed. "Tell me, I'm dying to know."

"Jimmy Federal was a big man on campus at UCLA, heavy into the Students for a Democratic Society, all that other fringe radical junk," Zalman explained. "But the problem with Jimmy was that he was flat paranoid, saw cops under the bed, poison gas in the air, thought there was going to be wholesale slaughter in the streets. So he decided to leave L.A. and go into a solid racket with a steady future. . . . He listed, Dean?"

"Yeah, I'll give him a jingle."

"So Jimmy Federal moves to Santa Barbara because he figures any town where they can burn down a bank is the kind of Brigadoon he's looking for, buys out this bail bondsman name of Lou D'Amato Never Sleeps, paints over Lou's name, and becomes Jimmy Federal Never Sleeps. Toss me a roll, will you, doll?"

"But if Jimmy Federal Never Sleeps was so paranoid, how come he became a bail bondsman? Hanging out with cops and robbers all the time?" Marie shook her head. "That's the last profession I would choose if I were a paranoid."

"Nuts have their own logic," Zalman said. "Jimmy figured that since the cops were going to put the entire world in jail, he might as well get rich by getting everybody out. He thought it was a growth industry."

"Hey, Jimmy!" McCoy's voice intoned happily in the background. "Long time, buddy! It's me, Doyle Dean McCoy! Yeah! Here in Santa B.! Yeah, and guess who's here with me!" he said expectantly. His face dropped. "Yeah, that's right. How'd you know, man?"

Zalman got up and took the phone from McCoy. "Jimmy, Jerry Zalman. I'm fine, you? Good. Listen, Jimmy, I need your professional expertise. . . . Not for me, you idiot! A client. Look, time to ante up, buddy. I'm here to collect on my marker. Yeah. The jail in an hour. See you there." He put down the phone. "Okay, I got it worked out. We're gonna go get Ed Robin out of the slammer, but I'm afraid there's one very big condition," he said gravely.

"You're going to put up the money!" Tracee chirruped.

"What's the condition?" Marie asked suspiciously.

Zalman smiled and rocked back and forth on his sock heels. "Somebody has to make me dinner," he said.

FORTY-FIVE MINUTES LATER EVERYBODY PILED INTO THE station wagon and rocketed down the hill toward the county jail. Zalman, who'd had a big plate of Caesar salad while Tracee and Marie were getting ready, was now gnawing on a shrimp kabob between bites of a French roll soaked in garlic butter.

"So how come Jimmy Federal, whom you haven't seen in fifteen years or more, how come Jimmy Federal Never Sleeps is willing to drop everything and meet you at the courthouse in an hour and generally be at your beck and call?" Marie said, handing Zalman a napkin.

"Owes me his life," Zalman said as he worked on the mammoth kabob. "Damn good, Yip. Oughta bottle this sauce, it beats the hell out of Paul Newman. Yeah, Jimmy Federal owes me his life," he said modestly.

"You're kidding!" Marie said.

"No, he isn't." McCoy laughed. He was sitting in the front seat wedged in between Yip and Tracee, who was driving as usual. Marie and Zalman had the back seat, and the dogs were in the cargo bay. "Back in the sixties, me and Jimmy sashayed into Jimmy's draft board one night," McCoy explained, "so's we could spread some ketchup around and destroy Jimmy's records, which we did, I'm proud to say. But as we're beating it out of there we find

214

out the cops are after Jimmy, so we head over to Zally's place, and he stashes Jimmy Federal in Tracee's hope chest."

"What?" Tracee squealed. "I remember that! You mean the police were after Jimmy? I never knew that!"

"It was a long time ago, Tracee, please," Zalman soothed. "All in the past . . ."

"I'm sorry I asked," Marie apologized.

"The police!" Tracee whined. "We could have been in real trouble, Jerry!"

"You never told me you knew someone called Jimmy Federal," Yip said moodily.

"I don't know him!" Tracee said. "Jerry knew him! There's a big difference!"

"I'm *really* sorry I asked," Marie muttered.

"And when the cops leave, Zally gives Jimmy the dough to blow town," McCoy said, oblivious to the discomfiture of the others. "We had a lot of fun in the old days, didn't we, Zally?"

"You should never have put him in my hope chest," Tracee wailed. "No wonder my towels were all muddy!"

"Look, goddammit!" Zalman exploded, "You want Ed Robin out of jail or what? Well, Jimmy Federal can get him out because he can front the bond because he owes me his life, right? You don't want to put up ten percent of a hundred grand, do you? I know *I* ain't willing to shell out for some lunatic lawyer who thinks he's young Wild West, so leave me alone about Jimmy Federal, for God's sake!" Zalman chewed defiantly on his sesame roll.

"The police!" Tracee humpfed as she pulled up in front of the jail. "I'll never forgive you, Jerry Zalman! There he is. . . ."

A tall, skinny, balding man with a long fringe of hair drifting down the back of his neck and a graying goatee trailing from his chin was leaning up against the fender of a brand-new four-wheel-drive Subaru, staring thoughtfully into the darkening night sky. He was wearing a blue polyzircon suit with skinny lapels and a string necktie with a big silver slide.

Zalman wiped off with his napkin, then jumped out of the car. "I'll handle this," he ordered. He slammed the car door behind him, the sharp crunch echoing in the soft night, and went over to Jimmy Federal Never Sleeps. "Long time, Jimmy. Hey, you look good." They shook hands.

Jimmy Federal smiled sweetly at Zalman. "Jerry, man, I'd know you anywhere. You look just the same," he said ruefully in a squeaky voice. "Still got your hair." He ran skinny fingers over his balding pate sadly. "I tried everything. Gonna go for the implants, I think." He looked over at the station wagon and waved at McCoy. "Yo, Dean," he called. "Hey, there's Tracee! Great gal! Nice that you two've stuck together all these years."

"We're divorced," Zalman snapped, trying to hide the note of relief he felt.

"Hey, good move," Jimmy Federal said without missing a beat.

Zalman explained the Ed Robin situation to Jimmy Federal, who sighed as Zalman spun the young lawyer's tale of woe. "I owe you, Jerry," he said when Zalman had finished, "and I'll get the guy out for you, no problem. But if he skips, it's half and half, yeah? I won't carry the whole freight if he books it, so you'll have to be ready for that eventuality."

"Jeez, the things I get myself into!" Zalman moaned. "I should be arrested! Yeah, yeah. Let's hope he stays put, okay?"

"That's what I always hope," Jimmy Federal said, clasping his hands. "Look, I'll take care of everything. Bring the guy over when he's sprung. It'll be a few hours, believe it. These mental midgets they got working the jail, they got their own way of doing stuff."

Zalman wrote down Yip's address and gave it to him. "Nice neighborhood. Real stable property values," Jimmy

Federal observed. "Say, Jer," he added with an angelic smile, "seeing as how you're tied up with the Knottes and all, you think maybe you can wangle me an invite for the big bash up at World O' Yip? My wife would die to go, but hey, we don't swim in the same pond, know what I mean? But like it'd impress the hell out of her, put me in good for a year, at least," he said hopefully.

"Consider it done," Zalman said. "Talk to me later."

JIMMY FEDERAL NEVER SLEEPS SHOWED UP AROUND TWO-
thirty that morning, a bedraggled Ed Robin by his side.
The house was quiet. Yip and Tracee had gone to bed long
before, McCoy had returned to the warmth of Molly
McCafferty's generous arms, and Marie, though she'd tried
valiantly to remain awake, had fallen asleep in front of a
rerun of "Cannon," the remote control locked tightly in her
fingers.

Zalman was barely managing to stay semi-awake by
concentrating blearily on the video exploits of the rotund
detective, who, in this episode, was investigating peculiar
goings-on at a cattle ranch. As usual, nothing could stand
up to the remorseless force of Cannon's personality, or his
gargantuan bulk. When Zalman heard the buzzer sound
from the gate down the hill he stumbled out into the hallway and punched the speakerphone. "It's Jimmy," a tired,
squeaky voice called. Zalman let him in, and a few minutes later, when Jimmy's Subaru appeared in front of the
house, Zalman was waiting on the front steps, his red silk
bathrobe over his pj's.

Ed Robin looked like a sad, wet weasel. His spiky hair-
cut had long ago lost its gel, and his sharply tailored suit
looked like it had been rolled up in a ball at the bottom of a
police locker for several days. His eyes darted around the

driveway, glittering with fear. "You gotta help me, Jerry," he whined as he climbed wearily out of the car.

"Call me Mr. Zalman," Zalman said. "You're working for me now, kiddo. Show a little respect." Just to soften the mood he offered Ed Robin a cigar. "Have one of these—calm your nerves," he said as he flipped open his leather case.

Robin took one with damp, shaky fingers, holding it close to the proffered flame from Zalman's gold lighter. "Thanks, Mr. Zalman. I like cigars, I think," he said uncertainly.

"Yeah? Maybe someday you'll be able to afford them, kid," Zalman said, staring around the shadowy driveway, lit with film noir contrast by a large, glowing moon. "Jimmy, I'd like to ask you in, but it's a little late. Talk to me tomorrow, pal."

"You haven't forgotten about the party?" Jimmy Federal said anxiously, lounging against a fender with his customary languor. "I called my old lady while I was hanging around waiting for Ed here, and she's all jazzed."

"No problem," Zalman said as he turned to go inside. "Ed, you're bedding down on Mrs. Knotte's sofa. I'll lend you a pair of pajamas."

"I gotta have a change of clothes tomorrow," the young man groaned. "I feel awfully—"

There was a sharp crack, the tinkle of breaking glass, and then the dim porch light went out, leaving only moonlight and the glare of Jimmy Federal's headlamps angling off into the trees. Zalman whipped around and instinctively ducked as he felt the second shot whistle through the air beside his head with the shrill squeal of a New Yorker hailing a cab. He saw Ed Robin's contorted face staring at him in the pale moonlight and saw the young man shudder as the third shot struck his shoulder.

"Damn," Robin said with the uncomprehending mildness of impending shock. "What's this?" He sat heavily on the ground, blood pumping down the arm of his rumpled

219

Italian suit. He struggled to get up, couldn't make it, and fell back again.

"What the hell!" Jimmy Federal yelped as he dove for the shrubbery with the slippery ease of a man who'd been practicing for this moment all of his life. He reached under his polyzircon jacket with his right hand and pulled out a .38 police special, then reached into his jacket pocket with his left hand and came up with a tidy little .25 caliber automatic. Crouching low to the ground, he blasted the .38 down the driveway and screamed like a bloodthirsty Viking. "You'll die for this," he howled. "I'm Jimmy Federal, and I never sleep!" He blasted off another round at the trees, waking a flock of nesting crows who cawed furiously.

"For Christ's sake!" Zalman yelled. "Ed, are you all right?" Jimmy Federal fired again. "Will you lay off?" Zalman snarled, snaking along the ground toward Ed Robin, who was feebly trying to press his handkerchief to his bleeding shoulder.

"I got shot!" the young lawyer moaned. "I can't believe it! I got shot! I'm gonna die!" he said in terror, struggling to get up off the ground.

"Stay where you are!" Zalman ordered as Jimmy Federal, still crouching low to the ground, ran across the driveway and along the side of the house, a weapon in each hand, looking like an improbably warlike Groucho Marx.

Inside the house, lights began to come on. "What's the matter?" Zalman heard Marie call. "Is everything all—"

"Stay inside, goddammit!" he hollered. "Call the goddamn cops! Call Primo, but stay inside!"

Jimmy Federal emptied the last of the bullets from his .38 into the trees. "You'll die for this!" he howled again. "Take a shot at Jimmy Federal, will you?"

"Oh, God," Ed Robin moaned, "I'm dying. Somebody help me! I'm dying, and I don't even own a house!"

"Shut up, you idiot! You're not dying!"

"How do you know?" Ed Robin whined. "I'm bleeding! I finally passed the bar exam, and I'm dying!"

"Are you all right?" Zalman heard Yip call. "What's going on out there? I'm calling the police!" he said stoutly. "The police are on their way. This is it! The police are definitely on their way!"

Jimmy Federal ran back along the edge of the driveway and crouched by his car. "I've got a slug with your name on it, sucker!" He yanked open the tailgate on the station wagon, rummaged around, pulled out a flare pistol, and fired off a cartridge in the direction of the shots. There was a solid *whump* as the flare sailed out into space, then a small explosion of white light in the distance, and immediately a large cypress began to burn furiously. *"Ah hah!"* Jimmy Federal howled manically. *"You can run, but you can't hide!"* He blasted off a second round from his flare gun, and a second tree went up like the Fourth of July.

"Jesus H. Christ on a crutch!" Zalman yelled. "Jimmy, lay off, for the love of God! Tracee, call the fire department! Call the police, for God's sake!" Summoning all his courage, Zalman leapt to his feet, ran across the driveway, and tackled Jimmy Federal around the knees just as he was slipping another flare into the big pistol. Jimmy Federal collapsed, and Zalman landed on top of him. Down the driveway, cypress trees burned merrily. Ed Robin continued to moan, and from inside the house Tracee's shrieks were more than audible.

*"My house! What are you doing to my Italian cypress trees, you monster!"* she cried as she came running out of the house in her nightie, blond hair floating in the air as though she were a demented sorceress. Her hands were outstretched like claws, and the light in her eyes glowed with radioactive hysteria. She was heading straight for them, and as he saw her coming Zalman realized there was only one possible course of action for a man in his position.

"You're on your own, buddy," he told Jimmy Federal as

221

Tracee bore down on them with the inevitability of a dreadnought. He rolled away from Jimmy and dove for a nearby flower bed, smashing dozens of primroses. Out of the corner of his eye he saw Marie, flanked by Rutherford, appear at the front door. Her eyes swept over the scene on the driveway, and she leapt for the garden hose without hesitation. Uncoiling the hose as she ran, Marie reached the end of the driveway and trained the water on the base of the burning cypresses, which were sparking, crackling, and spitting their sap into the warm night air.

Tracee had Jimmy Federal down on the ground and was pummeling him with her fists. *"I hate you!"* she bellowed. *"These are my trees!"* Jimmy Federal tried to protect himself. He'd assumed the nonviolent position and had his knees rolled up to his chest and his hands clasped over the back of his neck like the old war protestor he was.

Zalman heard a chorus of oncoming sirens in the distance, and in the sky there was the rumble of an approaching police helicopter, which suddenly burst into sight and trained its harsh white strobe light on the chaotic scene below. Zalman sat up cross-legged in the flower bed and searched for his cigars. There was only one left, a little mashed, but he managed to get it lit as he watched Tracee continue to pound Jimmy Federal.

Marie was doing a good job with the garden hose. She had the nozzle on high and was blasting away at the fire as Rutherford crabwalked and pranced around the driveway in a display of what looked like doggy breakdancing. The Doberman yapped and yowled in antic delight as the chopper continued to hover overhead. Zalman sighed and blew a perfect smoke ring into the now brightly lit night. As if to put a final touch on the wackiness of it all, Yip appeared on the steps of the house and looked around uncertainly. He carried a large silver tray set with half a dozen steaming mugs.

"Anyone for tea?" he called amiably, setting the tray down on the front steps. He stood sipping his own mug of tea and watched his wife pound the unfortunate Jimmy Federal, now begging miserably for mercy.

"Honey," Yip called gently. "Honey, don't hurt him, now. . . ."

The green *Exorcist* light shining in Tracee's eyes dimmed somewhat at the calming sound of her husband's voice, and her assault on Jimmy Federal subsided. She raised her head slightly, and Zalman thought for sure he saw a glimpse of fangs, maybe horns and a tail. She looked like something out of Stephen King's worst nightmares.

"Honey," Yip called again. "I've got a lovely cup of Yipnotic here for you. . . ."

Tracee wavered to her feet and looked over at her husband, standing placidly on the front steps, holding a mug of tea. The hook-and-ladder truck arrived at that moment with a burst of light, sound, and activity, followed by a couple of pumpers. Firemen leapt off the vehicles and began stringing hoses, to the further delight of Rutherford, who immediately teamed up with the crew's frisky Dalmatian. A burly fireman ran over to the trees and curtly pushed Marie and her garden hose away from the now-smoldering cypresses. The fireman began dousing the trees with a gargantuan stream of water, but there was really little left to be done.

Marie tossed the spurting hose on the driveway and dusted off her hands with evident satisfaction. "I'd say that was almost out, wouldn't you?" she asked the gray-haired fire chief, who was rumpling Rutherford's ears.

The chief nodded approvingly. "Damn good job, lady. Most dames—excuse me, most ladies—try to put out a fire at the top, but you went right for the base. Very good technique."

"I always loved Fire Awareness Week at school," Marie said proudly. "One time I found fifty-eight violations of the fire code in my own house! Boy, was my dad furious."

The chief laughed. "Hope they gave you one of them little silver badges," he said.

"I've still got it, too," Marie informed him with obvious pride of ownership.

At this moment an ambulance squealed into the driveway and two paramedics jumped out and ran over to Jimmy Federal, still lying huddled up in a ball on the ground. Tracee gave him a last kick, then walked slowly back to Yip for a mug of tea.

"Hey, you guys! What about me?" Ed Robin moaned pitifully. "I'm dying here! I'm bleeding!"

The paramedics looked at him scornfully and shrugged at each other. "Bitch, bitch, bitch," one of them complained as they went over to his side.

From his comfortable seat on the sidelines Zalman watched the show proceed. Then he got up, vainly tried to clean off his red silk bathrobe, now covered with dirt from the primrose patch, and walked over to Marie, who was still chatting with the grizzled fire chief. Zalman kissed her on the cheek and pulled her close. "Don't say we don't go to swell parties," he said.

"HONESTLY!" MARIE TOLD ESPINOZA WITH EXASPERA-
tion. "It's obvious who the sniper was after! What's the
matter with you guys? I mean, why would anybody in
their right mind want to kill poor Ed? He doesn't know
anything, he isn't doing anything! Who cares about
him?"

"Hey," Robin whined. "That's not nice." He was
slumped in one of Tracee's armchairs, and the two paramedics, Rick and Lance, were hovering nearby. They'd
done a lovely job of binding up his raveled sleeve. He'd
been very lucky; the sniper's bullet had merely cut his
upper arm, not even penetrating the muscle, and conse-
quently a compress and bandage were going to suffice.
Rick and Lance, who hadn't seemed eager to leave the
cozy warmth of the Knotte hearth, were now perched on
the edge of the couch, sipping mugs of tea and contentedly
munching Tracee's carrot cake.

"Love the Warhols," Rick said dreamily.

"And this entire room, it's just fab," Lance added.

"Oh, thanks," Tracee responded warmly. She'd recov-
ered from her fit and had agreed to let Jimmy Federal
into the house after Zalman had persuaded her that despite his torchwork on the trees, Jimmy was only trying
to help.

Espinoza opened his mouth to speak, but Marie bulldozed right over him. "That's not what I meant, Ed, you poor thing. Look," she said, turning back to Espinoza, "Ed was smoking a cigar, right? Well, the sniper thought he was Jerry, for Pete's sake! It's all obvious, Primo! Ed's the stooge! It's Ed who's up for Lisa's murder, right? Well, it's Jerry who's going to figure everything out, right? So it's Jerry the bad guy wants to bump off, right?" She wiggled in her chair in frustration.

"I am not a stooge," Robin protested thinly.

"Same diff," Zalman muttered, hoping to detour Marie from this uncomfortable line of dubious reasoning. "Look, sweetie, no matter who was trying to get who, there's nothing more we can do now. Whoever was out there—"

"I gotta a lot of enemies," Jimmy Federal said darkly. "There's a lotta guys out there who don't like me. Things like this have been tried before, you know." He was sprawled in an overstuffed armchair. Both his eyes were blackened, and one of the pockets on his polyzircon suit coat had been ripped away. Tracee had really tooled up on him.

"Right, right," Zalman backpedaled, hoping to soothe Jimmy Federal's paranoid ego. "But Primo's men have been all over the grounds, and there's no trace of anybody, just a few shell casings," he said. "Funny thing about this guy. He's very erratic. A real hit-or-miss kind of killer. He gets Lisa—"

"Lisa!" Ed Robin wailed. "I'll never forget you, baby. . . ."

Zalman ignored him. "He misses E.Y., he gets Mercer, he misses me—"

"Got *me* pretty good!" Robin said indignantly.

Zalman still ignored him. "Erratic, like I say. Misses his target, but he's cool enough to get away, even with Mr. Pyromaniac Federal over here doing his work."

226

"I know what I know," Jimmy Federal glowered through his puffy eyes. "Many men would like to see me dead. That's all I can say."

"I *hope* so!" Zalman said. "Well, cats and kitties, tune in tomorrow at World O' Yip. I'm willing to lay great odds that we're all gonna see plenty of action."

AT SIX THE FOLLOWING EVENING, ZALMAN AND RUTHER-
ford were sitting in Tracee's big living room watching *This
Gun for Hire* on TV. Alan Ladd was just telling Laird Cre-
gar that he was his own police, and Zalman, puffing his
cigar, mouthed the dialogue along with the abbreviated
actor. Alan Ladd was Zalman's fave rave.

Zalman was wearing a new dinner jacket which Yip's
tailor had hurriedly altered for the big boom bash, the
grand opening of World O' Yip, and Rutherford, who was
gnawing on a table leg, was wearing a pink scarf chosen to
accent his shiny black-and-brown coat. Down the hall,
Marie was putting the final touches on her own outfit, a
svelte, slinky black-and-gold sequin-and-beads number
that made the most of her luscious little figure. Yip had
been at World O' Yip overseeing the final details ever since
rosy-fingered dawn had stretched her lanky digits across
the horizon, and Tracee, who'd changed her clothes four
times by actual count, was showing Marie outfit number
five.

Down the hall Zalman could hear his ex-wife moaning,
"My hair is horrible! I look like a bimbo with this hair!
How could this *happen* to me?" Zalman, happily en-
sconced in *This Gun for Hire,* tried to ignore her. He fig-

ured that sooner or later Marie would straighten her out, and in the meantime he was having plenty of fun.

Cocktails were scheduled for seven, along with the world premiere of Yip's video, featuring, Yip promised enthusiastically, "an inside look at Santa Barbara, my hometown." At nine there was to be a gala dinner capped by the introduction of the new food fad and culinary creation, "Yip Cream, Dessert for the Discriminating."

Yip was in a complete dither and had been since morning, when he'd read, with horror, an article in the paper's food section proclaiming tofu as the least-liked food in America.

"What am I gonna do, Jerry?" he'd moaned. "Tofu is my life!"

Zalman had calmed him down, then given him sage advice. "Don't tell 'em it's tofu, tell 'em it's something else! Tell 'em it's chocolate pudding! Trust me, if you pump the press full of enough French champagne, they won't know what the hell they're eating, and what's more, they won't give a damn."

"But . . . but . . . that's . . . isn't that . . . *cheating?*" Yip breathed in anguish.

Zalman shrugged easily. "Aren't you the guy who said it's a rough, tough world? Tell 'em it's chocolate pudding," he urged again. "They'll lap it up."

Yip went off to World O' Yip muttering something unintelligible about the dubious ethics of merchandising.

Now Marie led Tracee out into the living room. Her fifth outfit was a clinging fire-engine-red dress which was slit all the way up her thigh and made her look like a lecherous sailor's dream. "What do you think?" she asked anxiously. "Is it me?"

Zalman smiled as Marie, standing slightly behind Tracee, made encouraging motions with her hands and nodded ferociously up and down. "You bet it is!" he said heartily. "You'll knock 'em dead, doll."

"Oh good," Tracee said, distracted. "I just have to get

. . . where is that . . ." She ran out of the room, teetering absurdly on four-inch heels.

"Thank God," Marie moaned as she sank down on the couch next to Zalman and fluffed up Rutherford's pink scarf. "I was afraid she was going to change again. Jerry, tell me the truth. Are we *ever* going to get out of here, or is this it for life? Weren't you the guy who promised to take me to Hawaii to get away from it all? Way back in the dim, dark days of prehistory, didn't you say we'd be off to Hawaii for a few fun-filled days in the sun? Wasn't that you, Jerry?"

"The same and none other, darling," Zalman said as he pulled her close and gave her a pretend knuckle-burn on the top of her head. "I swear it. We'll go hear Don Ho, we'll eat surf an' turf, I'll get you a lei. . . ."

"Keep it clean, buster . . ."

"We'll drink Zombie's Curse. . . ."

"Maiden's Ruin, I thought."

"Just help me out here, doll. Let's get through World O' Yip and see what happens."

"You think something's going to happen tonight, don't you?" Marie asked seriously.

"It better happen. I can't take much more of this," Zalman said. "I have my limits. Either the killer goes for E.Y. tonight or I hit the pike back to L.A. As far as the killer's concerned, he'd better strike tonight if he wants to lock horns with Jerry Zalman, Esquire!"

Half an hour later, Zalman, Marie, Tracee, and Rutherford drove up to World O' Yip in silence. Yip had been there since early afternoon checking out last-minute details, and Tracee was wringing her hands nervously.

"Everything's going to be all right, isn't it, Jerry?" Tracee asked hopefully.

"You bet, Trace. No question about it," Zalman said, hoping he didn't sound as insincere as he felt. Even though he'd made light of the situation with Marie, Zalman *knew* the killer would take another crack at E. Y. Knotte sometime during the evening. Hell, it was too good to miss. It *had* to be tonight—a big crowd, gaiety, distractions, party hats, plus the international debut of the dessert of the discriminating. Besides, the best place for a murder was in the midst of a laughing crowd, Zalman mused.

He wondered briefly where Yip had scrounged up the money for the opening. Not E.Y., that much he knew. And why was Yip so secretive about it? Zalman had asked him casually, but Yip had only laid his forefinger alongside his nose like Rumpelstiltskin and winked broadly. "It's a secret, Jerry. But I'll tell you later," he'd said.

Tracee? She'd been endlessly preoccupied, shrieking orders while her own huge statue was jockeyed into position, making arrangements for the buffet, the press releases, the flowers. "I've *got* to learn to delegate authority," Zalman overheard her telling Marie. "These details are driving me mad!"

"Wow," Marie said as they pulled up in front of World O' Yip. Tracee's nude statue, a true Botticelli clone, was illuminated in a pale, shifting curtain of pink and gold lights in the setting sun. A platoon of parking attendants, all dressed in vaguely Turkish tight white pants and flowing white shirts, leapt forward and wrenched the station wagon away from Tracee.

"Isn't it *dar*ling?" Tracee cooed over her statue. "Isn't it just the sweetest thing? My Yippie thought of it all by himself. I tell you, Marie, sensitivity is a wonderful quality in a man." She glanced sidelong at Zalman, then looked away.

Zalman glowered at her and stared up at the great winglike building in front of him. Flowers bloomed everywhere, Insta-Turf had been laid, trees planted. The local TV news camera crew was already setting up for the tagline human-interest story for film at eleven, and it was obvious that World O' Yip was definitely happening. Zalman helped the ladies up the broad steps and into the lobby.

The joint was jumping. It was still early, and only about fifty guests had arrived, but they'd already planted both feet in the trough in front of the buffet table and were chowing down before all the crab disappeared. The long lobby had been transformed into a veritable palace of hors d'oeuvres, each table featuring a different melange of cuisines. In deference to Santa Barbara's Old Spanish heritage, there was a table featuring an apparently endless selection of tapas, as well as the traditional salsas, tortillas, chimichangas, and menudo of Mexico, not to mention the cunning little mounds of refritos sculpted to look like sombreros.

Another table featured strictly health foods, yummy delicacies concocted out of soy milk, textured vegetable protein, and other vegetarian delights. Needless to say, there wasn't a soul at this table. In fact, most of the folks were lined up in front of the shrimp, crab, and lobster layout— living testimony to the culinary shrewdness of E. Y. Knotte.

Zalman looked around, trying to get his bearings and size up the crowd, which was predominantly A-league, he decided. Tracee took off in search of Yip, scurrying across the floor in her spike heels, her red dress shining like a spotlight in the ever-growing crowd.

"I'm hungry all of a sudden," Marie said happily, eyeing the lobster. "Gee, that looks good."

"Ummmm," Zalman said, still scanning the room. At the far end of the lobby he saw McCoy leaning up against a wall, an unlit Lucky dangling out of the corner of his mouth, looking bemused. McCoy was wearing a relatively clean pair of jeans, boots, and in honor of the formal nature of the occasion he'd donned an orange and black brocade smoking jacket with satin cuffs over a green Surf City T-shirt. He looked like an all-day popsicle. Zalman winced.

"I gotta talk to McCoy a minute," Zalman told Marie.

"Go lobster out, then join me, okay?" he said, pointing in McCoy's direction.

"Okey-dokey," Marie said, and she took off for lobster mountain. Zalman threaded his way through the crowd to McCoy.

"Dean," he said, distracted, "what's the word?"

McCoy fired a kitchen match with his thumbnail and exhaled a thick cloud of smoke. An organic-looking couple next to him gasped and moved away quickly. "Cigarette's getting to be better than a .357 for clearing out a room," he observed with a malicious grin. "I looked around, Zally," he said, turning serious. "Gave it the old once-over, and far as I can see, the joint's clean as a hound's back tooth."

Zalman opened his mouth to speak, but McCoy waved him down. "Hey, Zally," he said. "You gotta understand, these days you can't see much. Hell, a guy can make a little itty bitty bomb's gonna be so small you gotta have a microscope to see it. What I mean is, there's no big obvious sticks of dynamite or Boris-and-Natasha black anarchist bombs. No grenades in the ladies' lounge. Best I can say." He shrugged.

"Who's here?" Zalman asked. "More to the point, who's not here?"

"Looks like a cast of thousands," McCoy said. "Yip, of course. He's been going buggy for hours. You brought Tracee. Damn, she looks good in that dress!"

"McCoy . . ." Zalman warned as Marie joined them, a large plate loaded with seafood in her hand.

"Hi, Dean," she said as McCoy bent down to give her a kiss. "Hey, nice jacket! Nice lapel pin, too . . . celluloid, isn't it?" McCoy was wearing a large yellow saxophone with rhinestone accents on his chest.

"Yeah, Molly gave it to me. Told her I dug saxophone music, and she went out and got me this. Some great gal, huh?" McCoy said with a cloud-nine look in his eyes.

"Let's just attend to the business at hand, boys and

girls," Zalman suggested. "And yes, Molly is a lovely lady, and where is she?"

"Be here pretty soon," McCoy said, looking at his five-dollar black plastic watch. "Just getting off shift at the Blue Fin. Anyway, E.Y. and Rhonda ain't showed yet, that's one thing. I figure old Rhonda's waiting for the big moment to make her entrance. Make sure everybody's looking at her instead of the tofu."

"Oh, my God," Zalman groaned. "We gonna have to *eat* that stuff? I got my limits. . . ."

"Be polite, honey," Marie urged.

"Polite? There's polite and there's eating recycled pond scum," Zalman snapped. "I draw the line at pond scum." Suddenly the room lights dimmed slightly, and two huge projection TVs, one at either end of the room, lit up. A wide pan of the Santa Barbara coastline filled the screen, accompanied by the Beach Boys singing "Surfer Girl."

"What's this?" McCoy asked. "We got popcorn?"

"Looks like Le Film Yip." Zalman laughed. "Santa Barbara Babylon, here we come." He shrugged and tried to ignore the video, but it wasn't easy. The big images shifted back and forth between color, black-and-white, sepia, and an ugly, blotchy mishmash of tones that bore no relation to any reality except some inner recesses of Yip's tofu-crazed brain. The constantly swirling images had been spliced together at random, and the entire effect was that of a schizophrenic's nightmare. The huge Santa Barbara Courthouse, colored a nasty shade of post-atomic orange, faded into a purple surf and faded again into a full-screen close-up of Brunson the butler, grinning like a death's head. Images continued to come and go as the tape of the Beach Boys slowed down so that "Surfer Girl" began to sound more like "In-A-Gadda-Da-Vida."

"Boy, this is some fun, isn't it, guys?" Zalman muttered, trying to ignore the ever-changing screen. He nabbed Marie's fork and began to edge some lobster off her plate.

"You think there's enough here for both of us?" he asked. "This plate's big enough to feed the entire Italian army."

"This thing is making me queasy," Marie said, her eyes fixed on the TV screen. "Oh, no, I forgot Rutherford," she said. "He's still in the car! He was all dressed, and I forgot him! Here," she said, thrusting her overflowing plate into Zalman's hands. "I'll be back in a flash." She turned and scampered off into the ever-growing crowd filling World O' Yip.

Zalman and McCoy watched her go and looked at each other in amazement. "Tell me, Dean," Zalman said slowly as he munched meditatively on a lobster claw. "You're a bon vivant, sophisticated-man-of-the-world type guy. Do you understand women at all?"

McCoy shook his big head. "Nah, no way. Gave up trying 'long about high school."

"Sometimes I think that men and women exist in a parallel universe. Know what I mean?"

"Sure. I watch 'Dr. Who'! You think I'm a video illiterate? But me, I just keep hoping for détente in the sexual wars. Kinda your peaceful coexistence type of relationship."

"Wise idea." Zalman said. "Let's circulate, okay?" His eyes fastened on the projection TV as he saw himself down on his knees groveling for coffee that first morning at Tracee's.

"Nice performance." McCoy laughed. "I see you as having a touching gravity, yet you've married it with the fine, airy hand of a Lubitsch comedy. Yip made that all by himself, didn't he?"

"Give it a rest, McCoy. Yip's not a bad guy. God, I bet he's got that thing on a loop," Zalman muttered. "We're gonna be looking at that sludge for the rest of our natural lives, Dean old buddy." True to his prediction, the screen continued to slip and slide dizzily with an endlessly repeating series of images. Zalman shuddered. "This is awful."

Marie and Rutherford reappeared. Rutherford was still

wearing his pink scarf, though he'd managed to gnaw some of it loose and the edges were already beginning to look torn and tattered. Espinoza showed up, very well dressed in a conservatively cut dinner jacket. Art Carmichael, looking a little the worse for scotch, came solo. Ed Robin put his head in the door, but when he saw Carmichael and Espinoza he ducked into the whirlpool. Molly McCafferty came in and instantly glommed onto McCoy. Molly, who was wearing a flowing Mexican dress, was carrying a small white mouse in a cage.

"Isn't he just darling?" she gushed. "This little old lady came into the Blue Fin about an hour ago, and after she knocked back three straight bourbons she gave him to me. I'm going to call him Teddy. Oh, there's Carole, poor thing. Hold Teddy for a minute, will you, Dean? There's a darling. I have to talk to her for just a sec. . . ." Molly shoved Teddy's cage into McCoy's hands and snaked into the milling crowd, her white petticoats surging like froth.

McCoy lifted up the mouse and stared straight into his little pink eyes. The mouse stood up and wiggled its tiny white muzzle, and Zalman began to laugh.

"Don't say it, Zally," McCoy warned. "I know just what you're thinking."

"*Ooohhhhh*, isn't he cute?" Marie said as she bent down and tapped on the cage. "Hi Teddieweddie!"

"Teddieweddie?" Zalman mouthed in horror. "First it's ootsie-wootsie for Rutherford . . . and now it's Teddieweddie?"

"Keep trying for peaceful coexistence," McCoy advised.

"Easy for you to say," Zalman pointed out as he watched Molly on the other side of the room. There were now at least two hundred people packed into World O' Yip, and the noise was right next door to deafening. People were lined up at tables which were constantly being resupplied by more minions in white Turkish costumes, rushing back and forth in the throng. The bar was filled with folks lapping up screwdrivers, and Zalman could see that the crowd was spilling over into the other rooms. The big dining room held a flock of little tables, each with its own flower arrangement and tiny mock-up of Tracee's big bronze statue, and the crowd was gnawing feverishly on overflowing plates of chow.

A jazz quartet had taken up a position near the end of the bar, and the pianist began to tinkle "Route 66." Molly McCafferty had found Carole, a.k.a. Miss Kelp of the Coast, and the two women were deep in conversation, oblivious to the deafening throng. Carole was wearing a green one-piece bathing suit with seaweed festooned around it like a slimy green stole. She had a crown on, a three-pronged job with a clamshell on each point, and she was holding a scepter with a big starfish on the end of it. Marie, Rutherford by her side, ran over to them, and as Zalman watched from across the room the three women began to jabber frantically, all at the same time.

"Do they know what they're talking about, we wonder . . . ?" Zalman asked McCoy rhetorically, but McCoy wasn't paying attention. He was sipping a screwdriver and looking at Teddy, who was standing up on his hind legs and sniffing delicately at his Plexi-prison.

"Shouldn't keep these things as pets," McCoy said dolefully. "They're too damn little. How'd you like to spend your whole life in a Plexiglas box, for Pete's sake?"

"Hey, I'm a lawyer. My whole life is encased in Plexiglas," Zalman mumbled. "Ahhhh! The senior Knottes are making their entrance, I do believe. . . ."

Across the room, Yip signaled the jazz quartet to belt up and dimmed the lights. People from other rooms flooded in, people who'd been out on the balcony admiring the ocean's roar came in to see what was going on, and Rhonda Knotte made sure to give 'em a good show. She paused at the top of the stairs and struck a Betty Grable pose, one hand on the railing, one hand flung high. She was wearing an off-the-shoulder gold lamé Grecian goddess dress that looked like it had been laid on with a trowel, and rubies winked from her fingers and smirked from her ears. A diamond-and-ruby necklace that would have turned the Duchess of Windsor ten shades of purple adorned her bosom.

"Hello, everybody!" Rhonda called, flashing her great big movie-star smile at the assembled New Masses.

Her husband, in a black Western-cut dinner jacket and silver boots, stood proudly by her side. He had on a turquoise belt with a chunk of rock on it the size of a meteor and matching turquoise cuff links. He was holding a black Stetson in his hand and waved it graciously over the assembled crowd milling below him like peons. Zalman thought that if James Dean's Jet Rink had lived to attain geezerhood, he'd look just like E. Y. Knotte.

Rhonda accepted the crowd's ovation as her due, undulated her way down the stairs, and immediately began air-kissing everyone in sight. "Darling, you look kinetic!" Zalman heard her squeal to Tracee. Zalman set Marie's huge plate of lobster down on a long, low planter and turned to McCoy, still staring morosely at Teddy the Mouse.

"Look, Dean," Zalman snapped. "You're not Marlin damn Perkins, okay? Give *me* the mouse. You stick close to E.Y. You're the muscle in this operation, I'm the brains. You protect E.Y., I'll cogitate. Get it?"

McCoy reluctantly surrendered Teddy the Mouse to Zalman. "Take care of this little guy, Zally. When Molly comes back I want to talk to her about him. This mouse must go free!" McCoy sneered evilly and stalked away, assuming a nonchalant position behind E.Y. and Rhonda, mitigated by the fact that he made a V-sign with his fingers behind Rhonda's head.

Zalman sighed heavily and stared at Teddy. "How did this happen?" he asked the rodent. "A scant few days ago —and I must admit it seems like a decade—I was meeting and greeting in Beverly Hills. I was one of the elite, nature's nobleman. Now all of the sudden I'm trapped in the middle of a bunch of health food lunatics, holding a mouse." Teddy wiggled his whiskers and foraged in his bedding.

"Hey, Jerry, thanks a million for the invite!" a voice breathed in Zalman's ear. It was Jimmy Federal Never Sleeps. "Whatcha got there? Oh, a mouse, huh? Cute little guy."

Zalman turned to Jimmy Federal and stared at him balefully. "Right, Jimmy. A mouse. Walks like a mouse, squeaks like a mouse . . ."

"This is my wife, Moonbeam," Jimmy Federal said proudly, pointing to a tiny blonde with the smooth, unlined face of an acid casualty. Moonbeam smiled happily.

"Thanks for letting us in, Mr. Zalman. Wow, this is better than a Dead concert, for true. Jimmy told me all about you."

"Call me Jerry. Nice to meet you, dear," he said, switching Teddy the Mouse to his left hand. He shook hands gently with Moonbeam, whose vapid eyes fastened on the cage.

"Unreal," she said insipidly. "Cute mousie . . . say, can I hold him?"

"Sure," Zalman said gratefully, handing over the Plexiglas square. Teddy stood up on his hind legs and clawed feverishly at his prison.

"Poor little thing," Moonbeam Federal mused thoughtfully. "They shouldn't be kept as pets, you know," she told Zalman with a touch of severity. "It isn't nice."

"Yeah, I know, I know. I'm with you a thousand percent. It's not my mouse, see," Zalman said, looking around for Marie. "Just holding him for a friend." He saw Marie by one of the long tables, holding out a massive shrimp for Rutherford, who bolted it whole.

Moonbeam Federal peered thoughtfully at Teddy. Then, before Zalman could stop her, she flicked open the cage and let Teddy out into the planter. "Seek your freedom, little friend!" she said fervently. "Animals have rights!"

*"My mouse!"* Molly yelped from behind her. "That's *my mouse!"* She gave Moonbeam Federal a terrific clonk on the head, knelt down, and began to rummage around in the planter. Tiny Moonbeam staggered but managed to keep her feet.

"Mouse!" an elderly blue-haired woman behind Zalman shrieked. "They get in your hair!"

"That's bats," Zalman said helpfully, hoping he could calm her down. Inexplicably, the woman jumped up on a chair and began to squeal helplessly. "It's bats in your hair, not mice!" he explained again, although the woman wasn't listening.

McCoy came running over to Moonbeam Federal. "Gee," he said, pumping her hand, "I wish *I'd* done that. I wanted to, but I didn't have the guts."

"Animals have rights," Moonbeam said again, shaking the acid flashback out of her head. "We must protect our warm-blooded friends as we would our own young."

"Damn straight!" McCoy agreed staunchly.

"But that's *my mouse!"* Molly cried. "That's not fair, you guys! That's *my mouse!"* she moaned and sat down heavily on the planter, right in Marie's gigantic plate of lobster. "AAARRRRGH!" she said, jumping to her feet. "I sat in something!" She began to wipe furiously at her lobster-covered rear end with a skimpy cocktail napkin.

The blue-haired woman on the chair held her skirts up around her knees and shrieked even louder. *"Bats! Mice!"*

Marie and Rutherford came running over, and Rutherford began to lick feverishly at the lobster on Molly's rear end. "Jerry, what happened? What a mess! Who let the mouse out?"

*"What mouse?!"* Tracee cried, distraught. "We don't have *mice* here! World O' Yip is brand-new; everything is sanitary to the max! What about *mice?!* Who did this?"

"Oh, God," Zalman moaned, trying to escape the tight little knot of people growing ever larger around him, around Teddieweddie in the planter, around Rutherford still

240

licking hungrily at Molly, around Moonbeam Federal and the blue-haired lady on the chair. It was no use; he was trapped in a world of loons.

*"You again!"* Tracee howled at Jimmy Federal. "First you set fire to my house, now you try and ruin my business! *I'll kill you!"* Once again, the green *Exorcist* light began to glow in her pupils, and Zalman could have sworn her head was about to start swiveling. Once again, Tracee clamped her mitts onto Jimmy Federal's neck, but this time she hadn't reckoned on Moonbeam, who jumped onto her back without hesitation.

"Fascist swine!" Moonbeam Federal growled gutturally. "Yuppie bloodsucker!"

*"Yuppie! Me? You little bitch, who are you calling a Yuppie?"* Tracee released Jimmy Federal and roughly pushed him to the ground, then began to swing at his wife, who was clinging to her back like a frantic ant.

Zalman hopped up on the planter—carefully avoiding Teddy, who was curled up under a palm leaf—so he could get the hell out of the line of fire. Carole, Miss Kelp of the Coast, batted at the pair of struggling women with her starfish wand.

"Dean!" Zalman yelled. "Pull those dames apart!"

"Not a chance, buddy-boy," McCoy said, jumping up next to Zalman. "If you think I'm getting in the middle of those two, you're flat crazy."

"Why is this happening to me?" Zalman asked God. "I'm positive this is a parallel universe. . . ." Tracee and Moonbeam continued to slap at each other angrily, Molly was down on her hands and knees next to the planter searching for Teddy, and Marie, holding Rutherford by his pink scarf, was dissolved in a combo of tears and laughter.

Zalman's eyes swept over the room. More and more people were gathering around Tracee and Moonbeam, laughing and pointing. His eyes fastened on the big TV screen at the end of the room. Scenes of Santa Barbara flicked on and off—not exactly *Blood of a Poet*, but with

241

homemade video you take what you get, he thought abstractedly. Scenes of the past few days began to appear onscreen, and in spite of the two struggling women at his feet, in spite of the chaos around him, Zalman found his attention diverted. There he was, sitting on Tracee's couch on the first fun-filled day of this futile weekend of the damned. Another shot: Tracee and Marie deep in conversation on the deck. A point-of-view shot of E.Y. in his Wild West bar, shouting at his hapless son behind the camera. Another shot of Zalman on the deck groveling for coffee. A slow, wide pan of the Santa Barbara courthouse, then a sweeping shot of the lawn on the day of E.Y.'s fatal quick-draw contest intercut with Tracee and Marie waving frantically at the camera. Once again, the quick-draw contest, E.Y.'s aged pals grinning like a gang of death's heads, a big, fast close-up of a woman's hand reaching out behind her back for a man's hand, two hands reaching out for each other, reaching out surreptitiously, intertwined like a pair of snakes in love . . .

Zalman stared at the screen, but the image was gone. A shot of Brunson, sucking his teeth, filled the TV. "Yip!" Zalman hollered as things clicked into place. *"Yip!"*

Yip was plucking at Tracee's thigh-high red dress. "Honey," he said soothingly. "Honey, now don't do that, dear. . . ." Tracee had Moonbeam in an armlock, and she kept right on twisting.

*"Yip, goddammit!"* Zalman yelled from his perch on the planter. "Leave them alone and c'mere!"

Yip looked at his wife, who now had Moonbeam Federal down on the ground and was trying to yank her long, flowing hair right out of her skull, then looked helplessly at Zalman.

*"Now!"* Zalman yelled commandingly.

Yip Knotte abandoned his wife.

"Can you rewind the tape?" Zalman barked.

Yip nodded. "Sure, Jerry, but—"

"Do it!"

Yip flapped his lips together one final time and then ran for the VCR.

"Dean," Zalman warned, "if you don't dump a bucket of water on those two, I'm gonna do it myself."

"You go right ahead, Zally," McCoy said warily. "I'll just stay right up here where it's safe and watch you do it."

"Marie! Do something, will you?" Zalman called. By now Yip had reached the VCR and was rewinding the tape. Zalman signaled him to stop, and Yip pushed Play.

Zalman looked back at the screen. E.Y. shouting; the deck; the quick-draw contest; the courthouse; a hand touching another hand . . . a pale, long-fingered hand wearing a big fat ruby ring . . .

"Oh, jeez," Zalman moaned. "Dean, Dean, where the hell's E.Y.? You're supposed to be guarding him, remember? So where the hell is he?"

McCoy tore his eyes away from the women and stared around the sweating room. "Uhhhhh," he said helpfully, "I dunno. . . ."

*"Yeeowwwwwww!"* Moonbeam Federal shrilled as Tracee kicked her hard in the shin.

Marie came walking up to them calmly, an open bottle of champagne in her hand. "I've seen this at the Super Bowl wrap-up a hundred times," she said as she put her thumb over the mouth of the bottle and briskly shook it up. "I always hoped I'd be able to try it one day. . . ." With unruffled ease she aimed the bottle at the two scuffling women and released the champagne on them with a triumphant *whoosh*. Instantly, Rutherford abandoned the lobster on Molly's rear and began to lick the puddles of champagne with canine enthusiasm.

"So where's E.Y.?" Zalman repeated loudly, still scanning the room. E. Y. Knotte was nowhere in sight.

Tracee and Moonbeam abruptly stopped their brawling as Marie continued to squirt the champagne bottle at them. "It works!" Marie cried happily.

"I'm all wet," Tracee sobbed, her red dress dulled by the champagne.

"My hair," Moonbeam moaned.

"My mouse," Molly cried.

"Take care of 'em," Zalman yelled at Marie. "And don't forget Teddy! C'mon, McCoy," he said as he ran through the crowded lobby toward the big dining room.

McCoy at his heels, Zalman pushed past guests and waiters and stuck his head into the dining room, the bar, the oxygenation chambers, the whirlpool . . . no E.Y. "Where the hell . . . ?" Zalman said with exasperation. He made for the deck, McCoy right behind him, and yanked open the big glass doors.

The spray of the Pacific Ocean hit him in the face like a wet bar towel. Two men were struggling at the railing by the far end of the balcony, much, much, too close to the edge. . . .

It was E. Y. Knotte and Arthur Carmichael. Rhonda Knotte, a pistol in her hand and tired expression on her face, was leaning up against the wall. Her hand, the hand with the big ruby ring glittering in the night, was trembling as she pointed the pistol back and forth between the two men, wavering, trying to decide.

"Hold it, Rhonda!" Zalman barked as he pulled up short.

"Suffering cats!" McCoy exclaimed, nearly colliding with Zalman.

Rhonda's red head snapped in Zalman's direction, the gun still pointed at E.Y. and Art Carmichael. Her eyes darted back and forth between them. Then, Rhonda Warwick Knotte made her decision.

Just like the Amazing Kreskin, Carmichael read it on her face. He loosened his grip on E.Y.'s throat and took a step toward her. "Rhonda," he said, his voice gritty, "Rhonda . . . darling . . ."

Rhonda fired the pistol just as a huge breaker hit the rocks below, so for a brief moment it seemed like nothing had happened. But Arthur Carmichael took it full in the chest.

The D.A. looked at his lady love in surprise, took a faltering step forward, and caved like a collapsing wave, blood pumping all over the newly varnished deck. He picked feebly at his white shirtfront, looked down, saw it turning a deep, thick red, and died.

"Rhonda!" E.Y. gasped as he backed up against the railing. His hands opened convulsively toward her; his black Stetson lay crushed at his feet.

Rhonda looked at her husband, and a wild mania filled her green eyes as she lifted the pistol again. "I . . . I didn't know. . . ."

"You knew," Zalman said quietly, though he had to raise his voice so he could be heard over the roaring surf. He held out his hands, palms up so she could see he wasn't armed. "You knew. It was you and Art all along, wasn't it, dear?" he asked softly.

Rhonda's eyes filled with rage, and she kept a firm grip on the pistol, a nice lady-sized .38 snubnose. "No . . . I never . . ."

Zalman kept smiling and took another small step forward. "Give me the gun, Rhonda. Let's make this as easy as we can. Isn't that what you want? We don't want any bad press, do we, dear?" he asked her gently.

"It was Arthur. . . ." she told her husband, nodding hopefully. Her red hair and gold dress lit her up from within, and Zalman thought she looked like a Klimt painting, the way she glowed in the damp night air.

"Now, now," he said taking another small step. "It wasn't Arthur." He gestured toward the dead D.A. sprawled on the deck. "Art was only following orders, isn't that right, dear?"

E. Y. Knotte leaned on the balcony for support. "Babykins," he said brokenly, his voice shaking. "Babykins, how could you?" Still he held out his hand to his wife.

Rhonda shrank back, as if the thought of his touch was

death itself. "Nooooo!" she cried. "Noooooo!" The gun flashed in her hand like a star.

"It was Yip's video," Zalman said easily, still hoping to calm her down. He felt the deck rumble beneath his feet as another huge wave broke below. "I saw your hand in the video. Nothing much, just a pair of hands touching after the quick-draw contest. Well, a touch ain't much, but I've been married twice, and I know what that certain sort of touch means. Your ruby ring gave you away."

"Go easy, Jerry," McCoy murmured from behind him. "She's right on the edge. . . ."

"So why don't you just give me the gun?" Zalman continued. "That's the best thing to do."

"No, I won't!" Rhonda said.

"Oh, babykins . . ." E.Y. said, his voice shattered.

Zalman could see Rhonda's red-nailed finger tightening on the trigger of the .38, and he knew she was working up to it. If he could just stall her for a minute, get a little closer to her so he could make a grab for the pistol . . .

"Rhonda," he said desperately as he took another baby step, "Rhonda, look. You can stop now, you can stop anytime you want. Art's dead, but a good lawyer can get you off in a few years. Trust me, that's the way justice crumbles these days. A few years in Tehachapi, E.Y.'ll be waiting for you when you get out." He tried another step. Just another few feet and he could jump for her, try and wrestle the gun out of her hands before she drilled E.Y.

But Rhonda's eyes only widened, and her beautiful red lips twisted in contempt. "You're all the same," she snarled. "I've seen you guys at work all my life, and you're all the same. Lawyers and businessmen and agents and shrimp magnates and district attorneys, you'd say anything to get what you want, wouldn't you? But not this time. This time *I'm* the boss!" She swung the gun firmly in her husband's direction. "Art's dead, who cares? He was just following orders, like you said, Jerry. He was crazy about me, that's easy. Easy to make men crazy about me, isn't that stupid? God, it's so easy! All you district attorneys and shrimp kings . . ." Her face twisted in disgust. "All I have to do is wiggle around, tell you boys what you want to hear. It's disgusting! At my age! I should have had a better life. I should have had more!"

"More?" Zalman asked quietly. "What more could you ask for?"

"Babykins," E.Y. croaked. "I'd 'a given you anything you wanted, anything. You just had to ask."

Rhonda flipped her red hair over her shoulder. "That's just it! I'm tired of asking! I'm tired of begging and whining and pleading for what I want! If only *you'd* died in the pool! If only *you'd* died instead of Lisa, instead of Mercer! It would have been so much easier, and I wouldn't have to kill you now. . . ."

Rhonda aimed the gun, her grip firm and sure, and Zalman knew she was going to do it. He thought he felt the deck tremble again, and somehow, in the back of his mind, he was amazed he could feel so shaky, even at a time like this. He felt himself move into slow motion as he bent his knees and prepared to leap for the gun. He could feel McCoy right behind him, and both men left the ground at the same moment. The deck shook even harder as Rhonda, her hand jerking wildly, fired the gun at her husband and missed. Then the long balcony seemed to sway back and forth like a pennant in the wind, and as the ground cracked and shook Zalman realized that it wasn't Rhonda, it wasn't his own fear, it was an earthquake.

Rhonda spun toward him in surprise as her shot went wild, and E.Y. ducked and rolled along the shaking deck toward the dining room. Her hands went up in the air, and as she dropped the .38 it skittered along the shining deck and lodged tucked up tight against Arthur Carmichael's cold, dead thigh. Rhonda's gold feet grappled for traction on the wet and bloody wood, and behind him, like the devil's background music, Zalman heard screams from inside the dining room as the entire building heaved and

247

there was the sharp shattering of glass and the hideous crash of something big breaking.

Rhonda began to slide along the deck toward the railing and the crashing sea, her red mouth a great *O* of surprise and terror, and just as she came toward him Zalman saw the railing bend like a wet wonton and crumple into the ocean below.

He made a grab for her as she went past him, sliding now toward the jagged shards of the remains of the deck, and he felt his hands meet the soft flesh of her body, miss, then fasten on the gold hem of her dress. He felt himself fall facedown over the precipice and felt McCoy behind him latch onto his ankles.

There were more shrieks from within the dining room, and Zalman heard another terrific crash of glass. Out of the corner of his eye he saw a table come slamming through a window at the far end of the deck and saw it slide helplessly into the drink. He tightened his grip on Rhonda's dress as he felt the breaking deck bend again, and another tremor hit the Southern California coastline.

He wondered if this was the big one, the one comedians joke about, the one that'll turn Las Vegas into a great seaport, and he tried to get a better grip on Rhonda's dress. But through the crash of the waves, the crack of breaking timber, the shrieks of people inside World O' Yip, he could hear another sound, the tiny tearing of cloth as Rhonda's full weight pulled against the bunched fabric in his hands. Zalman felt her begin to go, and then there was a sudden rip and a great roaring noise as her gold dress tore away completely, and as he lay hanging over the edge of the deck, McCoy's hands clamped firmly on his ankles, Jerry Zalman saw Rhonda Warwick Knotte go headfirst into the crashing Pacific, tiny gold shoes kicking angrily to the last.

"Pull, goddammit, McCoy!" he heard his voice shout, and he felt McCoy's big hands tighten, and he realized he was gazing headlong into the abyss, the mouth of the water shrieking open below him like a bad, bad dream. Not like

Klimt anymore, he mused with disembodied objectivity. Like what was that guy, Munch? That Norwegian who did those awful drawings of open, screaming mouths—or was that George Grosz? One of them, anyway, and why the hell had he let Tracee talk him into this deal when all he'd wanted was his father's Toulouse-Lautrec lithograph back, for Pete's sake?

"Awwwww, cripes," he heard himself say in a very tired voice as he was pulled back to safety and his head took a whack on a four-by-twelve. He was bumped and scraped across some broken timber, and then Jerry Zalman passed out.

"An eight!" Marie breathed. "That's the biggest earthquake I've ever been through. She reached out and gently squeezed Zalman's hand. "We have them all the time in L.A., you don't even notice them after a while," she told Espinoza. "The last one was a six, I think. And the one out in Sylmar, the one in the early seventies? That was a six-point-something, wasn't it, Jerry?"

Zalman was stretched out on the couch in Tracee's living room, a big bandage taped to his head. "Yeah, I think so," he said, basking happily in the attention of his friends and admirers. Rutherford was crouched at his feet, panting like a pale imitation of a public library lion.

Despite the biggest Southern California earthquake in years, both Tracee's house and World O' Yip were still standing. They'd been built to withstand a ten on the Richter scale, but Knotte Pines hadn't been so lucky. Cracks in the foundation, a collapsed bearing wall, and a disintegrated turret had decided it; E. Y. Knotte was going to move in with Yip and Tracee as soon as Zalman and Marie left for L.A.

"Besides," E.Y. said, hunched down in one of Tracee's pale chairs, a steaming mug of Yipnotic clenched in his hand, "that house reminds me too much of Rhonda and all the terrible things she did!" He sighed again and shook his head. "How could she? Me, her own husband. She was so beautiful, and such a lady." E.Y. slapped disconsolately at his knees with the Dodgers cap he wore. He seemed to have lost his taste for Stetsons.

"Art did most of it. He was crazy about her," Zalman said, hoping to ease the double shock E.Y. had taken. "She planned the crimes, but she needed Art to do the dirty work. He fixed the brakes on you car, and when that didn't work, he tried to wire the pool."

"Tried to kill me and got poor little Lisa instead," E.Y. mumbled. "And then Mercer, my old saddle pal. And even tried to get you, Jerry, when you got too close. I know he did everything, but Rhonda planned it, just like you said, Jerry."

"People get greedy," McCoy said philosophically.

"She woulda had so much when I croaked," E.Y. said. "Just coulda waited . . . I wasn't such a bad husband. Fooled around a little bit on the side, yeah, but a man my age figures every day might be his last," he said with great sentimentality. "And after all, with no little nippers around, I gotta take my own shot at immortality, know what I mean?"

"Oh, sure," Zalman said incredulously. "Right. Immortality. It's a tough break, E.Y., but I know you'll pull through. You got a great family."

E.Y. shook his head and grinned at Zalman, fiddling with his Dodgers cap. "I'd be a damn goner, Jerry, if weren't for you and your pal over there," he said, pointing at McCoy, who was lying on the floor with Chester at his side. "And you won't be sorry for it on your way to the bank, like I said. My Shrimpkin business is yours for life," he cackled. "I'm getting rid o' those bozos I got in New York, and from now on you handle the whole shebang."

Zalman felt a warm, rosy glow spread over him at the prospect of a hefty increase in his standard of living. First the Shrimpkins, then who knows? Maybe the Crabster,

251

Zalman thought dreamily, and he made a mental note to suggest the Crabster to E.Y. at some future date.

Yip and Tracee came bounding into the room, both dressed in white jogging clothes that gave them a brilliant glow of health. "I have wonderful news," Tracee cried. "I just don't know where to begin."

"How's World O' Yip?" Marie said anxiously. "Is it going to be all right?"

"Fabulous." Tracee laughed. "The architect says we'll be ready to reopen in about a week, two at the outside. Except for the deck—which he's repairing at his own expense, I'll point out—the building took the earthquake right in stride. Just lost a little timber and some furniture and glass, that's all." She flopped down next to Marie and hugged her. "Aren't you thrilled?"

"I couldn't be more relieved," Marie said with a mock sigh and a hand over her heart. "I was afraid we'd had major damage, and now, just as we're starting, it would mean tremendous losses, not to mention the bad publicity. But we'll reopen within two weeks? You're right, Tracee, it *is* fabulous. We were awfully lucky, though."

"Huh?" Zalman said. "What's this *'we're'* thrilled? What's going on here?" he said, looking suspiciously at Marie.

Marie looked guilty and glanced sidelong at Tracee, who gave her an encouraging pat on the back. "Well, darling, there's a teensy little thing I forgot to tell you about World O' Yip."

"You *never* forget," Zalman said with a sinking feeling.

"Well, you know, a few days ago—God, it all seems so long ago now I can hardly believe it, can you, Tracee? I mean—"

"Marie," Zalman said sternly.

"Mmmmm, welll," Marie continued, "Tracee and I were talking after, um, after E.Y. didn't want to invest in the later stages of World O' Yip. Remember that, Jerry?"

"Marie . . ."

"Well. So when Tracee needed the money so badly and none of you would give it to her, well, I just called my banker in L.A.—he's been so helpful with my typing business, Tracee, it's so wonderful—"

"Marie!"

"So, well, Jerry, I took back a second mortgage on my house because, welll, it's almost paid up, because after my divorce I put down this huge chunk of cash so I could have low monthly payments, and of course I always pay more on the mortgage because it's just easier if you round the check off, and also I have one of those big lines of credit deals they send you from the bank where you can write a check for up to twenty-five thousand dollars as long as it isn't to finance securities."

Zalman stared at the love of his life with an open mouth. "Are you telling me," he said slowly, just to make sure he wasn't mistaken, "are you telling me that *you* . . . ."

"Ummmm, yes, I guess I am. Of course, Molly and Carole put in some money, too. E.Y. was so sweet to give Carole some money for Hawaii, and Molly's been very clever about mutual funds. She had the brains to get out at the top of the market."

"That's more than I did," Zalman muttered. "You mean that you and Molly and Carole the Kelp Lady—*you* three got the money together to open World O' Yip?"

"Wasn't that sweet, Jerry?" Tracee said happily. "That Marie is one in a million, and so smart with money, too. I talked to people all over town, and no one had the financial vision to see World O' Yip as a truly inspiring business opportunity. Marie saw it at once, and since she had the courage of her fiduciary convictions, so to speak, you won't be sorry. . . ."

Zalman had a bad feeling in the heartburn zone of his stomach. He stared at his ex-wife. "What do you mean, *I* won't be sorry?" he said slowly, the bad feeling rapidly spreading throughout his entire body. "What do *I* have to do with it?"

Tracee and Marie shot guilty looks at each other. Tracee gazed intently at a corner of the living room ceiling. "Oh, look," she said, "there's a big cobweb! I must get one of those long feather dusters. . . ."

"Tracee," Zalman growled.

"Now, Jerry," Marie said. "It was for your own good. You'll be rich."

"I *am* rich! What did you do? Huh? Go ahead and tell me. Maybe I won't kill you."

Marie smiled warmly. "I'm *so* glad, darling. Promise?"

"Tell me. *Then* I'll promise."

"Well, Jerry," Marie said, "even after I took back the second and even with Molly's mutual funds and Carole's little bit from E.Y., well, we still didn't have enough money, so . . ."

"I hate this," Zalman said, rubbing his stomach. "I haven't even heard it, and already I hate this."

"Well, dear, we sold your Toulouse-Lautrec."

"AAARRRRGH!" Zalman shrieked. "I knew it! I knew you did something horrible! How could you *do* this to me! I had a spot all picked out for it in my office! My father *gave* me that litho, and I'm damned sentimental about it! It was an heirloom! How much did you get for it?"

"Fifty grand," Marie said.

*"That's all!"* Zalman howled. *"I* would have given you fifty grand!"

Marie shook her head angrily. "No, you wouldn't, Jerry Zalman, so it's no good now turning around and saying that you would have before. You knew Yip needed the money, and you had your chance, and you didn't jump at it, but luckily I jumped at your chance for you."

"You've been spending too much time with Tracee," Zalman grumbled. "You're beginning to sound just like her."

"Why, thank you, Jerry," Tracee said. "What a sweet thing to say. You do understand, don't you, Jerry? We *had*

254

to sell the Toulouse. We didn't have any other choice! You men drove us to it!"

"It was worth more than fifty grand," Zalman said moodily.

"Oh, Jerry, you won't be sorry," Tracee said. "You'll make lots of money from World O' Yip, plus, of course, you'll get to do all the legal work."

"What a thrill."

"Plus, of course, the Shrimpkins. So you certainly won't lose anything by it in the financial realm, Jerry Zalman. Honestly," she said as she turned to Marie, "men are so venal! Oh, did I tell you that *People* mag called?" she said to Marie. "They want all of us to pose, isn't that divine? But anyway, that's not all I have to say, and I just wanted to be sure all of you were here, because this is a very important day in my life, and you're our favorite friends."

"Well?" E.Y. said gruffly. "What is it?"

Tracee smiled and grasped Yip's hand. "I'm pregnant," she said with maidenly modesty. "You'll have your nipper after all, E.Y."

E.Y. threw his baseball cap in the air. "An heir!" he yelled happily. "A little nipper!"

"Actually, Dad," Yip said with evident pride, "several nippers."

"Ever since we had this problem with not getting pregnant," Tracee said, "well, I've been running down to L.A. to this simply fabulous clinic they have and taking these fertility drugs. I'm going to have triplets," she announced, laying a maternal hand on her stomach. "So . . . several nippers."

"That's wonderful," Marie said. "I'm so happy for you!"

"Congratulations, Yip," Zalman said. "Have a cigar. Have three."

Yip opened a magnum of champagne and they all drank a toast to the impending nippers, whom Zalman was already beginning to think of as Huey, Dewey, and Louie. He sank down onto the couch with his glass and watched

255

Marie and Tracee jabber away about what they should wear for the interview with *People* and how much money they were going to make from World O' Yip and what they'd be able to buy with it. He sighed, thinking of his lost Toulouse-Lautrec. Rutherford got up next to him, rested his head on Zalman's shoulder, and gave him a tentative but comforting slurp on the cheek.

"Not on the lips," Zalman warned absently. But Rutherford didn't pay any attention to him. Zalman stared at the Doberman and thought about how much fun it would be to staple his pointy little ears to his head. Rutherford gazed at him adoringly and panted, drooling on Zalman's knee.

"Oh, well," Zalman said philosophically as he put his arm around Rutherford. "Looks like it's you and me, bub."

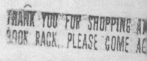